What the critics are saying...

4 1/2 Stars "Painter writes humorous dialogue and makes the most out of her modern-day heroine attempting to acclimate to vampire society in this excellent and hilarious offering. Characterization is strong, and the plot keeps the action exciting." ~ Page Traynor Romantic Times

5 Stars "...found myself turning page after page and didn't want to put it down! The scorching hot passion and tender love between Armondés and Danielle were beautiful, inspiring, and so arousing I found myself squirming in my chair... Sally Painter delivers an extraordinary story of love and betrayal..." ~ Lori eCataRomance

"Sally Painter is a rising new star for Ellora's Cave... a super, fast-paced thrill-a-minute from the get-go. Armondés has no intention of ever loving another woman after Danielle...Readers will chuckle and cry at the scene where the two lovers get reunited." ~ Angela Camp Romance Reviews Today

Rating 5.0 / Sensuality 5.0 "Immediately I was taken in by this book. Their relationship is immediate and so very hot. The interplay between the two throughout the book is exceedingly sensual and makes the reader want their very own Armondés." ~ Marina mon-boudoir

4.5 "Sally Painter has woven a story that I found I couldn't do anything till I finished the last page. Ms. Painter did one heck of a job and I look forward to reading more of her works in the future." ~ Laura Enchanted In Romance

SALLY PAINTER

ALL I NEED

ELLORA'S CAVE
ROMANTICA PUBLISHING

An Ellora's Cave Romantica Publication

www.ellorascave.com

All I Need

ISBN # 1419952307
ALL RIGHTS RESERVED.
All I Need Copyright© 2005 Sally Painter
Edited by: Sue-Ellen Gower
Cover art by: Christine Clavel

Electronic book Publication: February, 2005
Trade paperback Publication: August, 2005

Warning:

The following material contains graphic sexual content meant for mature readers. *All I Need* has been rated *S-ensuous* by a minimum of three independent reviewers.

Ellora's Cave Publishing offers three levels of Romantica™ reading entertainment: S (S-ensuous), E (E-rotic), and X (X-treme).

S-*ensuous* love scenes are explicit and leave nothing to the imagination.

E-*rotic* love scenes are explicit, leave nothing to the imagination, and are high in volume per the overall word count. In addition, some E-rated titles might contain fantasy material that some readers find objectionable, such as bondage, submission, same sex encounters, forced seductions, etc. E-rated titles are the most graphic titles we carry; it is common, for instance, for an author to use words such as "fucking", "cock", "pussy", etc., within their work of literature.

X-*treme* titles differ from E-rated titles only in plot premise and storyline execution. Unlike E-rated titles, stories designated with the letter X tend to contain controversial subject matter not for the faint of heart.

Also by Sally Painter:

All I Want

All I Need

Trademarks Acknowledgement

Dedication

Thank you to my neighbors and their icy driveway that made me slip and break my leg in five places last year. Had it not been for what appeared to be a horrid accident at the time, I never would have written ALL I NEED.

Also, I'd like to say 'thank you' to my long-time friend and critique partner, Lori Soard, who insisted I submit a manuscript to Ellora's Cave. So glad she's a good nag.

And, I'd like to thank Sue-Ellen Gower, my editor and her assistant Ann Leivelle! I owe so much to these two amazing professionals.

And, to my husband, Wayne, who always encourages me to test the waters of new adventures.

And, last, but not least, to Ellora's Cave for creating new arenas in the romance genre, for daring to flex a creative muscle and encouraging writers to do the same.

Chapter One

"I know you want to do this, Danielle." Her friend Amy smiled at her from across the bistro table. Danielle met the excitement in her friend's eyes with a feeling of dread. When they had suggested a night out to celebrate her thirtieth birthday, she had thought they meant something tame.

"Yeah, we *have* to do it." Lillian took a deep gulp of her drink as though she needed the liquor to steel her.

Danielle did not like this change in plans. It was bad enough they had coerced her to go out with them, but going to a new nightclub was not how she wanted to spend her birthday. She had heard rumors about the wild things that went on at the very exclusive club and it didn't sound like a place she would enjoy.

"We can do it right here," she said. "We don't have to make a big deal out of this." Danielle glanced about the bistro to see if anyone was listening to their conversation. She really wanted to dissuade her friends from seeing this through.

"You don't celebrate in a place like this. I mean not *this* kind of celebration." Amy flipped her long red hair over her shoulder.

"Amy's right. *Armondés* is wicked and the perfect place to cut loose. Come on, girl, this is the last night you can say you're twenty-something. Why, it's a milestone. You owe it to yourself to really celebrate." Lillian punctuated the assessment by downing her drink in one big gulp. She stared over at Danielle as though expecting her to agree.

"But isn't Armondés… I mean, I've heard about what goes on there, even you told me some wild stories after your first visit. It just doesn't sound like the kind of place I'd fit in."

Danielle wadded the cocktail napkin between her clammy hands.

"Oh, don't you just love that name? *Armondés*. I mean the name alone is mysterious and dark. As far as what goes on, girl, it's all pure fun!" Amy grinned widely as though *that* should reassure her.

"Oh yeah, I can just see it. This stud standing at the door, nearly busting the seams of his black tuxedo," Danielle groaned.

"Actually that's exactly how he looks, only it's a leather vest." Lillian waved at their waiter. The young woman came over to the table. "Another round and then the check, please," she said before Danielle could protest. "Just one last one for the road. Come on, Dani, you'll love it, trust me," she sighed.

She noticed Lillian's blue eyes sparkled when she spoke about Savannah's newest night hotspot. Her heart skipped a beat. They were not going to be easy to dissuade.

"Y'all didn't tell me you'd been back there." Just what had they been doing? She looked away, focusing on the rivulets running down the full glass of bourbon and ginger ale.

"Girl, Lillian practically lives there on weekends," Amy said and shrugged her shoulders at Lillian's intensive glare.

"I've been there a *few* times." She cleared her throat and glanced around the crowded bar as though searching for someone.

"So, tell her what it's really like." Amy leaned forward on her elbows. Her brown eyes widened expectantly. "You do a better job describing it."

"There are a lot of hot men there, Danielle. I've never seen such a convergence of male yummies anywhere. That's why we decided it was the perfect place for a woman turning thirty to well, you know, *celebrate*."

"And those yummies, Dani, they're all single," Amy said.

"Well, the ones we've met say they are," Lillian laughed and looked at the door once more.

"So it's set. We leave here and go to *Armondés*," Amy announced, sliding from the high bistro chair. She leaned against the tall table as though she were ready to leave.

"I don't know, Amy," Danielle hesitated with rising panic. She'd not expected this. She wasn't dressed for such a place. She had to prepare mentally. A club like Armondés wasn't somewhere you just walked into without being mentally, and fashionably, prepared. She frowned when the waitress set a fresh drink in front of her and handed the check cover to Lillian.

"Here you go." Lillian slipped her credit card inside and gave it back.

Dani swallowed the dryness in her throat. They were getting ready to leave. How was she going to get out of doing this? She stared at the fresh drink. Great, now she had two drinks, one with ice, and one with melted ice. "You two know it's been over ten years since I dated."

"God, Dani! You've been divorced for three years. What are you waiting on? Your life to pass you by? You need to get out and have some fun. You're too young to act so old!" Amy groaned.

"Thanks, Amy." Danielle tried to calm the anger roiling in her. They both knew how difficult it had been for her. Did they think it was easy to get over that pain? Why should she want to risk more misery in her life? How could she trust herself to ever judge any man's character accurately? Her confidence had been shattered.

"Amy, don't be cruel, how could Danielle have known about Stan? He hid it so well. I had no idea and I can usually tell when a guy's cheating."

"I'm sorry, Dani. I didn't mean it like that. I…I know it was horrible for you. I mean living with him for seven years and not knowing—"

"Stop it," Dani choked. "We aren't having this conversation tonight."

"No, we aren't, *Amy*." Lillian frowned at Amy, then continued. "You know Dani isn't like us. I mean, she's more...uh, well, conservative, but that's why we chose this place, Dani. It's time you saw how you could be living."

"And I appreciate what you're trying to do, honest. But, Lillian, that's not me."

"Exactly! It's not like any of us. And that's why we're going!" Lillian declared. "It's our birthday gift to you. How can you refuse a present? You wouldn't do that, would you, Dani?"

"Of course she wouldn't," Amy chimed in.

Danielle looked from one friend to the other.

"I just didn't know you meant *this* when you said you were taking me out on the town. I thought you meant dinner and maybe a show." Danielle was beginning to regret coming out with her two friends.

"Oh, please." Lillian downed the drink. "A thirtieth birthday deserves something spectacular!"

"Hey, girlies!" A woman in her early thirties, dressed in a sequined shell with leather slacks and spike heels greeted them.

"I was beginning to think you weren't coming," Lillian said and leaned to the side so the brunette could stand between them.

"Are we ready to party?" She sat down in Amy's vacated chair and leaned against Danielle. A little too close.

"Hi, birthday girl, feel like having some fun? Armondés awaits us!" She rubbed her shoulder against Danielle.

"Dani, this is our friend Minnie. We met her at Armondés," Amy introduced the woman.

"Hey," Danielle mumbled. The woman's dark, shoulder-length hair was stiff with spray, and her lips over-glossed. Floozy was the word her grandmother would have used. City-stylish was a nicer modern term.

14

"We're going to have a great time tonight!" Minnie grinned. "I had to show your two gal pals the ropes. Are you like your friends here, Dani? Are you a wild woman, too?"

"Wild? Me?" Dani looked at Lillian and Amy, thinking she didn't know them as well as she'd thought.

"We're wild?" Amy asked, seeming to stand taller as though Minnie's comment had been a compliment.

Dani stared at her friends feeling they were complete strangers. How had they kept this side of their social lives secret? And why? Why did they think she'd like this kind of entertainment?

"Look, Minnie, I was just telling Lillian and Amy that I don't think I'm dressed for Armondés. So why don't y'all just go on without me? Another time, perhaps." She ran a trembling hand through her long hair, thinking its brownish color was too average for such a place. She needed gold highlights and perhaps a shorter, sophisticated cut.

"Not go?" Minnie pursed her red lips into a pout.

"Oh no," her friends said in unison.

"Minnie?" Amy gave a look that indicated she was expecting something from their new friend.

"Oh, the gift!" Minnie rolled her eyes. "In the car."

"Can you get it?" Lillian asked.

"Back in a sec." She turned from them and wove her way through the crowded bistro.

"What gift?" Dread sank to Danielle's feet. This evening was turning out to be the most uncomfortable one she'd ever had.

"You'll see," Amy sing-songed and belted back her drink.

They were acting so odd. In almost fifteen years she'd never seen her friends so —

"How do y'all know that woman?" she asked Lillian, while nervously sipping the diluted drink. The liquor rolled down her throat and fanned in heated waves to her stomach. It helped to take the edge off a little.

"Oh, we met her the first night at Armondés, the hussy," Lillian said.

The waitress placed the check cover on the table and Lillian flipped it open, signed the receipt and returned her card to her purse.

"What?" She looked up at Danielle. "Don't you think she's the coolest chick you've ever seen? I mean, Dani, honey, this girl's got connections."

"You nervous, Dani? You aren't going to back out on us, are you?" Amy whined.

"Please go with us. We really put a lot of time and effort into planning this night, just for you. Let us do this for you," Lillian said.

"Here it is." Minnie reappeared behind her.

Danielle turned as the woman handed a large gift bag to Lillian.

"Wonderful!" Amy bobbed her head.

"So are you having a good birthday, sweetie?" Minnie licked her glossy lips with the tip of her tongue then reached over and took Danielle's drink from her. The woman's long nails didn't have the usual rounded or blunt cut, instead, they were sharply pointed. Her heart pounded harder. What an odd way to wear fingernails. She attempted to avoid Minnie's stare, but found herself captivated by the long-lashed brown eyes staring at her.

"Oh yes, you're going to have a wonderful time at *Armondés*." Minnie sipped the drink then carefully placed it beside the fresh one. "Thanks. That was delicious even though the ice has melted."

"Please, take this one." She shoved the other drink into Minnie's hand, with the ice clinking against the glass.

"Oh, you are too sweet," Minnie cooed then nodded to Lillian.

Danielle felt as though they had rehearsed all this. Before she could react, Lillian handed her the large gift bag.

"This is for you, Danielle, because Amy and I love you and want you to have some fun in life."

"Open it," Amy said.

"Maybe it would be better to do it in the ladies' room." Minnie's hot breath fanned over her.

"Why? What's in it?" The nervous fluttering moved from her stomach to settle into a choking knot in her throat. Why did Minnie suddenly seem to be in control of the party? Just who was this woman?

"You know it's all in *good* fun, Danielle. Now why don't you be a *good* girl and *let your friends give you this night*?" Minnie's voice was a melodic purring in her ear, even though it was a very noisy bar.

She tried to look away from the woman, but something about those dark eyes held her spellbound.

"Come on, Danielle. You *have* to do this!" Amy insisted. "Just say yes."

"That's right, Danielle, *just say yes*," Minnie droned.

"Y-yes," she repeated.

A cheer went up from the women. She stared at them, confused. What had she just done? Why had she agreed to do what they wanted? What was wrong with her? She didn't want to go to this club. Why had she said yes?

Panicked, she grabbed the bag and practically ran for the restroom. Amy was on her heels, with Lillian's laughter and Minnie's melodic voice trailing behind them. Minnie's voice sounded as though she were whispering in Danielle's ear.

"You can do this, Danielle. It will free you from all your fears about men. You *owe* it to yourself to *do this*."

The ladies' room was large, with a small salon adjacent to the toilet booths. Her legs trembled as she collapsed into the Louis XVI chair.

"Well, open it up," Amy insisted.

"Hurry up, Dani," Lillian joined in.

Danielle's pulse was a riotous drumming. Her hands shook when she removed the colorful tissue papers, revealing a large red box.

The box literally sparkled under the overhead lights. She lifted it from the bag and set it in her lap, tracing the embossed signature logo with a shaky forefinger. She had never had anything from Eloise. In fact, she'd never dared go inside the risqué shop, always walking on the other side of the mall just so she wouldn't embarrass herself.

"What's this?" she asked, looking up at them. Why would her friends buy her a gift from Eloise? Or rather, why would they have this Minnie person buy her a gift? The nervous quivering settled back to her stomach.

"It's your costume for this evening," Lillian smiled.

That was *not* what she wanted to hear.

"Here, sweetie, you look like you could use this." Minnie shoved the drink into her shaking hand. "Down it all real fast. You'll feel better."

Danielle did as told, absently wondering why she was listening to the stranger. Warmth flooded through her and the room spun around her. She'd never had that kind of reaction before. Her arms and legs tingled, feeling weak.

"Okay, enough drinking. Open the box." Amy moved slightly to let several women pass through the small room.

The box lid gave under her fingers. Timidly, she lifted it, revealing red tissue paper.

Amy stifled a giggle and fell against Lillian.

"What is this?" She pulled the tissue apart. The spaghetti strap dress was nestled against a deep maroon bustier trimmed in black lace complete with silk stockings. Her cheeks flushed hotter when she lifted the crotchless thong.

"Oh, I'm *not* wearing these." She looked at her friends, flashing what she hoped was an angry glare in the direction of their new friend. She was behind all this. The only thing Danielle didn't know was why.

"You have to wear it. Look..." Lillian grabbed the hem of her own dress and pulled it over her head.

"Lillian!" She looked about the restroom, relieved the other women had left.

"See?" Lillian tossed the discarded dress at Minnie.

"I've never seen that before," Danielle said, staring at Lillian's short red dress and the leather bra peeping above the low, scooped neckline.

"I don't wear it to the office, silly. Come on, get in the spirit of your party. Get changed." Lillian reached for her. It seemed like hundreds of hands groped her as she was ushered into a vacant stall, along with the party outfit.

"Hurry up. There's someone waiting for you at Armondés," Lillian laughed.

* * * * *

Their four sets of heels clicked in rhythm as the women walked from the parking deck toward the club. Danielle heard the music long before she could see the club. When they turned the corner, she paused and stared at the four-storied antebellum building. Large columns supported a series of balconies along the upper floor graced with intricate, wrought iron railings.

"Come on, Dani," Lillian called for her to catch up with them.

Danielle rushed across the busy street, prepared to join the others standing in the long line that wrapped around the building into the alley. Relief washed over her. They would never get inside. But the reprieve was fleeting when Minnie led them past the waiting partygoers, tossing a smile at the occasional disgruntled comment that they were breaking in line.

"Can we just cut in line like this?" she asked Amy, but her attention was quickly drawn to the elegant façade of Grecian columned archways and relief figurines of miniaturized mythological creatures plastered to the side of the building. The driving beat pounded from inside the club, vibrating the darkened windows.

"Come on," someone said, and dragged her past the crowd standing just outside the doorway. Danielle glanced up at the very muscular bouncer who blocked their entrance. He nodded to Minnie and opened the brass-trimmed door and they entered the marble-walled lobby. Shouts and groans ebbed behind them with several obscene oaths about breaking line.

Immediately, Danielle realized the rumors were true. Armondés was not an ordinary club. Her stare widened on the statues by the medieval-styled double doors. The alabaster lovers were frozen in their lovemaking, entwined within each other's embrace as another statue of a male with an erection stood over them—watching.

She reached out and let her fingers stroke the ribs of the male statue until Lillian shoved her toward another set of doors.

"Don't settle for that, Dani, the real thing's inside. Just wait, you'll see why I wanted to bring you here tonight. In this place, you can realize your deepest fantasies."

She was ushered through the heavy wooden doors into yet another outer room, smaller than the entrance and round. Red velvet and ornate gilded furniture decorated the mirrored room. Across from them was a third arched doorway with elaborate wrought iron gates instead of doors, and they were closed. She strained to see through them into the dimly lit, massive room with high vaulted ceilings. Above the dance floor were blue and yellow lights casting an eerie mood below on what appeared to be hundreds of undulating bodies. The music pounded out a throbbing beat and grew louder as they neared the entrance.

Her pulse spiked. The air was charged with an energy unlike any she'd ever sensed.

"Isn't it marvelous?" Lillian leaned over to whisper in her ear.

"You can have anything you want, Dani, *anything.*"

All Danielle could do was nod. A tall man wearing a sleeveless leather vest moved in front of the gates. His hard body seemed to bulge within the strict confines of the black vest and snug-fitting pants. His gaze swept over the women, and his lips spread into an appreciative grin. Danielle's cheeks rushed hot, feeling self-conscious under his regard.

"Well? Are you going to let us in, Frankie?" Minnie asked, her voice an octave higher as she strained to be heard above the deafening music. She threaded her fingers through the intricate wrought iron pattern and leaned into the locked gate. "This is *his* big date," she said in a lower voice, but Danielle caught the words followed by the second glance in her direction.

Frankie nodded, lifted the heavy key hanging from his belt and unlocked the door. Slowly, the iron gate creaked open upon its hinges, sending a warning chill down her spine. The women entered ahead of her, but she froze in her place. The excitement of the night shifted into a deep feeling of dread. There was something more about this place. Something just wasn't—

"Come on, Dani, this is all for you. Don't go getting cold feet. Not now." Amy grabbed her by the wrist and pulled her through the open archway.

Frankie's dark stare shifted over her when he leaned forward and closed the gate behind them. The heavy metal slammed shut. She jerked around, trying to shake the foreboding sense she'd just entered a prison. Of course, that was ridiculous.

"Oh man! What an incredible night this is going to be." Amy squeezed her arm.

"What do you think, Dani?" Lillian turned to grin at her.

Her stare widened on the three-storied high ceiling, the ornately carved statues and the gilded furniture. Even the tables were massive wood with marble tops. But most alarming were the suspended cages where men and women held in bondage struggled against their chains and leather collars. Dark booths were more like beds with red velvet draperies fringed in gold — some open, but most closed, revealing teasing glimpses of couples. Women with leather thongs twisted and moved over men dressed in leather chaps, while others wore Speedos. Danielle tried to swallow past the dryness in her throat.

"I bet you've never been to a place like this," Minnie leaned in to whisper.

"You bet right." Rising heat fluttered over her. A part of her was shocked, even horrified by what she saw, while another part of her found it just so…very exciting.

"What do you think, Dani?" Minnie used her nickname and gestured to the room.

"I think I've been out of circulation way too long, if this is what the single scene is all about nowadays."

This seemed to amuse Minnie for a moment then she simply nodded and moved away from them, disappearing into the surging crowd.

"Well, I guess most of the people at work would be shocked by this place," Amy spoke above the pounding music.

"I daresay any normal person would be shocked." Lillian gestured to the corner of the room where Minnie now stood waving at them.

"We have a booth?" Amy asked. "Wow, this woman knows how to make people snap to attention."

"Yes, she does," Danielle murmured to herself, staring at a man across the room. He stood out from the crowd, mostly because of his handsome looks, but also because, unlike everyone else in this club, he wasn't wearing black. She followed her friends to the procured booth, casting a wistful look in his direction. His dark gray suit highlighted his broad shoulders and attempted to disguise his muscular arms. He wore a red and gray brocade vest with gold, embossed buttons. The final touch was a black tie with a gold tie chain.

His unrelenting gaze smoldered over her face, searing down the length of her neck to the low neckline of her birthday dress. Danielle tried to look away, but she was captive to his presence. She willed her legs to take her in the opposite direction of the booth, where he now appeared to be waiting for them. Waiting for her. Quickening heat pumped through her.

He tilted his head slightly and her pulse jumped. He was staring right at her with a slow grin parting his lips. Excited shivers raced down her spine, tingling her nipples hard.

"That's Armondés!" Lillian grabbed her arm and squeezed. Amy pivoted to look at them with her eyes wide in an exaggerated expression of surprise.

"Oh my God! Do you see him?" Amy gasped. "Why is he watching *us*?"

Lillian looked past Amy then back to Danielle.

"He seems to be watching our birthday girl here."

Danielle recognized the name, *Armondés*. The owner of the club. Her knees weakened but she continued to walk toward him.

"Watching her? I'd say more like devouring her." Amy mouthed the words, *lucky you*.

"Come on." Lillian locked her arm through Danielle's.

"Please! Can we have a little bit of control, ladies?" She jerked free of her friends' armlocks. "You act as though I'm some kind of sacrifice to the guy."

"Sacrifice?" Lillian released her hold and flashed Amy a warning glare.

"Sorry, Dani." Amy relaxed the deathlike grip. "He's just the most eligible and desirable man ever. Other than that, he's nothing."

"You just don't understand, Dani. Amy has this big crush on him." Lillian sneered at the other woman.

"Oh, like you don't? Thing is, Dani, to have Armondés looking at you like that, I mean he's really interested in you. That's what all the women here are panting hot to have happen to them. You're just so lucky!" Amy literally trembled beside her.

"Amy, you have no shame. I swear, Dani, she's like some high-school kid. Gets all hot around Armondés. She's impossible to work with. If she keeps it up, I'm going to ask for a transfer across the street to your building. I'm serious, all she talks about is Armondés this and Armondés that. I have to listen to her all day long. You're lucky you don't work in our building!"

"Oh, like you don't talk about him?" Amy pouted. "I saw the way you went after him last Saturday night, but he took that blonde up to his suite, didn't he? Not you, babe."

"My turn will come, Miss Amy. You're just jealous that he bought me a drink and hasn't once noticed you."

"Am not! And so what if he bought you a little piddling drink. He still left you down here staring into your vodka."

"Look, Amy, do you want to make this about last Saturday or are you going to let it be about Dani?" Lillian challenged with restrained anger edging her words.

"You're the one who started it by saying I had the hots for him," Amy defended.

"Well, honey, you do," Lillian jeered.

Danielle stared at them unable to believe what she was hearing.

"Whoa!" She finally interrupted them. "Just what's wrong with y'all? You've never talked to each other like this. Ever since you first came to this place, you both act...well, different. Is there something I should know before we go any further?"

Chapter Two

"That's her." Minnie slipped her hand around the column of the booth and leaned toward him.

"I know," Armondés spoke, not daring to break his stare. He gauged Danielle Rivers to be about five-eight, and lithe, but very voluptuous with well-rounded hips, a small waist and larger than average breasts.

"They're real," Minnie spoke and shifted to stand beside him. "I can tell."

He ignored her, keeping Danielle's gaze locked to his. He watched the way her hips swung ever so slightly, teasing him with their unconscious rhythm. Something he'd not felt for several months stoked to life — desire.

"Do you feel resurrected?" she asked and once more he ignored her.

Danielle Rivers was irresistible. From her dark brown, long, silky hair and deep chocolate eyes to her full lips, currently pursed in a tense, uncertain expression, she was the woman he sought. If he must marry to save himself from the curse, then this woman would do nicely.

"She's lovely." He watched her move closer. Who would have thought he'd have survived to live two thousand years, much less seventy-five years beyond? He'd had two wives since his two thousandth birthday, yet neither had loved him. More importantly, he had not loved them, even though he had tried desperately. Lust's bloom did not last long enough when one was a vampire. Besides, he had not married them out of affection, but need.

He needed to avoid the curse placed upon the throne by his predecessor, the ancient vampire he had destroyed in order to gain control over the kingdom. Before Armondés' reign, very few of the clan had endured beyond a few hundred years, much less two thousand. He knew the longevity they now enjoyed was because of his reign as king. He had safeguarded against their natural impulses to hunt humans, which had exposed the clan to being hunted and slaughtered in retaliation. For the modern world, vampires were only a myth—partly because his clan, the largest one, was invisible. He had made it possible with a unique lifestyle. Armondés had literally saved the clan from being enslaved to their needs and desires while increasing life expectancy from hundreds of years to thousands. It had been his greatest gift to the clan, yet it was not perfect.

Not all of his people had survived. In spite of new counseling programs and training, some could not adjust to the "no hunting" law. For some, the vampire nature was just too strong to control. Armondés ground his teeth together. Guilt was an ugly companion and one he longed to shed.

"I believe she'll be different," Minnie said.

He ignored her, watching the way Danielle parted her lips as she listened to her friends. It was one of the sexiest gestures he had ever seen. He folded his arms over his chest and studied her, absently wondering how long desire for her would last. One year? Two?

His need for his last wife, Charisse, had lasted all of two weeks. He pushed the bitter memory away. He'd tried to comfort her, teach her, but she had been too wild. Her transformation had been the worst possible kind for a vampire. Being a vampire had not freed her. Instead, she'd been enslaved by the need to hunt. Trying to keep her safe had proven impossible and she had died before their second anniversary. The guilt had been too deep to consider taking another wife within the curse's mandatory one year. But now he must.

What kind of choice was it? If he failed to remarry, he would suffer the curse's wrath, and age to the physical appearance of two thousand and seventy-five years. Marriage was not a choice but a necessity. He closed his eyes against the memories of the two failed marriages.

"You won't have to suffer the curse," Minnie said.

"I have no intentions of doing that." Inwardly pushing the visual image of a walking skeleton from his mind, Armondés clenched his jaw tighter. Was that what a man over two thousand years old would look like if forced to age as the curse threatened? He should not have put this task off. Yet, he'd felt no hurry to recreate the same kind of marriage he'd suffered with his other wives.

He had to marry a human female and take her just before her thirtieth birthday, but there was no explanation behind this stipulation. His rival had survived just long enough to utter the curse before he crumbled beneath the stake. No one would ever know the whys, only that the ancient had cursed him and he had now lived long enough to be threatened. He had no intentions of testing the curse's validity. Ignoring it meant decomposition into a two thousand and seventy-five year old walking corpse. It was not a fate he was willing to test.

"But your delay has risked just that. Had I not found this one…" Minnie interrupted his thoughts.

"I think that's enough." He glared a warning in her direction. Minnie retreated behind the column then slinked back around to once more watch his reaction to Danielle.

He lowered his eyelids and blocked her intrusive probing. Minnie didn't know what it had been like for him. Although he had not loved Charisse, he did feel guilty about her death. His first wife was just as tragic a memory. Alexa had survived seventy-three years as his queen. Unfortunately, she had hated all things about being a vampire, especially him. Once the transformation had been completed she had refused to accept him as husband. She had lived the life of a recluse until one day she had stepped out onto the balcony at sunrise. His court had been quick to proclaim it an accident, but he knew Alexa had finally managed to do what she had so often threatened. Suicide.

Was he so unlovable? He looked at Danielle and longed to taste her luscious lips. Women hungered to make love to him. They poured into his club, openly propositioning him. But there was the constant risk his next wife would become just like Alexa or Charisse once turned. Any transformation was unpredictable. Some were little more than animals while others retained their intellect and personality. There was no way to predict the effects of becoming vampire.

"It's because, unlike us, brother, they began as humans. Humans just don't seem capable of accepting our *lifestyle*. Their transformations have too many variables."

"Can you blame them for not wanting to become what we are?" he asked. "If given the choice would you have been a vampire?"

"Better than being a *human* any day. Humans. They respond one of two ways, they either hate us and want nothing to do with us, or they end up like Charisse, wild with a thirst stronger than any of us ever had. She was my biggest failure. At least Alexa was calmer. I promise this one shall be different. As the Royal Mentor, I've fulfilled my sacred duty and delivered one most worthy to you. She is very different from the others. I feel it," she whispered.

"Do you?" he asked and let his gaze travel over Danielle, delighting in the deep blush that crept over her beautiful face when she noticed his stare.

"I believe you're pleased," Minnie purred in his ear.

"I shall let you know—later."

"My expectations have not changed, Armondés."

"And neither have mine, sister."

"Good. As long as we understand each other."

"There's never been any doubt that I understand what you want."

"And I, *you*." She moved again, molding her lithe body against the column. "She's very beautiful. Don't you think?"

"Indeed," he said, letting his stare linger. He knew her skin would be warm and soft under his touch. His gaze traced the gentle sculpting of bare shoulder, and the enticing arc of her neck. His attention riveted to the single throbbing heartbeat. He inhaled through flared nostrils, drawing in her scent as one would a fine wine. His mind buzzed with her seductive essence. If she were truly not yet thirty then she was perfect.

"Yes, she's perfect, and still twenty-nine. You have two hours," Minnie cooed, reading his thoughts, again. "*Plenty* of time."

"Enough! Stay out of my head, sister." His voice was like ice crackling over a frozen pond. He lowered his eyelids and threw what he intended to be a warning glare over his shoulder.

Minnie stiffened and quickly slinked away to sit down in the booth. Silent. Good. The less he had to deal with her intrusions the better. His sister's move to the city had proven more than he'd bargained for. While it was true he was running out of time and by royal right she held the position as procurer of his mate, it didn't mean he had to like it. Any more of her interference and—

"I heard that, brother. Were it not for my *interference*, you'd not have your prize this evening. Just remember that."

He released Danielle's stare and pivoted to glare down at his sister. Her eyes widened with a fear he'd not seen for a very long time.

"Do you flatter yourself to think only you can procure my mate? Is that what you think?"

"N-no," she said and looked away. "It's my job, though. You are obliged to accept my submissions."

"While that may be true, you should realize I can attain whatever woman I desire. You merely conduct a service for me, and we've yet to know how well you've done this time in the selection."

"As you said, it's my royal duty and I honor it by trying to find just the right mate. I scan them...I just felt—" she swallowed.

"Guilty?" He smiled slightly, hoping his contempt for her reflected in his expression.

"I do, even though it wasn't my fault. Charisse was—"

"Hunted down? Is that the phrase you seek?" he asked, "or was it more like betrayed?"

"You know that's not true. It's a vicious rumor started by those who envy my position as your sister. They wish only to drive a wedge between us."

"Spare me," he said, holding his palm in front of her. "Your duty is done, see about her friends. I don't want them knowing anything further about my club. Understand?"

Minnie nodded and slipped from the booth to greet the women.

"Come, ladies, I have a wonderful surprise for our birthday girl. Please, allow me to introduce Armondés Tresnávé." She turned to the man now standing beside her.

* * * * *

Danielle realized his charisma, across the room, had been diffused, because up close and in his presence the tingling sensation intensified. It was as though a slight wind tickled over her skin, awakening all nerve endings. It raced over her breasts all the way to her pussy in a hot ache. The wet heat flooded from her and an overwhelming need to feel him seared hot pulses to her groin. An urge to grind herself into him and feel him thrust—

"Danielle?" Amy asked.

She jerked from the daydream and looked about.

"I'm sorry, what?"

Her friends' nervous volleying of laughter echoed over the crowd.

"I asked if you've ever met a king before," Minnie repeated.

"Ah, no."

"Allow me, my sister is not very adept in introductions. I'm Armondés Tresnávé." The six-foot-plus, dark-haired man took her hand before she could react. He lifted it to his lips, but stopped, allowing only a soft breath to brush against her skin. Or had it been a sudden draft? She wasn't sure. It was so faint a sensation.

"Sister?" She looked at her friends who didn't seem shocked. A small detail they had forgotten to mention.

"And my sister is teasing about the king part," he said, straightening his muscular frame and sending a searing glare in Minnie's direction.

What was between these two? Sibling rivalry? Danielle considered them for a brief second before Amy and Lillian practically elbowed her out of the way so they could shake hands with the mesmerizing Armondés.

"I'm Amy and you have the coolest club I've ever been in," she gushed, not even trying to hide her desire.

"I think your reputation has exceeded your capacity. I noticed the waiting line tonight was almost to the corner. I'm Lillian, we met last weekend." She flashed a wide smile.

"Everyone wants to play at Armondés." Minnie's voice trailed off when her brother shot a warning glare. He shifted his attention to Danielle.

"But I'm very selective who gains entry." His lips parted slightly, and her heart flip-flopped. "Only very beautiful women and very few men." His laughter was sharp and held a darkness in its depths. A deep chill ripped through her. She took a step back, but was unable to break from his stare.

"Come, ladies, I have some of those very few men dying to meet you." Minnie grabbed Amy's arm and tugged on Lillian's long hair. "Let's leave these lovebirds alone. We have some real wolves to tend to."

"They're that wild?" Lillian's voice trembled with unbridled excitement.

"You've no idea," Minnie purred and left Danielle standing all alone with the mysterious Armondés.

"There now, I see fear in your eyes. Why should I frighten you?"

"I have no idea," she said and straightened her back, meeting his bold stare, daring him to challenge her further. She soon regretted her brashness.

"I find you irresistible, standing there trembling with your fists clenched so tightly by your sides. The last thing I want to do is frighten you." He leaned closer, letting his body brush against her. "Why do you feel so intimidated by me?"

"Are you serious?" She cleared her throat and turned her back to him, and struggled to focus on the chaotic dance floor. Strobe lights flashed blue then green across writhing bodies then bathed the crowd in red. The music throbbed with the partygoers, making it impossible to know if the music drove the dancers or if their energy created the music.

His presence was like a magnetic charge behind her. She sensed his stare travel over her, touching her head then her neck, slipping between her shoulder blades to sweep down the dip of her back. She was grateful the gown blocked his gaze.

His large hands molded over the mounds of her shoulders. Firm fingers massaged gentle circular motions over her flesh. A small groan escaped her. Danielle knew it was careless to embrace such abandonment, but a part of her didn't care. He excited her like no man ever had. While intrigue could truly create excitement, there was something else about him.

"You feel just the way I knew you would."

She swallowed the heat in her throat, but it raced past her attempt, bursting hot in her ears.

"I guess you're used to having whichever woman you desire. I mean…" she said, stammering over the words. "What I mean is, I know my own friends are blinded by your good looks and obvious wealth. And, the mystique surrounding a nightclub owner—"

He turned her around to face him, keeping her within the circle of his arms. Her knees weakened, but she managed to remain standing. His strong features stood out against the flashing colored lights, lending greater strength and an illusion of power she knew would flee in the brilliance of daylight. After all, he was a master at creating atmosphere, just look at the way the club was decorated and how he played the role of dark master of his little universe.

"And you're immune to me?" His voice reached her ears, pressing past the din of the club.

"I don't know if that's the word I'd use," she said, trying to infuse greater bravado in her tone. She would not allow him to dominate her so easily.

"I understand it's your birthday, today." His voice was melodic and held erotic promises in its seductive depth.

"No, it's tomorrow, the eighteenth, but my friends thought it better to celebrate tonight. I think they felt kidnapping me from work was easier than getting me to agree to this on a Saturday."

"Why did they feel they had to kidnap you?"

"It's a long story." She managed to pull slightly from him, placing a little distance between them. That was better. She lifted her chin and stared up into his handsome face, noticing the way his dark eyes masked against any probing gaze. What was he hiding?

"You're so young, yet so very wary of the world. What causes one to become so frightened at such an early age?"

"I'm not frightened nor am I that young, thank you. I'll be thirty in," she said, pausing to glance at her wristwatch, "one hour and forty-five minutes."

"Oh, that's different. In that case, we should have some champagne to toast you into the next decade of your life. Don't you agree?"

She smiled, not because she felt relaxed in his presence, because she certainly didn't. It was because he honestly thought thirty was young. Here she'd been agonizing over leaving youth behind her and this gorgeous man thought she was too young to be jaded about life and wary of what? Men? Well, after that man she'd been married to, she had every right to mistrust the bastards. Perhaps in Armondés' world—she glanced about the club, flashing a quick look at the couples moving about the dance floor—she was an enigma. None of these women seemed to distrust men. She watched a dominatrix crawl into one of the corner booths, leading a man wearing a dog collar.

"Ceirdo?" He called to the man who stood nearby, trying to look nonchalant, but obviously there to await his boss's orders. He responded by turning and disappearing through the pair of ornately carved wood doors, leading to what she assumed was the kitchen. Never mind that the music was deafening, or that he had stood nearly ten feet from them and could not have overheard their conversation, much less Armondés' summons. Perhaps it was a standing cue between them that it was time for him to retrieve champagne.

"Come, allow me to treat you the way a queen should be treated." He took her hand in his. The contact of his flesh sent a rush of new sensations through her. She tottered on the edge of something. Unsure she was ready to take the plunge he so obviously expected her to take, she cleared her throat.

"Queen?" She pushed the word past trembling lips.

"Queen for the day? For those who celebrate their birthdays?"

He guided her toward a draped booth. Danielle hesitated, glancing about the other booths, closed from view by the heavy, red velvet draperies, but it was evident what was going on behind them. The silk-covered mattress glared at her.

"But your booths don't have any tables," she argued.

"Of course not. Didn't you notice the motif throughout my club? It's Romanesque, of sorts, with a mixture of medieval. The

Romans were great loungers. They ate from couches, beds actually. What? Do you find it uncomfortable?"

"Well, yeah! I don't know you. Don't you have a regular table or something?" She looked around for one.

"Here, you don't have to lie down. Just sit on the edge, like this." He pulled her down onto the thick mattress beside him.

Her stomach fluttered. Even though he made it sound so natural and almost innocent, it was anything but.

"Master." The bulky man dressed in tight leather pants and a very gothic-style vest held the tray in front of Armondés.

The bottle was already opened and two glasses rested on the tray. She squinted against the dim flickering light, realizing Ceirdo had already poured their drinks. Her pulse quickened. She knew about date rape drugs and well, she wouldn't put much past anyone in this place, especially its owner, whose employees called him *Master*! He really did get into character for his club. Nervously, she looked around for Amy and Lillian. How could they just desert her like this? Did they think this was a birthday present? Armondés?

"Does drinking champagne always upset you so?" he asked. She was sure amusement danced in his eyes, but when she raised her stare, it was fire that flickered in those depthless pits. Her breath latched in her throat.

"Do I appear upset? It's just this is all so strange. I've never been to a place like this."

"And you find it unnerving?"

"Yes," she said. "I truly do."

"What do you find uncomfortable? Tell me and I will change it."

She laughed, but the hard look in his eyes assured her, he meant it.

"It's just a bit, well, I don't want to hurt your feelings." She took the tall flute of champagne he thrust into her hand.

"My feelings are not easily bruised. Please, it's your birthday, you may have whatever you desire."

His voice was strong and deep. It seemed to vibrate through her, racing to all her tender places. She lifted the champagne glass to his. It was as though the club froze, as though no one moved and the world didn't exist. It was just him. He was all there was. And she was with him, staring into his intense, dark eyes. His square jaw clenched then released as his lips parted slightly into a very satisfied smile.

"Happy Birthday, Danielle, my queen of all I possess. Now *drink*."

Heat rose in her. She tilted the goblet back and let the bubbly liquid enter her mouth and rush toward the back of her throat.

"*Drink*," he said again.

She hesitated then swallowed with a wave of acceptance that startled her. It was as though she watched herself from somewhere secluded, aware her body was responding to something beyond her control. She should have been frightened, but panic was quickly replaced with a burning need. It radiated through her entire body, sending heated throbs radiating to her clit. She squirmed in the seat, crossing her legs, but that only intensified the erotic spasms. If she didn't know better she'd swear she was having an orgasm. She squeezed her legs tighter. Her pussy pulsed harder.

"What would a queen desire for her birthday?" he asked and nodded to Ceirdo, who took their glasses, then handed Armondés a long jewelry box. As though she were drugged, her eyes seemed to cross as she tried to focus on the wrapping. It appeared to be a silk-like material with three rosebuds serving as a bow.

"Oh, my God, what is this?" she asked, feeling a little lightheaded. The purple gift blurred in front of her.

"Just a small token from your king."

"You're really good at this game," she said.

"Do you think I'm playing a game?"

"Of course. You're this grand club owner who's used to having whatever woman you want. You have money, obviously. Don't mind spending it. Like to play the role of a king."

"Are you criticizing me for planning ahead of time for your visit to my club? I had hoped my hospitality would be something pleasing, not insulting. When my sister told me about their plans to bring you here tonight, I thought I could make it a nicer evening for you. I see I haven't done that. I'll leave." He stood. Her heart sank.

"No!" She jumped up beside him, grabbing his hand. The room spun slightly. She staggered, but strong arms came around her waist. She didn't pull from his hold. His hard body felt good against her. "I didn't mean to insult your thoughtfulness. You've just taken me by surprise. That's all. I didn't know this was all planned."

"It's okay, Danielle." He lifted his other hand and threaded long fingers into her hair. A small groan escaped her lips. He tugged her hair, pulling her head back, angling it to receive his kiss. What was it with this guy? He seemed to cast some kind of spell over her every time he touched her. She waited for the touch of his lips. She knew it would be a powerful kiss, an all-consuming heat. She longed to feel him. Her lips ached to touch his, but the kiss never came. She opened her eyes.

"Then you will accept my birthday gift?" he asked and held the purple silk box adorned in white rosebuds in front of her. Slowly, he relaxed the hold on her hair, but didn't move his hand. Instead, he ran his fingers through its length.

"Of course," she said, feeling stupid for making such a big deal over the evening. Her fingers gripped the silky wrappings. "It's so beautiful." She sat back down, placing the gift in her lap. He moved with her, sitting easily beside her.

"What's inside is even more beautiful," he whispered against her ear, sending chills tumbling down her back. "Just as I'm certain what's inside you is even more beautiful." Firm fingers pulled through the length of her hair again then moved to trace imaginary circles along her bare shoulder blades. His hand slipped over the back of the dress, gliding down the material. Fire radiated from his touch as he pressed his palm into the small of her back. Excited streaks of pleasure coursed to her groin and she licked her lips.

Her pulse pounded in her ears, drowning out the frantic rhythm of the music. Trying to focus on untying the satin ribbon that held the roses to the package, she noticed her hands were trembling against the knots.

"Allow me," he said, and leaned so close his scent rushed toward her as though it were a living entity. An enticing mixture of old-world aromas she instinctively knew were rare, yet commonplace for him filled her nostrils. The headiness seeped into her very pores and intoxicated her. Touching the tip of her tongue to her lower lip, Danielle glanced up into his handsome face. She swallowed hard. His lips were just inches from hers. The need to taste those soft moist lips overpowered all thought. Just a small taste wouldn't hurt. She tilted her head slightly then stopped. And once tasted, would she be sated or would be become addicted? Would she need to trace the length of his chest with her tongue all the way to his cock?

Her own thoughts shocked her and she struggled to clear the seductive haze encircling her, but his nearness unsettled her with an edgy, excited need. She felt the package slip from her and heard the ribbon give under his efforts, but her eyelids were leaden. Her lashes fluttered closed. She tried to open them wider. The sound of the box opening on its hinges seemed to break the spell. Her stare widened on the contents, nestled against the deep purple lining.

"Are those real?" she asked, quickly feeling foolish for uttering yet another insult. The diamond necklace sparkled under the flashing lights. Shards of brilliant prisms pierced right into her line of vision, blinding her momentarily.

"I never give anything that's not real." He moved to fasten the necklace around her neck.

"I can't. Really. These must be worth a fortune."

"Yes, they are, and fit for a queen, don't you think?" He released the necklace.

It weighed heavily against her chest. The diamonds and gold were cold against her skin, but quickly warmed.

"Hand me the mirror," he said, turning to Ceirdo, ever-present and waiting for the next order. Armondés held the mirror up to her. Her vision filled with the incredible diamond necklace that rested against her ivory skin looking as though she'd always worn it. She brushed her fingertips over the diamonds.

"This is part of the birthday joke, I know, but I would love to wear this necklace for the evening. It's gorgeous."

"You may wear it every evening if you choose. It's yours."

"I can't," she protested again, but this time her words were silenced by chilled lips brushing against hers. Her pussy quivered and wetness rushed between her legs. All he had to do was look at her, barely touch her, and she was a frenzied mass of heat and need.

"I want to see what you have hidden under those panties," he whispered. The husky edge of his voice sent excited shivers over her and her nipples hardened in response.

"I think we're moving too fast," she said, struggling to keep the trembling from her voice and trying to shift from him, but she couldn't move.

"Baby, I don't do it fast. I like it nice and slow." His breath blasted hot against her ear. Her heartbeat thumped harder and she finally stumbled to her feet, moving slightly from the booth. She staggered but regained her balance, staring at the sea of faces streaked with flashing lights. Where were Amy and Lillian? Just wait until she caught up with them. She reached underneath her hair and tugged against the necklace clasp. His hand covered hers.

"Keep them. They belong to you."

"They're not worth the price you ask." She jerked from him and tried to unclasp the necklace again, but his hands covered the attempt once more.

"I wasn't asking you to pay for them, Danielle," he whispered against her ear and she suddenly found herself standing in his embrace. How had that happened?

"Really? It sounded like proposition to me." She turned in the circle of his arms and flattened her hands against his chest, determined to push from the hold.

"Stop struggling so." He brushed smooth fingertips against her forehead.

Her knees weakened. The lights spun around her and a loud ringing filled her ears.

"What have you done to me?" she asked. The room darkened and she slumped forward over his arm.

Chapter Three

"Where am I?" Danielle asked, blinking at the unfamiliar room. Realizing she was lying on a bed, she sat up. The sudden movement sent her back to the pillows with a groan. Searing pain pierced the residue clouding her mind, and she massaged her temple with clammy fingers against her temple.

"Here." Armondés kneeled beside her, holding a glass of what appeared to be water.

"What's that?" Her own tone of voice unnerved her.

"I'm only trying to help you. You fainted." He held the drink in front of her. "Let me help you sit up, but take it slowly." He gripped her upper arm and steadied her onto the edge of the bed.

"I suspect it was a combination of excitement and champagne," he assessed.

She took the glass from him, feeling more than a little embarrassed.

"You're a tad dehydrated. You'll feel better once you drink." He tipped the glass to her lips. As though she were his puppet, Danielle drank the water, only it had a bitterness that at first she thought was lime then realized it wasn't. She pushed the glass away.

"What's in it?" She narrowed her stare on him, unsure if she should be angry or frightened.

"Just a small remedy made of aspirin and herbs." He moved the rim to her lips.

"Herbs?" she asked and pushed the glass back into his hands. "I want to go home." She tried to stand but staggered into his arms. Her face scraped against his hard muscled arm.

Her pulse spiked. What had she gotten herself into? What had Amy and Lillian gotten her into? Fear was not even an adequate word. Terror. Yes, that came closer to what she felt when she lifted her gaze to his. His was a mixture of coldness and heat. Her mind groped for something, anything, to anchor her to the real world, but reality was a cloudy illusion of thoughts and emotions.

"Have a care, now. Sit." He gently deposited her back onto the edge of the bed, setting the glass on the antique nightstand.

"Where are we?" she asked, deciding to sit until her mind cleared. Had he drugged her? Was that what had happened? The thought quickened her breathing. She must leave!

"This is my home. I live above the club."

She tilted her head, but couldn't hear the ever-present pounding beat she remembered from the club.

"I spent a lot of money soundproofing it." He pulled the nearby chair beside the bed and sat across from her. "Are you allergic to alcohol?"

"No, why would you ask such a question?" She frowned over at him.

"I've never seen anyone react quite this way." His voice dropped off. "I mean, it was a good year."

"What?"

"The champagne vintage. It was from my best collection. Did you know fossils have been recovered proving wild vines thrived as far back as a million years ago?"

"Huh?" She blinked, confused.

"Champagne. I was telling you about it just before you collapsed. Do you not recall? Well, it doesn't matter. The world almost lost French wines due to a Roman decree that all the vineyards in France be dug up so as not to compete with the Italian wines. My family's roots have been traced back to that period, around 92 A.D. during the reign of Emperor Domitian. But he failed to understand the French passion about our vineyards. The vines were hidden and cultivated in secret. For even then French wines, especially those from Champagne, were prized above all others."

"Your family had a vineyard?"

"Has."

Realization struck her.

"Oh, how stupid of me. Tresnávé Champagne and Armondés Vineyards are world-renowned." She felt stupid. How could she not have connected it before?

"Oui," he said. His shoulders squared, and he seemed to literally grow taller. Clearly he represented an ancient bloodline, old money and old traditions with a business tossed into the mix. She could only imagine such lineage and knowledge of one's past. The only family she had was an aging aunt.

"The champagne I served you is quite antiquated. This particular vintage is believed to have been lost centuries ago during a fire. But my family managed to rescue it and decided to keep for use on special occasions."

"Oh my, and here I fell ill to such an expensive gift. Please forgive me."

"Not at all. It's rare for one to react in this manner, but it's foolproof."

"Foolproof?"

"It's the champagne used over the centuries to test for compatibility. It saves making mistakes."

"What?" she asked, feeling as though she must still be cotton-headed, because he was making no sense.

"The men in my family open one of these bottles when they meet the woman they feel destined to be their, well, wife."

She must have turned pale because he rushed to catch her, but she steadied herself, bracing against his hard body.

"If the woman is truly the man's mate, she shall grow ill and faint. Just as you did."

"It's definitely time for me to leave." She stood, and he rose with her, but held her upper arms between his large hands.

"You think I am eccentric?"

"No, just a tad rusty on the one-liners. The last thing I want to hear right now, on this day, is a marriage proposal, whether merely a pick-up line—"

"I see. You had a bad marriage?"

"I did. I ended it three years ago, but the experience left me more than a little cynical about the whole institution of marriage—especially the male component."

He nodded, but didn't relax his hold. He stood staring down at her with an expression not of the expected anger at being rejected. Instead, his eyes held warmth and well, a consoling softness that totally disarmed her.

"Tomorrow marks the one-year anniversary for me."

"I had no idea. I'm sorry. Divorce?" she asked, unable to believe any woman once ensnared in his bed would ever leave.

"She...died."

Danielle nodded. It explained so much. He was grieving. Probably looking for someone to confide in. Maybe his need was more a longing, like hers. Just not wanting to be alone, only she didn't want to admit it to anyone. Still, it was odd that they should share such a common painful experience, although the circumstances were quite different. Not at all what she had expected of a man like him. It was difficult enough to end a relationship like she had, but to have it taken from you without a choice must have been horrible for him. Sympathy for his loss overwhelmed her.

"I'm sorry for your loss," she said and touched his arm. "I truly am, but I must be going now." She brushed past him, focusing on the door.

"You can't go."

She turned and found him standing in front of one of the broad tapestries suspended from the high vaulted ceiling. His footfalls were silenced by the thick Aubusson rugs covering the rich hardwood floors.

"It's late." She tried once more and turned from him, dodging the gilded marble table jutting from the wall. Her mind screamed for her to leave, but something inside pleaded for her to stay. It was unlike any feeling she'd ever known. Absently, she glanced up at the painting as she passed, but the texture and color brought her to a halt mid-stride. Soft golden light fell over the oil canvas, but it was the style that gave her pause. She knew it so well, like any good art student would.

"Renoir?" she muttered then turned to glance over her shoulder at him, only he wasn't behind her. She turned back around and cried out when she found him standing in front of the door. How had he done that?

"Yes. It's part of my collection. I like to keep them in a safe place, but every so often just ache to have one grace my home."

"You own a Renoir?" she asked, taking a moment to study it again.

"Several actually. I have most of them on loan to museums. Art like this needs to be shared, but I admit I'm rather greedy when it comes to my private collection. I like to bring them back home every now and then to enjoy all by myself."

"And the one over there is an Antonio Pisanello?"

"Very good, you are an art connoisseur?"

"No, I studied art in college."

"And your favorite?"

"Erotic art always intrigued me." She wondered why she had shared that with him. She had never revealed to anyone her secret love affair with erotic art. Would it have mattered to her husband if she'd told him? "Erotic art seems to be something most artists avoid. I'm not sure why, perhaps it is too personal. The Greeks and early Romans however even portrayed it in their pottery," she said then stopped, feeling she'd revealed too much about herself.

"Yes, almost decadent by the twentieth or even our twentieth-first century social expectations. Come see my favorite." He led her toward the center of the room where a large round painting, spotlighted by a soft golden hue, hung on the back wall of the elegant room.

"It has to be a copy, the original's in the Louvre," she said, marveling at the painting.

"So they say," he said and moved to stand closer to her. So close, his body slightly brushed against hers. "But the truth be told, I could not part with this one. Pierre Masterique's best work," he said.

"You *own The Restless Harem*?"

"Yes, but I assure you, none of the women in the harems were quite this white." He laughed.

"You've seen a real harem? Actually been inside one?"

"This painting certainly did create a stir of gossip when Pierre first unveiled it in 1725."

"You sound as though you knew him," she said and let her gaze wander over the painting.. It was truly a masterpiece of nudes that seemed to undulate and entwine like serpents. She wanted to touch the canvas so badly, instead, balled her hands into hard-knuckled fists by her sides.

"No, it was created to be felt by more than just your eyesight." He reached out and gathered her fist in his hand.

"Unclench your fist," he said, and she complied with his command. "Good, now then, very carefully." He held her open hand inside his larger one and guided her to the scene of light and dark shadows. She tried to count the number of hues the artist had used for flesh color, but found it impossible. The nude women seemed to flow from one pose to another.

"You know what it feels like, don't you?" he asked.

"What?"

"To take the basic materials and mold them into something different, yet so beautiful. Transform it into something more than it was intended to be."

"I...I don't know." Her hand trembled in his as he pulled her toward the painting. She wanted so much to touch it, yet feared she would harm it. She'd always wanted to explore the paintings in museums, but they were roped off, kept at a safe distance, with "do not touch" signs, which only made her long to feel them more.

"You have my permission to touch this painting, Danielle," he whispered in her ear, sending cascades of delightful shivers down her back. "Just imagine, your fingertips touching the paint laid down by the master's hand."

Her fingers tingled and a thrill so deep, she knew not where it resided, emerged when the ends of her fingers brushed against the hard surface, ridged with colors and movement.

"Oh my God!" she gasped and allowed him to move her fingers over the scene of the nude woman, sitting in repose on the red rug with several other nude women. This one leaned back with her arms bent over her head, so her breasts rose high above her waist.

"Imagine what she felt like, lying there naked. Of course he used the same model for most of the women, so she posed in different positions under his gaze as his brush penetrated the paints and ground them against the pallet. What do you think she was doing when he brushed the oils onto the canvas and gave her the expression you see?" He guided her hand to the woman's rounded face, tilted upwards. Pressing her fingertips against the woman's rosy splotched cheeks, he guided her to caress the smooth paint, then slid to trace the gazing eyes only to drift back to the slightly parted smile.

"And as he watched her writhing there on the rug, naked except for the necklace, his brush moved faster and faster in a desperate attempt to capture the fullness of her breasts. See how he painted their bounty by giving light and shadow with the soft flesh hues?"

Her pulse throbbed.

"And with a delicate stroke to the fullness, he created two nipples, erect and poised for eager lips." He lifted his other hand to her breast and thumbed over her nipple, teasing it to hardness. Her pussy moistened.

"Then his masterful strokes fleshed out the narrow waist, fanning to the part of the female that a man most worships. Her shaved pussy." He breathed heavily in her ear. She licked her lower lip.

"And did she shave it for the artist?" she asked, surprising herself with the question.

"Yes. He demanded she do so. Pierre wanted to see it. How else could he paint it in all its feminine glory?" His fingers threaded through hers and locked in a firm grasp as he slid her hand to the woman's pussy. "Do you think she grew moist as she lay there, letting his eyes move over her while he painted the canvas vigorously, longing to capture her essence?"

"I…I…" she stuttered.

"I want you. You're going to belong to me." His words sent a scorching heat over her face.

"I don't know you," she gasped, her words barely audible to her own ears.

His fingers spread over her breast, and his large hand cupped it.

"I think Pierre grew more and more aroused as he guided his brush to recreate her beauty. He knew every inch of her voluptuous body but professionalism prevented him from tasting her. Oh, he longed to taste her. He would run his own tongue over his lips as he watched her ease her forefinger into her pussy and spread herself while he watched." He squeezed the fullness of her breast in his hand.

Her clit throbbed, longing for his fingers to travel down her belly and beneath her panties.

"And he maintained his self-control as best he could, until his hand shook so much, he could no longer guide the brush in even strokes. Then, he would take a break, turning quickly on his heel to hide his erection from the model. He'd disappear into the privacy of his cottage where he would long for relief, the kind only a woman can give a man." He lowered his head, letting his lips touch her neck ever so lightly. Her breath latched in her throat. His arm wrapped around her waist, and he jerked her against his hardness.

"See how hard I am for you? So he was for his model."

"Mmm." She touched her tongue to her lips, anticipating his kiss.

"Do you think he should have taken her? Fulfilled his deepest longings?" He ground himself into her, brushing against the rawness of her wet pussy.

Her body was not her own. She wanted him. His hard cock teased the heat between her legs. His sleek, rock-hard muscles brushed against her again. She needed him. She knew she should run from him, escape this strange place, but she wanted him. She wanted to touch him. Taste him. Feel him deep inside her.

Danielle groaned between heated kisses, and pressed into him.

"And so one day, overcome with the unsated need to know what it felt like to be inside her, Pierre seduced his round-buttocked model. Under her enchanted spell, he fucked her as no man had ever fucked a woman. Poor Pierre couldn't stop even when he longed to stop. Possession was his greatest need. He had to be inside her, for when he was not, his very soul seemed to rip from him."

Danielle groaned, needing to feel Armondés inside her. The dress's zipper gave under his deftness and she moaned when her dress didn't slip from her fast enough. A rush of cool air raced in its wake as it finally fell around her feet.

He lifted his face so he could look at her. Suddenly, she was glad she'd worn the bustier and crotchless thong her friends had given her.

He captured her lips with his. She lifted her leg around his hip and pulled him closer. He pressed into her, pushing her against the marble table. Her garter straps stretched and cut into her thighs. He ran his hand up her leg, stopping at the top of her black silk stocking. The elastic tugged against the lacy garter followed by a muffled snap. The tension released, sending the strap to her waist.

"I think Pierre's model would have been very jealous of you," he said with a deeper tone filling his voice.

"I think all women would be jealous of me if they knew I was with you," she said with labored breath, and held his face between her hands and met his hungry kiss.

His tongue darted between her lips and claimed her tongue, twisting around it as though afraid she would change her mind and try to flee. The last thing Danielle wanted at that moment was to leave.

His hands grasped her bare buttocks. The thong she wore pressed harder into her as his fingers tightened against her flesh, grinding his hard cock, trapped within the trousers, into her.

Deliberately, he eased her onto the marble top. The shock of the cool stone against her ass sent excited shivers racing through her.

"I want you," he breathed in her ear. Delightful quivers cascaded down her back, sparking an aching need between her legs.

She gasped, and raised one leg to his shoulder.

"My beautiful Danielle." He pressed chilled lips against the curve of her calf and slipped the stocking down her leg, tracing the path with unhurried kisses.

Danielle groaned, tilting her head back to lean against the wall, grateful for the solid support.

"I shall take you, Danielle, in many ways. I want to make you mine. Will you let me?" He released her leg, letting it slip to his side, and spread her legs wider.

"Yes. I'm yours."

Slowly he lowered his stare to where the bustier stopped and the crotchless panties now gaped open. From his deep groan of obvious appreciation she knew the sight of her shaven pussy, glistening with proof of her excitement, aroused him further.

The heat of his stare was almost a caress against her flesh. She squirmed, longing for his touch, and was rewarded by a look of intense hunger glazing his eyes.

She ached for his firm fingers to travel to her exposed moist heat. Her desperate, short breaths charged the very air as she waited for fulfillment. Instead, he stroked gentle trails down her arms with the back of his hands. Lightning streaks shot through her.

"Take me!" she begged.

Without warning, those same gentle fingers bit into her flesh and Danielle found herself thrust against the fine material of his pants. He grasped her hips and lifted her from the table, cupping her buttocks.

The movement created a rough friction between material and flesh that massaged the aching pulse between her legs. A demanding need to free the hardness trapped inside his pants tortured her.

"I want you, Danielle." His hand slid over her bare thigh, pulling the remaining stocking along the length of her leg. His stare followed the silky path. Her flesh scorched under his touch. She willed his hand to travel over her abdomen to her pussy, but he continued to tease her by running it down to her ankle then slowly back up.

His power seemed to radiate around them. All the blood rushed to her head when his firm lips, tasting like cool champagne, finally covered her trembling ones. She welcomed the demanding kiss, wanting more, desperately needing release from the fiery excitement devouring her.

His tongue teased against her moist lips then slipped inside to claim her mouth. Danielle moaned and savored the possession, entwining her tongue with his, then thrusting her tongue deep into his mouth. She writhed under the fervent rhythm as his hand trailed the curve of her hip, teasing the path down her leg again. But this time he paused. Anticipation, need and the aching expectation of his touch had made warm juices slip from her pussy. He shifted slightly and at long last cold fingers met throbbing flesh. Ragged breaths rasped from her as the edgy longings pulsed stronger under the firm strokes. His fingers pressed harder into her soft heat. Her moan vibrated against his kiss.

Armondés pulled from her clinging embrace, pressing quick kisses to her lips. Fluttering against a leaden tug, her eyelids opened to be met by a devilish look, one full of appreciation and desire.

"You're full of surprises, my Danielle. Your passion runs deep," he whispered, then glided his hand over her thigh toward her pussy. She lifted slightly from the table, arching into firm fingers as they pressed into her swollen nub. A deep sigh of pleasure trembled over her lips.

Danielle found herself lying on her back as he lifted one leg onto the table so she was spread open to his gaze. His deep hungry groan fell over her. Breath held, her pulse drummed a riotous beat, until at last he leaned over and flicked his tongue against her clit in quick rhythm. She moaned and bit her lower lip. Never had any man been so adept a lover. Each lash against her swollen clit sent a volley of heat coursing through her. Pressing her hand against the cold marble, she leaned back, captured by his expertise. Wave upon wave of pleasure and sensation inflamed her. Ravenous with desire, she whimpered and squirmed under his flicking tongue. His fingers probed her opening, teasing, entering then retreating, each withdrawal extracting a throaty moan from her. She needed him to finger-fuck her.

With his free hand, he dipped into the leather bustier and his fingers found a hardened nipple, pressing the roundness between thumb and forefinger with just enough pressure to send jagged streaks of pleasure to her groin. Danielle moaned under the additional sensation and he finally thrust his fingers into her pussy, his tongue whipping against her clit while his fingers fucked faster and harder.

She moved against the invading fingers as pulse after pulse radiated through her, bringing the edge of climax closer and closer. A shaky breath escaped her and muffled into a deep moan when his fingers withdrew.

"Don't stop," she begged.

She shifted to get closer, but he moved his hand and plunged those talented fingers into his mouth and sucked, groaning as he tasted her.

"Your juices taste like the finest wine. And I am the last man who will ever taste you, Danielle."

Her pulse pounded when he pulled the wet fingers from his mouth and reached down to softly caress her swollen lips, teasing with circular motions that brushed against her opening. Her clit was molten fire, radiating just beyond his strokes.

His gaze devoured her partially exposed body. Heat followed his stare, driving her beyond any point of self-control. She grabbed for him, but her fingers slipped and he moved.

"Why..." She swallowed the dryness, trying to sit up.

"Did I stop when you were so close to coming?" he asked, finishing her question.

"Yes. God, yes." She slid closer to him.

"Because I want you to see what is soon to be yours."

"W-what?"

The unmistakable sound of a zipper made her heart drum harder. Rising onto her elbows, she bit her lower lip and watched as the fly parted and his hard cock eased through the opening.

"Oh my!" she gasped at the very large cock. She ran her tongue over her lips, longing to taste him. A deep groan vibrated from him as those same strong hands now stroked the length of his thickness. Bracing himself with long legs locked in place, Armondés stood in front of her, a lazy smile spreading over his lips, making sure she could see him. Wildfire lashed against her swollen clit and she caught her lower lip between her teeth, wondering if she could take all of him.

"I want to fuck you, Dani, but it's going to be slow. Do you know why?"

She gulped and shook her head.

"Because I want you to come right at the moment of your thirtieth birthday." He nodded toward the large clock in the foyer.

Her vision blurred then sharpened on the Roman numerals. It was 11:45 p.m.

"Are you serious?" Her eyes widened on the teasing cock he still rubbed, denying her the pleasure of touching or feeling it plunge deep inside her.

"Very serious," he panted. She watched each stroke move up and down the thick shaft and pressed her lips together, longing to feel his cock thrust deep inside her.

"You're torturing me," she rasped, and leaned forward to touch him.

Her fingers closed around the hardness and moved up and down, gliding her hand with his. He leaned over and kissed her cheek, then moved one hand to lift her chin to meet his fiery stare.

"Patience, my love. You will thank me when you're thirty."

Chapter Four

"I don't understand," Danielle murmured, noticing the way his handsome face contorted in the dim light. It was an illusion of shadows, she told herself. She needed him to finish what he'd started, but he turned and her grasp around his cock slipped. Frustration bubbled inside her, yet before she could complain, he turned around, holding a silver chalice in front of her.

"Drink this," he said, raising it to her lips. The thin rim of cold metal pressed against her trembling lips. Expecting chilled champagne, she pursed her lips against the goblet, but was shocked by the warm, creamy liquid. The mixture slid down her throat, racing in a blazing trail to her stomach.

"What was that?" she asked and started to comment on the taste, but the buzz came fast and she slumped forward in his arms. The world spun around her, threatening to fade into unconsciousness.

"It's the last part of the ceremony." He brushed stray tresses from her face.

Fiery streaks shot to her feet as the liquid coursed throughout her system. She lifted her face and pressed her lips against his. The raging need returned with a pounding urgency that burst, moist, between her legs.

"I need you," she said, feeling groggy. Was it the wine?

"That too is part of the ceremony."

"W-what ceremony?" She pulled from him then paused. She really didn't care what he was up to, she just wanted him to fuck her. Now!

"You'll see." He pressed her backwards onto the table once more. "Do you know what happens when you turn twenty-nine, Danielle?"

"Hmm. I'm turning thirty. So far, frustration." She reached for his kiss, unconcerned about what he was saying. Her mind was numb from the wanton passion and an overpowering need to feel him inside her. "Come here." She surprised herself with the demanding tone that vibrated in the words.

"In a bit. This is a very significant time for you. Socrates said we gain our souls during our twenty-ninth year. Come midnight, you will own your soul."

"Good. I have but one question, are you going to make love to me or talk?"

"In time, my love. As part of the ceremony, I'm obligated to make sure you understand the ramifications of what we are about to do."

"I do. I understand how ramming is part of fucking," she giggled, feeling freer than she'd ever been. She would never talk this way in a sober frame of mind. The giddiness overrode all inhibitions. "And the ramification will be release and satisfaction when you finally fuck me," she gasped. Had those words really tumbled out of her mouth?

"So you understand then? Once you own your soul, Danielle," he breathed, "I'm going to help you relinquish it—in exchange for immortality."

His words penetrated the fog drifting through her mind. Did he just say he was going to take her soul?

"This is what you agree to when you ask me to take you."

"Uhm." She reached for him. "Enough talk."

"Are you certain this is what you want?"

"Oh, God, yes, I'm begging," she cried. "It's what I want, Armondés." She needed to feel him inside her. When she looked up into his handsome face, she met the dark piercing lust unmasked in his eyes. Her pulse raced.

Armondés leaned over and pressed his strong lips to hers. At last! She moaned, wrapping her arms around his neck, afraid the teasing was not over and he'd slip away once more. She had never been so determined about anything as she was that he was going to make love to her. Now!

His lips slid from hers to claim the curve where neck and shoulder met, pressing tender kisses into her flesh. She squirmed under the seductive trail of tingling sensations. His lips parted, sucking tender skin between them. She struggled to clear the haze holding her mind prisoner. Was he giving her a hickey?

"I was seventeen the last time I had one of those," she murmured. The pressure from the suction as her tender flesh slipped deeper inside his mouth sent sizzling currents to her pussy. Juices rushed between her legs, just as a new sensation of pain and pleasure radiated from the kiss. She jerked, moaning with the bite clamping deeper into her skin. What had he just done? Heat extended from the wound and coiled around her, wrapping her in deep sensuality. He sucked the wound, his tongue lashing her skin.

Her ears roared with a deafening flutter and an irresistible soothing flushed over her as though she were slipping into a warm bath. Her heart pounded faster. The sensation of her own blood coursing through her veins startled her. Groggily, she realized this was more than an ordinary kiss and pushed against his chest, but he caught her wrists and pinned her arms above her head, pressing her harder against the table.

"What are you doing to me?" she asked, surprised at how slurred her speech was.

"Making you my mate," he said and slid between her legs, his hard cock brushing her thigh.

He thrust into her and she gasped from the rough entry as it seared a tender path. Relaxing against the penetration, she moved to match his rhythm slowly at first, then faster. Excited, spellbound with heavy eyelids fluttering closed, she rolled her hips. He groaned against her neck and again found the tender spot. Her gasp grew into a cry when his teeth pierced the wound once more. Soreness was quickly replaced with an odd mix of pleasure and ache.

Hips tilted to greet his thrusts, she rocked against him, returning each plunge with a rotating grind. Her clit brushed against him with each contact, sending a frantic need to press harder against the raw heat tingling to her pussy. She cried out in frustration. His large hand slipped from her wrists and goose bumps trailed along the path of his fingertips. A rush of heat moved over her waist and stomach. She shifted to allow his hand between their joined bodies and arched her back, anticipating the urgent touch. The clock chimed. Groping fingers sought her pussy and finally brushed the swollen clit. She gasped at the welcome relief, wiggling against the rapid movement. He moved faster and increased the pressure. She ground into him, seeking release only the frantic rhythm could bring. The clock chimed loudly from the hall.

"I take you as my wife." The words huffed against her ear as he rammed his thick cock into her.

Heat surfaced. She pumped against him, needing it all. The ache snaked up her spine, rose to her head and burst bright against the darkness behind her closed eyelids. Release quaked through her, throbbing in a series of short spasms.

He groaned and drove deeper. The walls of her pussy clamped around the heated shaft. She grasped his buttocks and rolled her hips into each plunge. Wrapping her legs around his narrow hips, Danielle locked her ankles and rode him with wild abandon. The familiar slapping sound as his balls smacked against her, excited her further. His back muscles flexed under her hands as he pounded harder, hammering his cock deeper into her pussy.

The clock chimed again. She clung to him with heat flashing from her clit and racing up her spine. Armondés ground himself into her, pumping faster. Release teased her. Denied her. Then, suddenly, burst edgy fire raced to her head.

She shuddered in a wave of spasms. Undulating spikes of pleasure quaked through her in a final intensity.

"Now you belong to me," he said, driving himself faster until he, too, shuddered against her, releasing a groan of deep pleasure just as the clock's last stroke chimed. "My Danielle," he breathed, "according to the laws of my kingdom, we're now husband and wife. >From this moment you will now call me husband and I shall call you beloved wife." He moved in a gentle slow rhythm, still deep, but settling into a warm rocking as he pulsated inside her.

"Married?" she asked groggily.

* * * * *

"Is it true?" Minnie's high heels clicked against the marble floor. She marched the short distance from the landing and stopped in front of the man guarding her brother's suite. "Answer me. Is it true?"

"The king is resting, Princess, please." He held his hand up in front of her. "Do not cause a disturbance so late in the evening."

"It's almost sunrise, you imbecile. I need to talk to my brother while I still have time. I heard he finally succeeded in procuring a mate. Is this true?"

"I have orders he's not to be disturbed, Princess." The tall man didn't move.

"Stand aside or be dust." She drew a stake from behind her back.

"You have such a sense of humor, Princess." The guard took a step back.

"You think I'm kidding? Ask your predecessor. Oh, wait, you can't because he's dust. I want to talk with my brother, now!" She held the stake poised to strike the guard. He raised his arm, as though the large metal cuff around his wrist could shield him. Minnie watched the fear rising in his eyes.

"What's going on here?" Fredrick Van Cantrep, Armondés' best friend and business advisor, glared at the guard, who lowered his arm and nervously raked his hand through his blond hair, trying to appear undisturbed by the princess's threat. He resumed proper decorum with his hands clasped behind his back.

"Freddie, be a love and tell this ogre to step aside so I can talk with Armondés."

"The king is not to be disturbed, Minnie." Fredrick stood across from her with dark blue eyes glinting with a familiar look. She stiffened her spine, not daring to let her gaze dip below his waist, yet she was drawn to his groin like a magnet. The bulge confirmed her suspicions—her threat to destroy the guard had aroused Freddie. He was such a good masquerader, hiding from everyone but her just how much he loved to watch her hunt or in this case destroy a simple-minded guard.

"I just need to know if the rumors are true, Fredrick? Did he make that Danielle woman his mate?" she asked, trying to keep her voice from stretching an octave higher in her panic.

He grabbed her underneath the arm with fingers digging into her flesh a bit harder than necessary, yet she didn't try to jerk from his hold. She rather enjoyed the way he became all possessive and intense whenever he thought he was in control. She allowed herself to be pulled into the hall parlor. Fredrick released her with a shove and she came up against the wingback leather chair by the fireplace. She stood watching as he hurriedly closed the doors behind them.

"What are you up to?" he asked.

"I'm trying to find out if my brother is still youthful or if he turned into the ugly, ancient vampire he is. What the hell is wrong with you?" she asked and rubbed her arm, pretending it was bruised.

"I'm doing my duty. Our king doesn't want to be disturbed," he said, turning from her to pace over to the window. Minnie's gaze took in his strong Roman nose and powerful square jaw. Desire seared her and she reached for his arm but stopped a few inches short, imagining the feel of his muscles beneath her hand. The wanting always proved more exciting than the getting.

"The sun threatens." He nodded toward the cityscape of old buildings and beyond, where the river snaked along its path toward the ocean. A thin thread of lighter gray was beginning to emerge along the skyline.

"So speak fast before we must retire." She started across the room, pausing at the doors to glance back at him. A slow smile twisted his lips and she jerked the double doors open. Her stride quickened with her heels clicking against the marble floor as she hurried down the dark corridor to her suite. His footsteps resounded behind her.

He caught up with her inside the room and spun her around. Before Minnie could say anything, his lips covered hers. A deep longing ignited in her. Drawing her arms around his strong neck, Minnie molded her body to his. Fredrick released her and grabbed for the long velvet drapery, paused as though playing "chicken" with the sun, and then jerked the heavy material closed against the first rays of morning.

"You do love playing this game, don't you?" he asked.

"I thought you enjoyed my version of 'run for the coffin', Freddie?" She moved to the bed, longing to feel its comfort beneath her. "Tell me now. Is it true? Did he take that woman? Is my brother still the youthful-looking, handsome king, or did he miss the deadline and transform into the two thousand and seventy-five year old vampire he really is?"

"He's still the handsome young king. The civil ceremony will be in a couple of weeks or whenever the transformation is complete. Armondés informed me early this morning. I tried to find you so I could tell you, but you must have been busy with those two friends of the bride's. I hope you didn't kill your food this time, love." Fredrick shed his tuxedo jacket and tugged on the bow tie, all the while keeping his stare centered on her.

Minnie smiled, liking the way his gaze moved over her.

"I don't think Armondés meant for you to kill Danielle's friends." He tossed the jacket on a nearby chair and stood a few feet from her.

"Oh please, Armondés could care less about those twits. He's too enamored of Danielle."

"I'm sure he will care." His wicked smile assured her Fredrick had no real concern for what had happened to the women.

"Well, I don't care." She kicked off her shoes, aiming for his groin, but the two high heels sailed over his head. He glanced at the shoes, then shook his head. A menacing sneer settled over his sharp features.

"So why are you wearing the tux?"

"Armondés wanted the civil service performed earlier this morning. I didn't know if I'd have time to dress later."

"Oh, gawd! My brother is such a hopeless romantic. A wedding ceremony complete with tux? Did he really think she'd be in any condition this morning?"

"It appeared she was until about thirty minutes ago."

"And what happened?"

"The usual. She's a real mess."

"Well, good. Do you think her transformation will be as advantageous for us as the last bride's was?" She stood beside the bed and let her dress fall to the floor.

"Only time will tell, my love." His lips lifted into an appreciative grin as he pulled the tie from around his neck and moved closer. Minnie curled one leg underneath her and sat on the edge of the bed—waiting. She had fed all night, and was now ready to make love to Fredrick all day. Gliding her hand up the spiral post, she leaned forward so the fullness of her breasts pressed over the low-cut bra. The pose induced the kind of reaction she'd wanted when he reached out and grabbed her by the arms. Roughly, he dragged her from the bed into his powerful arms. Minnie laughed at the rough play, staring up into his eyes, blazing with hunger.

"My kills always excite you, lover." Minnie drew her arms around his hard muscled back, poised to receive a ravenous kiss. She would ride him until he begged for mercy.

* * * * *

"Wake up, my love." His voice was golden sunshine piercing into the abyss. "Come, Danielle, it's time to awake." Her mind was a jumble of images flashing from one scene to another. She groaned and pushed the dreadful dreams away. Weariness weighted her to the bed. Where was she? She snuggled deeper into the pillow. Arms encircled her, and pulled her tighter against him.

"Where am I?" she asked, opening one eye against the dimly lit room. Soft lamplight glared, sending sharp pains to her head. "What time is it?" Realization shocked her awake. She blinked against the red and gold bedroom décor, trying to place it.

"You're in my bed." His lips pressed against her shoulder. Delightful tingles cascaded down her back.

"Oh my. What happened?" She dared not turn to face him. She was naked. His hard cock was hot against her ass.

"You wound me. Surely you recall last night. Our marriage?"

"Our what?" She sat straight up in bed. Pulling the silky sheet with her, Danielle dug her heels into the broad mattress and managed to slide from him. She scrambled to the end of the bed and stared at him.

"Our marriage." His lips stretched into a slow, sexy grin as he held up his hand. The gold band reflected the light and pierced a brilliant shard right into her eyes. Fragmented scenes ran through her mind. Scenes remembered as dreams. It wasn't possible. How could she have done this? She forced a glance at her left hand and gasped. The wide gold band butted snuggly against a large ruby surrounded by sparkling diamonds.

"How? I don't understand," she whispered.

"We fell in love." He shrugged and reached out, but she pulled from his touch.

"That's insane. People don't just fall in love and get married on their first date." She looked at the wedding rings on her finger. The diamond had to be three, maybe even four carats. How did a man just happen to have such a ring on him? She was definitely still asleep. She'd wake up in her own bed. All she had to do was wake up. She squinted and tried to will herself awake.

"What are you doing?" he asked. The bed gave under his weight. She opened her eyes to find him on his knees in front of her—with an erection. Her stare widened. Had she taken that big thing inside her last night? Excitement tingled to her pussy. Moist heat rushed between her legs.

"This isn't real. I'm dreaming."

"It's as real as it gets, Danielle. Last night I didn't just make you my wife, I made you the queen of my clan. A clan of immortals."

The last part was too much for her. She was on her feet, searching the room for clothes, any clothes would do. His chuckle brought her frantic search to a halt. She gripped the sheet and turned with breath latching in her throat at the impossible image he made. He lay on his stomach, arms folded in front, resting his chin on them.

Her gaze slid over the handsome face, moving past broad shoulders to the slight, firm rise of perfectly formed buttocks. A scene flashed in front of her of grabbing his ass and shoving against him. She widened her stare.

"It wasn't a dream," she gasped. Realization crashed around her. She lifted a trembling hand to her neck but flinched from the searing pain radiating from the tender area. Danielle stumbled over to the dresser mirror and twisted her head to expose the ugly bluish marks. "You *bit* me. Why would you do that? That's not a hickey, that's a *wound*." She leaned forward, but froze when she realized the light from the lamp behind her was filtering through her stomach region.

"What is that?" She glanced at the lamp then back to the mirror. Her reflection was faint, like a ghost.

"It's okay. Really, we don't lose our reflections entirely. That's a myth of sorts. And your pallor will improve once you've had some blood."

She'd *not* heard that right. Her stomach rumbled.

"Yes, I could use some breakfast."

"We'll take it slowly at first. It's such a transition for most. A shock. I want to ease you into your new life."

"Look, this has been fun, but I really need to get home. If you could get my clothes..." She stared at him, longing to flee, yet wanting to feel him inside her again. His dark eyes held mysterious secrets offered in a brief glimpse last night. His touch remained imprinted in her memories. If this were a dream, then one more time with him would not matter. And she was certain it had to be a dream. Or, was it?

"Your clothes were ruined. I'll buy you new ones more suited for the new you. As Queen, you'll need appropriate attire. Don't you understand, my Danielle? Everything about you is different. As my wife, you now have certain royal duties. Oh, there's plenty of time to worry about those later. Once your transformation is complete Minnie will train you, teach you about the court and what is expected of our queen. Certain social etiquette. It's her duty as Court Mentor to serve us both in all social and courtly obligations. But, as your husband, I'll be your teacher in all other things."

She tilted her head slightly and stared at him, wondering if she had really heard what he had just said. He was playing a strange game and clearly was not the man she had thought he was. His sense of humor was more than merely different, it was downright bizarre. And he appeared to really enjoy the king and queen role-playing. It was time to go.

"I'm a very patient teacher. You'll see, my Queen," he added as though expecting a reaction from her.

A short snort-like giggle escaped her attempt to keep from bursting into laughter. She cleared her throat and fought to regain composure.

"Not that I'm not flattered, because I really am. But I have a million things I need to do today. It's Saturday. That means I have grocery shopping to do, dry cleaning to pick up, and the garbage can to roll from the street back into my yard. Well, you know the kind of things most Americans do on Saturday. Laundry? So if you'll forgive me, I'm going to find my clothes and just leave."

"Go ahead. Leave. You'll burn in the sun."

"Oh, I think I can survive without sunscreen, even if I'm going out in that very horrid dress my friends bought me. And speaking of them, where did my gal pals go?"

"Minnie introduced them to some guys."

"It figures." She wrapped the silvery sheet about her and put one hand on her hip, hoping he'd get the hint. "This has been a very exciting way to celebrate my birthday, but seriously, Armondés, I need to go. Where are my clothes?"

"Until I can take you shopping this evening, I'm afraid you must resign yourself to wearing that sheet." His eyes danced with excitement.

"This is no longer amusing. I need to go." She folded her arms over her chest.

"All you need, I can give to you. Come back to bed with me and let me make love to you. I will be a good husband to you, Danielle. You'll see. Being my queen can be very rewarding." He lifted himself up on one arm and swung his legs over the side of the bed.

"Oh, that is such a sweet line. Truly it is—" she backed toward the wide double doors, "—but as you can see, I'm not playing around."

He stood from the bed and took long strides toward her. Danielle looked away from his tall, naked body. She knew that just one look at his muscular frame would find her ensnared in his sheets again. He grabbed for her and got the sheet instead as she twirled out of it, lunging for the door.

Panic gripped just as his hand closed around her wrist and she slammed into the door. His hands were strong and turned her so her back was pressed against the door. He lifted her from the floor and spread her legs to straddle his hips. His hard cock plunged inside her and Danielle gasped. The entry seared a tender path until she relaxed around him. Grasping her hips, Armondés moved in and out, slowly at first, then faster. The roughness of the taking sent excited trembling over her. Aroused by his urgency, that drive to complete possession, she surrendered to her own flaming desire. His groan vibrated against her neck and once more his teeth sank into her flesh. Her moan grew into a cry but the soreness was quickly replaced with pleasure and liquid heat.

"We're going back to bed. This is our honeymoon."

"We are *not* married," she slurred, feeling giddy and stimulated by his strength.

"Then where did you get the rings?" He held up her hand with the jewels glinting from her finger.

Scenes and snippets of conversation crowded her mind. The room suddenly grew hot. She licked her lips against the sudden thirst, a drying heat that choked until tears streamed down her cheeks.

"Here," he said and cradled her in his arms, stroking her face with the back of his hand. "You're going to make yourself sick. You can't skip your very first meal. It's dangerous."

"First meal?"

"Yes, me." He held her effortlessly against him. His hard cock still inside her.

Her pulse throbbed at the thought. What kind of power did he hold over her? It had to be drugs. His lips brushed her forehead and her eyes fluttered closed, again. Try as she did, she couldn't open them. He showered kisses all over her face and carried her back to bed, walking slowly, balancing her as he remained deep inside her. Once by the bed, he stopped and lowered his face to capture her lips. The fervent kiss stole her breath and she gasped against his lips. Slowly, he withdrew, slipping her from the hard shaft. Danielle whimpered softly, reluctant to have him pull from her as he lowered her to the bed.

The warmth of the sheets greeted her and Danielle opened her eyes, surprised at how easily they opened when only moments earlier her eyelids had been weighted shut. He stood watching her lay naked in his bed, unashamed. Her pulse quickened. In fact, the way his excited gaze touched her breasts made her nipples harden. And when his stare slid down over her abdomen and paused at her pussy, she writhed in anticipation of his touch, but it didn't come.

Rocking her hips in a seductive circle, attempting to beckon him to take her, didn't budge him from where he stood with one hand firmly locked around his large cock, seeming to enjoy her agony. Even spreading her legs, opening herself to his gaze didn't make him come to bed, so Danielle slipped her fingers into her mouth then moved to her pussy where she spread the lips so he could see her clit. And still, he did not move to take her. She stroked a forefinger against the swollen nub, enjoying the molten sensation the movement created. His hand stroked his cock harder and she rubbed faster to match the rhythm. Moist urgency radiated from the friction created and she moaned. Determined to drive him wild with lust, she opened herself wider and inserted two fingers into the opening and plunged deep, rolling her hips provocatively.

A possessive throaty growl came from him and her hand was pushed aside. She smiled, satisfied the seduction was complete. Bracing his body with his hands flattened against the mattress, Armondés lowered his face to her pussy, flicking short, fast strokes against her clit. She wiggled under the teasing and pushed against him, hips moving to the tempo of his tongue. His forefinger plunged into her and the aching need eased, then rose. She ground against the pressure, moving to meet the finger-fucks.

Suddenly, she felt herself being lifted from the bed and turned onto her stomach. The mattress dipped as his weight eased behind her and he spread her legs apart. His hard cock rammed into her pussy and she pushed onto her knees to receive each powerful thrust. Strong fingers dug into her undulating hips as he pumped into her.

Excited surges trailed his hand as he slipped around her hip and cupped her pussy. New heat throbbed to the swollen nub. She bit her lower lip, longing for those long fingers to splay over her, spread her lips and rub her raw until she came.

Frustrated, she grabbed his hand and guided him, but he pulled from the attempt and once more cupped her. She shoved her hips into him and Armondés rocked backwards onto his knees, pulling her up into his lap. Finally, his fingers uncurled to drum staccato thumps against her clit, sending her into a frantic rhythm of need. Danielle pounded harder against his cock and suddenly found her legs lifted above her head. In one swift movement, she was sitting face-to-face, straddling his lap with his hard cock still inside her. Overwhelming new sensations quaked alongside the urgent yearning, different than anything she'd ever felt. Was it hunger? The gnawing surged from her groin, mingling with need and desire, growing in a fluid heat, burning a path to her eyes.

"Here," he said and shifted so her face was buried into his neck. "It's time for you to feed." He pressed her head toward his neck and she opened her mouth. She planted kisses along the strong line, sensing that was what he wanted, and then remembered the fierce hickey he'd given her. Of course, he wanted the same. She had experienced moments during sexual heights where she'd felt like biting, but this was stronger and completely different. Could she do it the same way he had done it?

"Feed, my love."

What did he mean by *feed*? Surely he wasn't suggesting—Her stomach pitched at the thought, but a low growl vibrated from her abdomen, born of a craving stronger than any she had ever experienced.

"Don't be afraid, it's part of our blood-bonding."

"I can't," she whimpered, tracing circles with her tongue against his neck. His cock pushed harder into her, arousing a driving need to taste him, a desire as strong as any sexual urge. She longed to take his flesh between her lips and pressed her mouth harder against his neck, sucking it past her teeth. The sensation was unbearable. She wanted to bite down, hard.

He rubbed her clit faster, thrusting his cock deeper. It was like a drumbeat as he pounded harder and harder. The heat built and rose like a furnace blast. She ran her tongue over his flesh, tasting him, wanting more, needing more. She nibbled, timidly at first, testing for his reaction. He pumped faster, driving his cock farther. She tightened the walls of her pussy around it and he throbbed under the grip, groaning.

Blood rushed to her head, nibbling gave way to a series of tiny bites, each growing harder than the previous. She longed to clamp her teeth into his flesh. Her clit hardened beneath his fingers. The moan vibrated against his neck as electric currents coursed up her spine. She cried out, panting, longing to taste him. The rising sexual hunger peaked and Danielle clamped her teeth against her release. Hot, sticky fluid rushed into her mouth. She jerked. Armondés fucked her harder, pounding and pumping until she cried out and sucked his neck, reeling under the torrid sensations. Her climax rose then burst in soft heat with relief rushing between her legs like fire. She groaned, eyelids fluttering shut, and sank into a liquid pool of ecstasy.

He jerked and quaked in orgasm and spilled his hot seed into her. Danielle released the clamping bite, exhausted and more satisfied than she could recall. Armondés pulled her down onto the mattress with him. She straddled him as he lay on his back, still throbbing inside her. This awareness sent her pulsating into another climax. She ground her hips hard with her teeth sinking once more into his neck, deeper this time. She sucked against the wound, drawing the velvet richness into her mouth.

"Danielle," he groaned and pushed her away, holding her face between his hands. She screamed and struggled for his neck, ravenous to feel his flesh against her lips but he was stronger and pinned her to the mattress. She thrashed underneath the restraint.

"Let me go! Let me go!" she screamed.

"Enough, Danielle! You'll drink me dry. Then I won't be able to please you."

She stopped struggling and looked up at him, blinking at the dark flow trickling down his neck.

"Drink?" The wound glared at her. "What have you done to me?" Horrified realization ripped through the drugged haze and released in a scream that reverberated against the windowpanes and echoed down the outside corridor.

Chapter Five

"What the hell was that?" Fredrick broke from their kiss and lifted from the bed, but Minnie was quick to pull him back.

"Sounds like Danielle just found out she's a vampire." She tried to capture his lips once more, but the moment had been severed.

He pulled away and rolled onto his back, resting his head on his arm.

"Damn my brother, he always robs me of what I need." Resigned to the interruption, she turned on her side, tracing imaginary lines over his chest.

"Do you recall when you found out you had been transformed, Fredrick?"

"I awoke to find your brother had brought me a whore from the village for my first feeding. Our king, in all his kindness, saved me from torture and persecution. It would have been more merciful to have let Charlemagne's court kill me." His eyes glazed in memory.

"But then you'd never have known me, baby."

"Right." He shifted and gathered her in his arms.

"So what do we do now, Freddie?" She planted a kiss on his cheek, tracing the line of his square jaw with her finger.

"We wait."

"Wait?" She rose up on her elbow and leaned over him.

"Yes, to see how good your new sister-in-law is at dodging assassins."

"Do you think he'll stay in Savannah now that he has his mate?"

"Armondés will return to his castle and vineyards where it's safe." He flashed her a devilish smile.

"And what if the assassins follow?" she asked, staring down at him.

"Then we'll have to warn Danielle of the dangers that await any new queen in our unsettled kingdom. And of course, Armondés will want us to go back to France with him. You'll be expected to train her in all things queenly. It's your royal duty, you know."

"We've been prisoners too long, Freddie," she pouted and pulled her knees to her chest, resting her chin on them.

"Patience, Minnie. We'll win our freedom soon enough. Don't do anything stupid."

"I want to hunt so bad I could scream. It's not natural to force us to drink from his Private Label. We were created to hunt. It's part of what we are. Our instincts, desires, needs…we have the right to be what we are."

"I promise you soon, very soon, you will hunt again."

* * * * *

When Danielle awoke, it was night. She turned over in the bed, but the place beside her was empty. She must leave. Now! She kicked off the covers and swung her legs to the floor. She stood and immediately regretted it. The room spun. She groped for the bedpost but her knees buckled. Her cry echoed against the high ceiling as she fell to the floor. The thick rug cushioned the fall, but she was too weak to stand.

Running footfalls came in response to her cry followed by a door opening and slamming shut.

"Danielle!" Armondés picked her up and placed her back onto the bed. "You're too weak to be walking about."

"Wha…what's wrong with me? What have you done to me? I want to go home," she murmured. Chills wrapped around her like an icy blanket.

"It's normal. It'll pass in a few days. You're in the process of transforming. It takes a while for the cycle to complete."

"What are you talking about?" she asked. Her focus centered on his neck where the bruise and bite marks had discolored his skin, but it was flawless. She reached out to stroke the area. How could that be? She touched her own wound, prepared to recoil in pain, but there was none.

"Your neck has healed, too," he stated and shifted the pillow underneath her head. His dark hair fell around his face, creating a mysterious and very sexy look. Her breathing quickened.

"I need to call my aunt. She worries if she doesn't hear from me every day, and my friends must be wondering what happened to me since I never returned from my birthday party."

"I got your laptop from your house and sent emails from your account. They won't be worried. You can call them all later." He stroked her face with his hand and leaned over her. His lips touched hers ever so lightly. An electrical current shot through her. She jerked and immediately felt better. "But first you must rest. Grow stronger. Then we'll talk."

She started to protest but he held up his hand and moved it over her face. Her eyes closed against her will and once more she fell into an abyss of fragmented thoughts, sounds and vignettes of dark scenes. She wanted to scream, to get up and run for the door, but she could not control her body.

For the next few days, Danielle felt as though the world had turned into a thick fluid through which she struggled to move. Every movement was labored as though in slow motion. Armondés was always there whenever she resurfaced from the fevers. Each time she opened her eyes, she attempted to rise from the bed with only one thought—to get away from him. Each time, he would give her the silver chalice to drink from and she'd fall back into a deep slumber.

Her senses were heightened and each featherlike touch from him was intensified. She could even feel the satin sheet against every tiny place it touched her flesh. The material's sensuality sparked deep longings, causing her to writhe and lust for him. Slowly, she emerged from the haze when he entered the bedroom. She groped for him and he eased into the embrace, drawing her against the length of his hard body.

"There, my love, the worst is over." He stroked her hair, pressing her head against his chest. "Now you shall grow stronger." His lips pressed against her forehead and he drew her deeper into his embrace. Her body cried out for his touch. She needed to feel him inside her and wrapped her leg around his. She rocked her hips so her pussy brushed against his leg.

"Not yet, my precious wife."

She groaned and thrust harder into him, needing to feel him respond to her need.

"Tonight. Tonight," he whispered and stroked her hair. "Sleep now."

Her eyelids were lead weights and closed once more despite her efforts to keep them open.

"Sleep." His voice moved over her like a warm blanket.

* * * * *

Armondés glanced across his club, quickly noting Fredrick and Minnie sitting at the bar, surveying the crowd. He started to hail them, but paused when Fredrick leaned in a little closer than necessary to whisper something to her. Minnie angled her head and slightly brushed her hand over his knee.

So, they had become lovers. He wondered why the realization shocked him. After all these centuries, he had often wondered why the two had not been drawn to each other. Instead of pleasing him, as he'd often anticipated, the thought of Minnie and Fredrick together worried him. Why should he have such an odd reaction? What could be better than his best friend and his sister becoming a couple? It could only strengthen their clan. Or, he considered his sister, it could rip their clan apart. Minnie could be volatile.

"Can I get you anything, Armondés?" the petite waitress asked and flashed a generous smile at him.

"Non, merci." He shook his head, still watching Fredrick and Minnie. Their heads angled toward each other, they appeared to be critiquing the couple who had just entered the club. Were they hunting in secret? Anger scorched him, but he quickly dismissed the thought. They knew better.

He heard Danielle cry out before she opened her mouth. Her words echoed from their chamber, and he turned from the club, walking quickly, not waiting for the guard to open the door to his private entrance. When he reached the staircase, he lifted his arms and flew to the top floor of his suite, bursting into the room just as she slipped from the bed. He caught her and cradled her against him.

"Let me go, please. Why are you doing this to me?" she asked, still half-asleep.

He carried her to the chair beside the cold fireplace and draped a blanket about her.

"You need some blood." He pulled the tapestry cord along the wall. The response was instantaneous.

"Yes, Your Highness?" the uniformed butler asked, standing in the open doorway.

"Private Label for the Queen."

The servant bowed and closed the doors behind him.

"There, my love, it shall all be better very soon."

"Armondés?" she asked, lifting her pale face to squint up at him. The pained look in her eyes made him feel as though his heart would burst. "Why is this happening? What am I becoming?"

The butler returned with the black wine bottle and two goblets. She sniffed the air and straightened in the chair as the servant placed the silver tray on the table beside her. Danielle growled and grabbed the bottle, lifting it to her lips to gulp its contents with a hunger he recognized all too well. He waved the servant away.

"Slow down, sweet Danielle, your first bottle should be savored, not gulped."

She pulled the bottle from her mouth and swiped at the blood trickling from the corner of her mouth.

"First bottle?"

"Your first real meal."

"You call this a meal?" she asked. Anger grated in her voice. Deep, smoldering rage rose in her eyes. "I call this disgusting!" She tilted the bottle to her mouth once more and didn't break until it was empty. She glared up at him. "I need another one."

He shook his head and tugged the bottle from her grip.

"Give me another," she demanded and stood from the chair. The blanket fell from her, but she didn't seem to notice.

"You can't have another just yet. It takes time. It's a process. You can have more in a few hours."

"I said I wanted another. Give it to me, or I will take it directly from your veins. I really don't care." She stood with hands on hips. The vision she cut, standing naked in front of the large window against the backdrop of city lights below made him halt mid-stride. The gentle curve of hips and her long slender legs, parted slightly to reveal a shaved pussy, set his desire raging. He turned to find the blue gown he'd bought earlier that evening. Minnie had been very cooperative in helping select a suitable wardrobe for his new wife. Opening the dresser drawer, his hands shook as he reached for the silk gown.

"Here, put this on before you become chilled." He handed it to her, but she refused to take the garment. Instead, she glared at him. Armondés shook his head and tugged it over her head, drawing her arms into the sleeves. It fell around her curves to the floor.

"There now, you look gorgeous." He brushed his lips against her forehead.

"I need more of the Private Label," she murmured.

"Your reaction is normal." He drew his arms around her, but she pulled from him, backing into the corner. She stared at him sideways and hissed as though she were a trapped animal.

"My poor love, this shall pass. I promise. By tomorrow you'll feel much better." He had said the same thing before in what felt like forever and still she didn't get better. He was concerned she would slip into the baser level like Charisse.

"I want to go home."

"I can't let you go, Danielle. You belong with me now."

"How long have I been imprisoned in your bed?"

"You're not my prisoner—" he started to explain, but she interrupted him.

"How long?"

"You've been here a little over a week."

"What?" she asked. The harsh angry glint in her eyes dulled. "A week? How many days exactly?"

"Twelve days."

She tightened her stare on him.

"The transformation has its own timetable. It can't be rushed." He shrugged.

"Just what are you turning me into?" Fear hid beneath her bravado. He could smell it cowering in her. It lurked in the shadows of her torment. He longed to quicken the process for her, but knew no one could. "Tell me, what am I becoming?"

"I think you know."

"I want to hear it from you. Tell me."

"Vampire."

The air rushed from her, and she stumbled back into the chair.

He kneeled beside her, taking her hands in his.

"I thought it was all a myth." She bowed her head with tears spilling down her cheeks. "Why did you do this to me, Armondés? Why?" she asked.

"I had no choice. You were destined to be my mate. It was time to take you." He longed to wipe the tears from her eyes and assure her everything would be all right, but he couldn't. It was too early to tell if his beloved Danielle would survive her transformation.

"My birthday. I remember now." She rubbed her temple.

"You will remember more as time passes. You'll discover this new life is not so bad." He lifted her hand to his firm lips. The sweet scent of her flesh sent waves of longing pulsing in him. She was ripe for the tasting. He touched the tip of his tongue to her skin and groaned, slowly lifting his stare. "We have eternity to explore each other."

"Yeah, right. And in the meantime I'll be going out at night hunting and stalking innocent people and killing them." She paused when he started laughing.

"That was true in the past. But my clan lives in the twenty-first century. We're a bit more sophisticated than that, my sweet wife." He picked up the empty wine bottle and turned it so the label was facing her.

Her look narrowed as she read it aloud.

"Armondés' Private Label. Yes, I read it earlier. So, you create this?"

"Yes along with my team of chemists. It's our clan's label. No one else can purchase it."

"Transition Douce?"

"Smooth Transition. This is blended just for those who are going through transition."

"Just how many do you convert?"

"I, personally, none. Except you. But many in my clan fall in love with non-vampires and then wish to have as a mate. There's a certain protocol for obtaining permission."

"Permission from you?"

"Yes. There now, enough questions for the night. This blend will sustain you until your transformation is complete.

Then you shall simply drink any of the Private Label varieties, there are many. Don't worry, Danielle, things will grow clearer for you now."

"So where do you get the...the blood?"

"We have people who are very willing to keep us supplied. We pay them well for their services."

"But how can you keep this a secret?"

"The same way our very existence is kept secret. We've cloaked ourselves with legends and myths for centuries and have allowed mortals to come close to the truth only to tear it apart so no one knows what is true and what isn't. When confusion reigns it's easy to disguise the truth."

"I want to be alone," she interjected abruptly.

He watched the emotions shadow her expression. His hope that he was reaching her shattered. She hated him.

"I know it's confusing, Danielle. But you'll see, this is a wonderful gift I've bestowed upon you."

"Is that what you call it?" She pulled her knees up to her chest and rested her chin on them. "I don't know who I am anymore. You've robbed me of my life, Armondés. How is that a wonderful gift?"

"It's normal to feel the loss. You should mourn it, because it has fallen from you forever. In exchange you have immortality." He reached over and covered her hand with his. She jerked from his touch.

"Get out! I can't bear to look at you," she wailed and buried her head in her hands.

He started to console her but decided she needed time to adjust. Only she could face the next few days. She must work through it—alone. He would remain by her side to answer questions and lend support, but ultimately, it was a solitary path.

Danielle hugged her knees tighter, wanting to cry, but she'd shed all the tears she had over the past hour. Slowly, she uncurled from the chair. The thick Aubusson rug enveloped her toes, tickling the soles of her feet as she walked across the bedroom. Stopping in front of the window, she stared across the city.

The lights along River Street outlined the Savannah River, joined by twinkling lights from ships and barges as they moved down the snaking waterway. How she loved the city. But how different it all was to her now. The club faced River Street with the back overlooking Factors Walk, not at all where one would expect to find such an erotic nightspot. How she adored walking along the cobblestone street and shopping among the many stores lining the river.

She opened the door and stepped into the night, resting her hands on the wrought iron railing. The early spring air wisped about her face, carrying evening scents of azaleas, gardenias and jasmine on the warm breeze rushing toward the river. She took a deep breath, letting the heated aromas fill her senses. Closing her eyes, she recalled all the wonderful springs she'd spent walking through Savannah's almost magical garden squares.

When she opened her eyes, it was to the snaking Savannah River and the multitude of lights outlining its long, curving path. The Olde Harbour Inn had always been one of her favorite historic places along the riverfront and from here she could see its roofline, shadowed in the streetlights' glow. She walked along the balcony, following it around the back of the building which overlooked Factors Walk.

Those same streetlights revealed moss-covered oak trees dancing in the rustling evening breeze as it moved through the city. From her vantage point she could see several city squares bursting with flowering azaleas, shaded by crepe myrtles and palm trees. Suddenly, the magical moment crumbled around her. She would never be able to enjoy the sun warming her face as she sat on one of the numerous park benches eating her lunch.

"This is insane," she said and hugged herself against the abrupt waves of hunger. It wasn't like normal hunger that radiated from the stomach. This hunger came from a place lower. As powerful as any sexual need, it consumed her. She gripped the iron railing, wrapping her fingers around the cold metal, but the need kept rising in her until she threw back her head and released a primal roar. Her cry was muffled by the city sounds below, but echoed loudly in her ears. Even though she knew it was her voice, it sounded separate from her.

"I hate him!" She leaned forward and jerked against the railing. The ironwork groaned under newfound strength and popped from its base. She stood holding the heavy section of metal as though it were plastic and not several hundred pounds of iron. "Look what he has done to me!" she wailed with tears filling her eyes and scorching her throat. She was tempted to hurl it crashing into the window behind her, but thought better of it and leaned it against the other railing. Her heart filled with sadness.

Standing in front of the open section, she looked down at the crowded street through blurry eyes. The weekenders partied in the vibrant town, oblivious to her. Unaware that within the city vampires disguised themselves as businessmen and women. No one knew that Danielle Rivers had been transformed from a human into a bloodsucking creature. How she envied them. How she longed to return to her own mundane life.

In the distance a female voice sang the lyrics to an opera. The melody was pining and sad. Somehow it complemented her desperation. What if she plunged herself to the ground? She remembered all the vampire lore from books and movies. It would probably take more than a fall of several stories to kill her. Perhaps everyone already thought she was dead. She bowed her head. The opera replaced the night around her, pitching higher then dropping, only to rise higher once more in a wistful composition of music and voice. It seemed to float through the air and stop in front of her as though in concert just for her. Tears welled in her eyes and spilled down her cheeks.

She was dead to all she had ever known. Her thoughts moved to the night of her birthday party. A harmless night on the town had turned her life into a living hell. Was anyone looking for her? What about Amy and Lillian? Surely they had contacted the police and reported her missing. Someone had to be looking for her. She thought of her aunt and knew the elderly woman would be concerned that Danielle had missed a week of daily calls, although Armondés said he'd sent emails. Was he lying? No, he was too smart to lie. The last thing he'd want would be police showing up and asking questions and probing into his life. To the world he was a millionaire winemaker and club owner. He would not risk everything when a simple email would suffice. She was certain he'd made sure no one missed her. She retraced her steps around the balcony and went back inside. She'd be damned if she'd give in to him so easily.

There had to be something modern medicine could do for her. The gnawing gripped her harder. She doubled over in pain. All she had to do was find a phone and call Amy and Lillian. Her mouth watered with a need for another bottle of Armondés' Private Label. She hated herself. She knew it wasn't wine, but she could not allow herself to believe she had such a thirst for human blood.

"It's too powerful to resist," Armondés said and moved from the shadows by the door. How long had he been standing there, watching her?

"I have great willpower. I've done all the diets. I've fought off urges for chocolate and carbohydrates," she tossed back at him.

"This isn't like a food craving or a bad habit. This is just as strong as the need to breathe, although you no longer do that."

"I don't?" she asked, recalling how she'd smelled the flowers.

"It's more habit than necessity. In time you will let it go, just as you will release other human needs."

"I see. Does that include sex?" She flashed what she hoped was a look of hatred in his direction. She watched the way his jaw clenched. His steely look wavered under her assault. This vulnerability surprised her.

"Come. I have another bottle ready for you, perhaps this time you shall use the goblet?" He lifted the bottle and slowly poured the rich liquid into the glass.

She snapped alert. Her nostrils flared at the intense pleasure the smell brought to her. Blood! The need overpowered her once more. She rushed to the side table where he stood. Her hands shook when lifting the goblet. The sight of the thick, dark liquid was as sensually pleasing as gazing upon Armondés naked.

"You find me so pleasing?" he asked from behind her.

A chilling current ripped down her back.

"So you can read my mind?" she asked absently, intent upon the goblet. She raised it to her face. She allowed the smoothness of the glass to caress her lips and sniffed. It was as rich and fragrant as any wine bouquet, only this reminded her of rich, liquid chocolate. Sweet. Addictive. And so pleasing. She stuck her tongue out and touched the creamy mixture. The sensation was immediate. It traveled down her throat to her belly and fanned out into her body in an electrical shock. She tilted the goblet and devoured the contents. When finished, she licked her lips and held it out to him.

"More."

"There is more, my love, but you must pace yourself. Come sit with me and talk, then I will share a glass with you."

She wanted to scream at him, but knew it would probably only make him withhold her next glass longer. He sat down on the loveseat, tucked into the corner of the suite. Reluctantly, she joined him.

"Are you feeling better this evening?"

"No."

"You look as though you are."

"Looks are so deceiving, aren't they?"

"I suppose. Then you're still angry with me?"

"I shall be angry with you, Armondés, for the rest of my life."

He laughed.

"You find this all so damn amusing, don't you?"

"Not at all. The rest of your life is eternity, that will be a very long time to remain angry at me."

"It won't be long enough for me to show you how much I detest you and what you've done to me. You had no right!" she said, venting her anger on him full force, and silently vowed she would never allow him to make love to her again.

"You gave me the right." His dark eyes glinted with open ardor.

"I did not!"

"You did. I asked before I took you. I would never take anyone against her will, especially the woman who would be my queen."

"Okay, I give. What's with this king and queen thing? Are you saying you're King of the Vampires?"

"I am King of my clan, which is—"

"Oh wait, I know this one. Damned. Right?" she asked and giggled giddily. She realized the blood had an intoxicating effect similar to alcohol, but she didn't care right now. All she wanted to do was let Armondés know just how much she hated him.

"You're angry now, but soon you'll realize the advantages to being immortal, and the greater ones to being my queen." His stare was intense, with sparks of unspoken promises of pleasure.

Desire stoked hot and threatened to tear down her resolve to deny him.

"I'll take your word for it. In the meantime, I want to return to my apartment. I need to call my aunt."

"That's not possible. Not just yet. You need to be fully acclimated to your new lifestyle before contacting your former friends and family."

"Former? I'll have you know they are still my friends and family."

"Of course." He put his arm around her shoulders and drew her to him. "I can help you with your anger. If you'll let me."

"How?" she asked, trying to shake the ardent need rising in her. Why did she feel overpowering desire for such a despicable creature?

"Perhaps it's because you too are now just as despicable," he said.

"You did it again. You *can* read my mind?" She jumped from the loveseat.

He stood and in one swift movement took her into his embrace, brushing her lips ever so lightly with his. She had never received such a tender kiss. It was as soft as a rose petal. Her body responded as though she were a mere puppet under his control.

"Take off your gown and let me see you naked, Danielle. I want to kiss your pussy and make you scream out my name." Before she could comply with his instruction, his hand glided over her shoulder and slipped the strap down her arm. The bodice gave and the gown fell from her.

She trembled, standing naked in front of him as his gaze devoured her slowly. His hand brushed against her breasts and he leaned over to capture a hardened nipple between his lips. Sucking it, fiery twinges sizzled down her abdomen to her pussy. His hand cupped her other breast in a slow kneading motion. The warm touch moved from her breast down her leg and to the soft folds of her pussy where his fingers parted her lips to stroke her clit. Frenzied cravings coursed through her while her mind screamed against the overpowering sensations he brought to her so easily. She could not control the intense need to feel all of the erotic pleasures he offered. Helpless as though under his spell, her body responded to his every touch.

"You like it when I touch you like that," he said and eased her onto the armrest, spreading her legs to either side then bending over, teased her with short, fast flicks of his tongue against her clit.

"Oh, God!" She grabbed his head between her hands and thrust her pelvis against him.

"You are mine, Danielle." He lifted from her and unbuckled his slacks, unzipping and dropping them to the floor. He stepped from the folds and hastily shed the briefs.

Her stare was immediately drawn to his hard cock. She touched her tongue to her lips, craving the pleasure only he could give. Armondés stood in front of her and reached for his shirt. Thinking he was going to slowly unbutton the dress shirt in a tease, Danielle shifted her perch on the velvet arm to prop her back against the wall. His muscles arms flexed and the sound of rending material quickened her breath. She watched the fabric give under his supernatural strength and rip from his hard muscled torso. She let her gaze move over his sculpted six-pack and taut chest. He pulled the remains of his white shirt from him and tossed it aside.

"Oh, my," she whispered with the heat coursing through her body choking off her words.

He reached down to let his fingertips caress her rosy-tipped breasts. Hardened nipples tingled beneath his touch and moist heat surged from her pussy. She reached for his cock and stroked him, luxuriating in the feel of his hard flesh. His desire seeped from his cock beneath her firm movement and she rubbed his juices into his flesh, longing to feel him inside her. Anxiously, she spread her legs and guided him to her. Armondés grasped her hips and pulled her to him, positioning her to receive his entry.

Her eyes closed. Rolling her hips in a persuasive rhythm beneath him, Danielle grabbed his firm buttocks and thrust against him, meeting his pumping.

Her own vigor startled her. She needed him as badly as she'd needed the bottle of Private Label. Sensing her urgency, he shifted, lifted her from the velvet arm and sat down on the loveseat with her straddling him.

"Oh, I like this better," she gasped and moved against his cock, now free to grind into him, tilting her hips, and pulling from him. She hovered over the tip of his shaft.

She moaned. Waves of pleasure shot through her as his cock moved against tender flesh, driving the need to ride him harder and plunge him deeper with each movement. He gripped her buttocks and pumped his cock into her. She arched her back and pressed against him. The excited urgency zigzagged up her spine. The frenetic sensation quaked through her, drawing the walls of her pussy to clamp around his cock in a hard rhythmic squeeze.

She felt him come inside her, throbbing and pounding his orgasm as he clutched tighter and jerked in a powerful release. New sensations pounded to her clit. She shuddered with the driving pleasure searing through her. He sucked one of her nipples, prolonging the throbbing jolts and heightened pleasure. Like from tiny electrical shocks, her body jerked with each new wave until, exhausted, she slumped against him. Spent. Fulfilled. Taken to a new sensual awareness, she marveled at his ability to strip her of all defenses and leave her with a longing for his touch so deep that a new need emerged, one only he could satisfy.

Chapter Six

"Hello Aunt Sue... Yes, I'm fine... I know. I'm so sorry for all the confusion. Did you not get my emails?" she asked, referring to the ones Armondés had sent from her laptop. "I would have called sooner, but I've been sick... No, I'm much better now. A friend of mine has taken great care of me... I don't know when I can come to Virginia. Maybe in the fall. So how have you been?"

The conversation with her aunt was long and often repetitive until she finally convinced her aunt everything was okay. With that accomplished, she called Lillian, but got her voicemail. She decided to call work, but was shocked when someone else answered Lillian's extension.

"Oh, sorry, I thought I'd dialed Lillian Thompson's extension."

"I took her place, may I help you?"

"Took her place?" she asked with panic seeping into her tone.

"Yes, may I help you?"

"Ah..." This was not what she'd expected to hear.

"Hello?"

"Wh-When did she leave?"

"She quit about two weeks ago. Is there something I can help you with?"

"Quit?" Her heartbeat pounded out her rising fear. Lillian would not give up her job. She loved her job. She'd been there for fifteen years. The only way she'd ever leave the bank would be if she were fired or laid off. She'd never quit. Recruiters had tried for years to pry her away, but Lillian's family had deep roots in Savannah and at the bank itself. "Do you know where she went? Do you have a number or the name of her new employer?"

"From what I understand, Ms. Thompson moved to France."

"France!" Danielle's fears were confirmed. Now she knew something was very wrong. Lillian would never move to France or anywhere. She had lived within five miles of her childhood home all her life.

"Is there anything else I can do for you today?"

"No." She hung up. "France?" She shook her head. "Armondés!" She stomped across the room into the foyer. "Armondés?" she called again, but still no answer. She went back to the phone and dialed Amy's work number and received her voicemail.

"Amy, this is Danielle. Call my cell. I need to talk with you about Lillian." She hung up.

"Did you call me?" He appeared in the doorway. How did he move so silently? She had to learn to move like that.

"Do you know anything about Lillian moving to France?"

"No."

"That's all you have to say?"

"What do you want me to say, Danielle? I don't know anything about her. That night she brought you to my club was only the second time I'd seen her." He wore a pair of dark slacks and a white dress shirt and stood with his arms folded over his chest.

"Yet she was a frequent patron of your club and a good friend of Minnie's. Minnie! I need to talk with Minnie." She started for the hall.

"She's not here. She went to Atlanta for the weekend with Fredrick."

"Oh? And who is Fredrick?"

"You met him on our wedding night. You shall meet everyone next week, once your transformation is complete. I shall present you to them all during our wedding celebration."

"And when were you going to inform me about all this?" She planted her hands on her hips.

"I just did."

She gritted her teeth and paced across the room to the windows. That was it! She was going to end this right now.

"What are you doing, Danielle?" he asked, closing the space between them.

"What I should have done when I first realized what I'd become." She slipped her hand between the draperies. The pain was instant. The sun scorched her skin as though she'd placed it on a stove burner. A small stream of smoke rose.

Armondés reached her before she could open the drapery any further and jerked her from the widow.

"Don't *ever* do that again!" he demanded.

"I'm sorry," she cried and collapsed against him. "I'm just so frustrated. I'm exhausted. I can't think clearly. The transition hurts. I ache all the time. It's disgusting to crave blood. What I wouldn't give to be able to eat a hamburger and fries. Anything other than blood. I miss food. I miss the sun. Oh God, I just miss my old life." She lifted her head and grabbed him by the sleeves. "Please, Armondés, I don't want to be a vampire. I hate myself! I hate being this horrid creature! Can you undo it? Please?" Tears streamed down her cheeks. "Please undo it!" Ragged sobs jerked from her.

"It can't be undone, my love," he said and stroked her hair, letting his hand cup her face. "You will feel better soon, I promise, and then you can do some of the things you used to do. Why, you can even see your friends. You can go out with them at night, again. You'll see, things will get better."

"I don't believe you. I feel I will be like this for all eternity. I would rather burn in the sun than—"

"Shh," he said and kissed her forehead. "That kind of talk is forbidden. Do you understand?" He held her tighter and she rested her head on his chest once more. "It is a normal part of the transition. Your body is adjusting to the changes taking place. It's a process. But it does have an end. You'll see. Soon, you will feel better and can go shopping with Lillian and Amy and do all kind of things just like before."

"Are you sure I didn't have any emails from them?" She pulled from him slightly to meet his stare. She would know if he was lying. She was beginning to be able to sense his moods and sometimes it felt as though she could hear his thoughts.

"You may check your email." He held her face between his hands and kissed her cheek.

"I did earlier. That's why I called them." She pulled from him, hugging herself against the chill that had settled in her chest. Something had happened. She sensed it.

"I didn't delete anything. I only sent out emails to keep people from becoming suspicious."

"Yeah, I read my resignation letter." She threw him what she hoped was a disgusted sneer. "Thanks a lot. It took me two years to work my way up in the marketing department, and you took it all away from me in one quick click."

"I'm sorry, it had to be done."

"Right. You're too good at this, Armondés." She considered him for a moment. "Just how many wives have you had?"

"Why do you want to know that?" He folded his arms across his chest.

"I think I have a right to ask."

"Perhaps."

"What was the longest you were married?"

"Long enough." His laugh was bitter and guarded.

"What's that supposed to mean? Long enough for what? And, why me? Why now? What was so damned important that you had to get married and to me of all women?"

"I had to get married or suffer an ancient curse. It wasn't until my two thousandth birthday that I had to first marry... It's a long story. A curse placed on me because I won the throne. But it only became active when I turned two thousand years old."

"Two thousand?" she asked, feeling as though he'd struck her in the stomach. Her knees turned to water and she stumbled into the nearby chair. "You're two thousand years old? Oh God! That's incredible. How? I mean. Oh, God."

"I am two thousand and seventy-five, actually. It's something of a record. My kind used to survive only a few hundred years."

"Only a few? So, what made your two thousandth birthday so special?"

"I don't actually know. My predecessor was two thousand when I beat him in Tournament."

"Tournament?"

"Tournament is what we call the act of challenging the king. When another seeks his throne there is a tournament, a fight. The king chooses the location and weapons if any are used. Generally a sword is the choice of weapon."

The thought of losing him had not occurred to her. What would become of her if he was destroyed? Would she want to live eternity without him? She depended upon him, but that didn't mean she loved him, Danielle silently reasoned.

"Is the king challenged often?" she gulped.

"It's never happened to me." He smiled with a devilish glint piercing his eyes.

"Good," she sighed with relief. "So, your wife who died last year, you were married for seventy-five years?"

"No. Only two years."

"Oh...so you've had other wives. How many?"

"Only one other."

"You were married for seventy-three years? My God! You must miss her very much."

"It was not that kind of marriage," he rushed to assure her. "None of that matters, Danielle. You're my wife, now. And I've fallen madly in love with you as I never have with any woman." He reached for her, but she pulled from his touch.

"Whoa there, Dracula, I want to talk about this wife thing first. Then we'll deal with the love thing."

His laughter filled the room with its deep rich baritone echoing against the high ceiling.

"I don't find this funny, Armondés. I want to know about this last wife. What happened to her?"

"I don't know for certain. It's believed she was killed by a vampire stalker."

"Oh God, what is that?" Her anxiety level elevated to the highest alert. Not only did she have this new way of life to contend with, but now she was discovering it came with several built-in enemies. Enemies who would want her dead. "Is a stalker like a slayer?"

"Very similar to those portrayed in movies," he answered, but without any outward sign of grave concern.

"Are there many of them? I mean, do I need to worry about being stalked?" she asked, turning her head slightly because she really didn't want to hear the answer.

"You don't need to worry, my Danielle. There are only a handful left in the world and most of them are in South America."

"Why South America?"

"The largest vampire clan reigns in Brazil." He stated it matter-of-factly but she still found it all incredible.

"Then do vampires exist all over the world?"

"Yes."

"That's amazing! No wonder all cultures have legends about vampires. Only, I guess they aren't really legends."

He shrugged. She worried he was trying to lead her off topic and quickly regained control of the conversation.

She sat down in the nearby chair and waited, expecting him to spill the story when in fact, he appeared very reluctant to divulge any of it. In spite of herself, Danielle admired the way his crisp cotton shirt fitted his broad chest and how trim his waist was. She mentally shook herself and returned her focus on her next question.

"So now tell me about the other wife. The one you say you didn't love but were married to for almost three quarters of a century."

"Like you, she was thirty when I made her." With hands clasped behind his back, he paced in front of the cold fireplace.

"Made her? Oh, that's what you call it when you bite the victim and she goes through transition?"

He nodded but didn't offer further explanation. She gritted her teeth. This was not going to be easy.

"So why thirty?"

"It's part of the curse. I have to take my mate during the last minute of her twenty-ninth year."

"Oh. Yes. I vaguely remember the clock. So is that it? That's all there is to fulfilling the curse?" She crossed her legs and sat back in the chair, feeling calmer yet determined to get the entire story even if it meant pulling it from him piece by piece.

"There are also a couple of tests for compatibility."

"What kinds of tests?"

"Like the special vintage champagne."

"The one that made me sick?"

He nodded.

"That was part of the tests?"

"Yes. The other was tasting the Private Label."

"Oh my God, you did have me drink blood before I was transformed. Before I needed it!"

He shrugged but made no apologies.

"And had I failed the tests?"

"You would not have grown ill from the champagne and the other test would not have been necessary."

She watched the emotions slip past his attempt to rein them, but the look in his eyes betrayed the passion he held in check. Desire licked hot flames over her, but she closed her eyes to his hypnotic stare and regained control.

"So, what was her name? The wife you were married to for seventy-three years."

"Alexa. She was my first wife."

"Did you love her?" she asked with held breath. Of course he'd loved her. Why else be married to someone so long?

"No. I tried, but she hated being a vampire. She hated all things vampire, especially me. It was a marriage in name only."

Relief washed over her. Absently, she wondered why she cared so much. So what if he'd loved another woman. It wasn't like she was in love with him.

"So what happened to her?" she asked, struggling to ignore the way he moved, each gesture was a subtle seduction to her senses.

"She killed herself," he mumbled and bowed his head.

"Oh." Danielle watched the emotions move over his face once more. She was surprised that after a couple of thousand years he couldn't hide emotional reactions any better than that. Unless it was vampire thing and somehow being his mate allowed her such glimpses. Perhaps he was not the coldhearted monster she so desperately needed him to be. He'd shown her tenderness over the past weeks and had seen to her every need, yet he had also robbed her of the life she'd had as a human. She rubbed her temple. It was too complicated to sort out.

"Why was your second wife hunted by the vampire stalker?"

"I'm not sure. It's still under investigation. But Charisse took too many risks and it was just a matter —"

"Charisse? That was her name?"

"Yes."

"What kind of risks, Armondés?"

"She was not careful, that's all."

"I see. So what kind of danger does her death place me in as the new queen?"

"None. You're safe as long as you stay with me."

"Ah, that's the truth of it, isn't it? I mean, that's the whole point of all this. I'm to be your sex slave."

"No. Never a slave." The hurt in his voice struck her full force, but she was determined to block all emotions. She couldn't afford to let empathy cloud her judgment since it was obvious his spellbinding powers already had a strong influence over her.

"I need to think about all this. I just don't know what to make of you or myself for that matter. Nothing is the way it's supposed to be." She gnawed on her lower lip.

"I ask you, Danielle, was your former life so wonderful? Was it filled with a man who adored you as I do? Did you have a skillful lover whose only desire was to please you?"

"Well…I didn't have that, no. But I had other things that were just as valuable."

"Such as?"

"There was my job. It was a good career path."

"Did you truly have a career path? Were you going to be promoted beyond assistant manager?" he asked, revealing once more how one-sided this marriage was with him knowing everything about her and Danielle knowing only the few things he had chosen to share.

"I might have made manager. Just because I didn't have a four-year degree didn't mean I wasn't going to go back to college and get one. I had plans."

"Plans? What plans? When were you going to do that?"

"Someday." She hedged the question. It was true, she had not really made any plans to enroll in college and probably would have let it slide past her.

"Do you still believe your old life was better than what I can give you? Do you think growing old is a gift? Did you look forward to growing old without a husband and children? Without grandchildren? I know you thought about these things. I know they were not things you had found, and were not likely to find a man who could fulfill all your fantasies."

"You don't know me. You have no idea—" She looked away from him, fighting the tears threatening to spill over her eyelids and stream down her cheeks.

"But I do know you. I know everything there is to know about you. You hate licorice. When you were in the first grade you stood up to the class bully, and your first sexual encounter was with Billy O'Hara who lived two blocks from you."

"Stop!" She stood and paced across the room, putting as much distance between them as she could. "That is mental rape! How dare you steal into my thoughts and memories like that."

"It's what a vampire does, my love. You can enter my mind just as easily if you try."

"I don't want inside your mind!" she screamed and held her hands to her head. "I don't want anything. All I need is to be set free. Let me go. Let me go back to my old life."

"Why? Because it was safe? Comfortable? Boring?" His eyes seemed to darken and she sensed he was reading her thoughts, again. She mentally blocked him, visualizing a wall rising between them.

"Maybe it was all those things, but it was *my* life, Armondés. It belonged to me." She trembled when she met the longing in his gaze.

"The life I've given you belongs to you, my sweet Danielle. All you have to do is claim it." He rose and moved toward her, seeming to practically float.

"It is not the life I choose. Don't you understand?" she cried. "I no longer know who I am. What I will finally become once the transition is complete. I'm lost, Armondés. Lost."

"No. You are just finding yourself. I promise you. You will find this new life better. Please, at least try."

"Why? Why should I?"

"Because I love you, Danielle. I've never loved anyone in my entire life. But, I do love you." His words sent waves of comfort and warmth over her. It had to be part of his ability to manipulate her thoughts and emotions.

"Love?" she asked, opening her eyes. "How can you call this love? I don't know you. You don't know me. This isn't love, Armondés. It's lust."

"I've known lust all my life. This is new. This is different from anything I've ever felt. I know you. I know everything about you and I love everything about you."

"You've lived all these years and never fallen in love?" Her resolve to refuse him and the life he had given her threatened to crumble under the intense emotion radiating from him and engulfing her like a physical embrace.

"I didn't believe it was possible for me…for a vampire to love." His voice deepened with pain resonating in its tone, but he continued, "I always thought it required a soul. But maybe that too is a myth."

Danielle was so confused by her conflicting emotions. One moment she despised herself and him, then the next she was overwhelmed with the compulsion to draw her arms around him and soothe the longings of a loveless lifetime. Perhaps transition was similar to hormonal fluctuations. Perhaps that was accountable for the sporadic mood swings and emotional roller coaster she found herself riding.

"I don't understand," she finally said, clasping her hands together in front of her.

"I thought I'd never know love. It has been claimed that vampires don't have souls. But, there's something inside me that you've stirred to life, Danielle. I can't explain it. I don't understand it myself, only that it's an intoxicating feeling and I know it must be love. I want us to build a life together."

"I can't build anything with you, Armondés. This is insanity. I had a marriage. I tried to build it into something that would last. It didn't."

"That isn't important. I don't want to know about your previous love life." He turned his back to her.

"Really? That isn't very normal. Most men would want to know about my previous marriage at least."

"I am a vampire." He faced her once more. "I've been a vampire for two thousand and seventy-five years. Do you think I could possibly react as a human man?" He faced her again.

"I guess not." She stiffened when he moved to stand just a few inches from her and trail his finger along her jaw, tracing an imaginary line down her neck.

Her pulse quickened. Even though she knew that, according to him, she no longer had a heartbeat, she certainly felt a pounding in her chest. Perhaps he wasn't a vampire and the concoction he'd given her was not blood but a drug. Yes, that would explain so much.

"You're not drugged, sweet, unless you call my lovemaking a drug." He scattered a string of kisses down her neck, following the path of his finger until he came to the V neckline of her aqua shirt.

He unbuttoned it and slipped his hand beneath her lace bra. His fingers found a nipple and rolled it between them, squeezing gently. She moaned. Immediately, it hardened, sending sharp sensations to her groin. How did he do that to her? How could he break through all her anger and fear and make her desire him? He buried his head between her breasts and deftly moved to unhook the bra. She lifted her arms as he peeled the blouse and bra away in one swift movement. He looked down at her naked breasts, nipples hard and erect. A warm blush fanned over her.

"You are so beautiful, my Queen," he whispered and stroked her breasts with the backs of his hands, caressing in light tender touches.

"Am I under a spell? Is that why I can't resist you?"

"Would that make loving me easier to accept?"

"I don't love you."

"Oh, you do love me, my Danielle. I can feel it."

"I don't want to love you," she whimpered as he planted tiny kisses along the column of her neck.

"But you do. You want me." His hands glided over her curves, leaving tingling trails of fiery sensations in their path.

"I don't want to—" She could no longer struggle against the powerful feelings coursing through her. The internal war made her weary. She longed for release. Peace. If that meant accepting him, then she must try for her own sanity.

"Give in to your feelings, my love. There's no reason to resist what you feel."

"If I do, then I'll lose myself completely," she sighed. There, she'd voiced it. Now he knew the one thing she feared even more than being a vampire.

"As I said, you lose only the human frailty, nothing more. And, you gain so much. More than you can imagine. All you have to do is embrace our union. Accept me as your husband. Your lover. It's the last part of transformation, Danielle. The acceptance."

"Acceptance?"

"Yes, of who you now are," he whispered in her ear. "Acceptance of me. Of us."

He moved behind her, drawing her back into his chest, trailing his fingers down her arms.

She leaned into him and he released a deep sigh, cupping both breasts in his warm hands. His touch eased the longing, and she willed herself to accept what she was, what he was. She now knew she needed the release she could only find in complete transformation. No longer trapped between two worlds, two sets of emotions, one human and the other unknown—vampire.

"That's it," he soothed, pinching her hardened nipples between his fingers. "Let it all flow from you. Accept your new life."

She groaned under the excited pulses radiating from her nipples to her clit as he squeezed harder, but she needed to feel his lips sucking her nipples. As though having spoken her need, he obliged by turning her around within the circle of his arms and lowered his face to her breasts, closing his lips over a nipple. He tugged and suckled it. Liquid fire pulsated to her clit.

"Armondés," she gasped and raked her hands through his long dark hair. Why should she try to resist him? It always ended up the same, she wanted him. She needed him. It was a moment of conscious choice. She chose him. She needed to believe he loved her, otherwise, nothing made sense. So for the moment she pretended they were in love, a typical newlywed couple.

He flicked his tongue against her nipple then moved to the other. Desire clouded her thoughts with unrestrained impulses. She moaned and tried to press against his cock. A low growl vibrated in her, as lascivious longings surged inside her.

The essence of her being rose from within the deepest part of her and took form, stretching into the places of anguish, transforming uncertainty into decisiveness. She moved her tongue over her teeth, touching the sharp pointed canine teeth that protruded beyond the other teeth. A feeling of power surged through her as her tongue slid over her new fangs. She gasped and flexed with the growing wave of energy as it claimed muscles and tissues, strengthening her arms and legs, quaking and trembling until it possessed her body completely. A new realization burst into consciousness as the emerging vampire within claimed new life.

Danielle pushed him into the nearby chair, surprising both of them.

"You have reached acceptance." A wide grin spread over his handsome face as he sat waiting in obvious relief and excitement.

She stood over him and danced in rhythm with the new hunger snaking up her body. He grunted his pleasure and sat watching as her breasts heaved in her arousal. Bare-chested with her skirt askew, she knew the effect her undulating hips had on him. She saw the longing move over his face and flicker like wildfire in his dark eyes.

A slow, grinding tune vibrated from her without forethought as she swayed and twisted in front of him. Her reward was a deep mumbling and smoldering stare. Incited, she rolled her hips with the molten energy radiating and building between them. Untamed and wild, the desire shaped her movements. Danielle reached behind her to find the skirt zipper and the material loosened, falling from her. She stepped from it, bracing her legs wide apart, aware the thin, lacy panties revealed her shaven pussy. He unbuttoned his shirt and stood.

"Not so fast," she said and pushed him back, placing her bare foot on the arm of the chair so his face was only a few inches from the thin veil separating his tongue from her flesh. He reached for one of her breasts, but she leaned back so his fingers merely grazed a nipple. "Did I say you could do that?" she asked, all too aware of the power she held over him.

"Your emerging self seems to be quite a tease," he said and relaxed in the chair with a very satisfied smile spreading over his lips.

"And you enjoy being teased, my King."

"Sometimes."

"Hmmm…" She moved and wiggled her toes against his broad chest, trailing her big toe down to his flat belly and to the bulge inside his slacks. Slowly, she massaged his cock in circular motions.

"I can unzip it for you," he offered.

"No." She flattened her foot against his chest and shoved him back. "I'll do it."

His smile widened, and he moved his hands aside, allowing her complete control Waves of excitement coursed through her. He'd always been the aggressor, it was now her turn. Resting her foot on the arm of the chair, she bent over him, and allowed a most advantageous view of her crotch. His stare scorched her, sending a rush of heated wetness to her panties.

She reached for his trousers with the fine material brushing her fingers and slid a finger between the zipper and cloth flap. He shifted in the chair and she knew he felt the same kind of excited anticipation she always felt whenever he undressed her. His hands balled into hard fists. The newfound power to titillate him emboldened her and she shifted to her knees. Spreading his legs apart, Danielle settled between them and lifted the metal tab on the zipper. His groan impassioned her and she tugged on the zipper while he hurriedly unbuckled the belt.

"No." She pushed his hands from the buckle before he could release it. "You can't do anything unless I tell you. Understood?"

He muttered something unintelligible. Danielle leaned over and unzipped the pants. His cock, still trapped within his underwear, bulged through the open fly, and he mumbled once more, shifting in the chair to push his pelvis upward. She knew he ached for her fingers to stroke him, longing for that needed touch.

Instead, she glided her fingers over the underwear, ever so lightly touching his hardness beneath. A throaty sound vibrated from him. The rush was stronger than she'd anticipated. The need for fulfillment strained against his grip of the arms as he struggled to contain the urgency. He sought release from the pulsing fire coiling in his belly, a release only she could bring.

His need flashed like fire through her, radiating to her pussy. Slowly, she worked the belt buckle and let it fall free, and quickly unhooked the slacks. The fly opened wider and his grip on the arms of the chair turned white-knuckled.

Her fingers slipped beneath the underwear band, he flinched as she brushed against his flesh and dipped deeper to curl strong fingers around his cock.

"Your hands feel good on me," he whispered when she exposed his balls, cupping them within her hands. Strong, even strokes against his hardness drew a deep breath from him as she moved up the shaft, slowly at first, then faster, building tempo. His groans of pleasure filled the room. Satisfied he was sufficiently aroused, she leaned forward and took the hard cock in her mouth, pressing firm lips around its stiffness.

He moved under the teasing, having waited as long as he could. His excitement sent sharp waves of arousal flashing over her. Flicking her tongue over the end of his cock, she sensed the touch set his need to the very edge of control.

"I want to fuck you," he said with the fullness of desire rasping in his voice.

His hands closed over her shoulders and she quickened the rhythm, stimulating his cock with encircling fingers as she sucked harder. Suddenly he shifted and her reign was over. Danielle found herself lifted from the floor with strong arms supporting her while they floated toward the ceiling. She tightened her arms around his neck, fearing the fall would come at any second.

"Shh, my sweet. I've got you. Besides, you can fly or even float, too."

"What?" she asked, kicking her feet, longing to touch solid matter, knowing she was helpless to keep from crashing down.

He must have realized her fear overrode any passion she'd felt and quickly lowered them to the bed, settling onto the mattress. She shivered.

"I'll teach you how to float later. You'll find it a most enjoyable way to make love." He stroked her arms, letting long fingers trail down to her thigh and the moist softness between her legs.

"You need to be welcomed into your emergence in a proper vampire fashion." He moved one of her arms over her head and pushed it toward the bedpost, then the other arm. At first she lay there thinking he expected her to comply with his demands as she had required him, but when he spread her legs and placed each at the same angle to the posts, she immediately knew bondage was in store for her.

"I don't think I'm ready for this," she said, licking her lips, not daring to admit just how arousing the intimation of bondage was.

"Ah, but that is the point, isn't it?" He stood, dropping his remaining clothes to the floor.

Danielle started to sit up, but he held his hand up as though to stop her. She giggled at such a lame excuse to prevent her from moving, until she realized she could not move. It was as though her limbs were lashed to the bedposts.

"Now relax, my tempting wife." His voice was rich, with sexual energy vibrating in each word. "You are going to learn a lesson about control, my love."

"How did you do that?" She strained against the invisible bindings. It felt as if leather strips cut into her wrists and ankles each time she struggled to sit up. "What is this, Armondés? How is this possible?"

"I'm a vampire. Remember? I can do a lot of things mortals can only imitate, rather clumsily at that."

A titillating anticipation rose deep from within as she struggled against the tethering. He walked toward her, his cock erect and buoyant with his movements.

She stopped struggling, transfixed by his naked body, so close, yet so far from her touch. The desire was excruciatingly wonderful as she watched him sit on the bed by her.

"There now, that's how a vampire likes to see his prey. Defenseless and wanting." His lips slid into a wicked grin with the same burning desire mirrored in his eyes. "You do want me, don't you?" he asked, opening the bedside table.

She strained to see what he was retrieving, but found even her head was held against the pillow by the same force making her practically paralyzed. Paralyzed but not numb. Every nerve ending in her body sizzled with anticipation. The drawer closed and she caught the white flicker as he brought the boa plumage in front of her.

The feathery boa looked as though it had been broken from a very large wrap and absently she wondered where it had come from and why it had been stored in the nightstand.

"So many questions racing through that lovely mind of yours," he droned and dragged the soft feathery wisps over her face and down her neck to brush her breasts. Already peaked and hardened by the arousal of being bound and at his mercy, the touch of the boa sent burning strokes over her abdomen to her pussy.

She struggled against the invisible ropes, writhing as the feathery string trailed over her abdomen and swirled against the lips of her pussy ever so softly. She looked up and was surprised to see the boa moving by itself. How was that possible? Armondés' stare moved about her body and the instrument of her arousal shifted to travel the length of her leg. When it slipped around her ankle to tease the sole of her foot, the electrifying touch sent her into a frenzy. She writhed but her body didn't respond, held immobile by his power. The frenetic energy gripped her body, heightening with her inability to move. She released a throaty gasp.

"You want more?" he purred in her ear, letting his tongue flicker along the opening. Shudders roared in her ears and down to her feet.

"Y-Yes," she rasped.

"What about a cold stroke like this?" he nodded and an icy chill tickled between the lips of her pussy and brushed her swollen clit.

Her moan vibrated deep inside her.

"Or perhaps something a bit harder?" he asked.

The thickness moved between her legs and slipped inside her opening.

She gasped, pulsating in every imaginable area of her body. Incredible waves of pleasure gripped her. She bit her lower lip, longing to move with the urgent sensations tantalizing her, but he still held her immobile.

"I can do a combination of things to you, my love. You just have to let me know what you want." His hand moved over her leg. Firm fingers spread her pussy enough to allow a gentle stroke against her clit. He lowered his head to suckle one of her nipples. The intensity of the stimulation was too great and she cried out, longing to thrash against the sensations.

"Please release me," she breathed.

"In time, I want you to have a few moments of this intense teasing then I am going to fuck you hard."

"Yes, please."

"Not just yet, what if I allow you to move your torso, would that help?"

Suddenly she could raise her head and managed to lean slightly forward, but her arms were still tied to the post with invisible bindings.

"No! It's the lower part that needs to move," she agonized as he leaned over and pressed a tender kiss against her pussy. She quivered and burned for more. She tried to wiggle her hips.

"Yes, I can see that is the area," he groaned as he lashed her with his tongue then stopped.

"Oh God, what are you doing!" she gasped, needing more.

"It is an art form, you know." His fingers entered her pussy, plunging deeply, the sensation making her toes feel as though they were curling in response.

"Please, Armondés," she begged, collapsing back into the bed.

He didn't stop, quickening the strokes.

She swallowed against the raging fire building her, demanding the touch that would free it, but he withheld himself from her.

He shifted so he was inside her spread legs and lowered his lips to her pussy, blowing a heated path along the soft mound and folds.

She moaned, longing for his tongue to taste her, lick her, but once more he tempted her and withdrew.

"Do you wish to anger me or arouse me?" she asked, feeling a frustration greater than any she'd ever experienced.

He moved his hand and her torso was freed of its bonds. His finger slipped between the folds and she moved with relief against his strokes, pushing her hips so her clit could brush against his finger. He quickened the rhythm, driving the friction deeper into her flesh until, arching her back, she shuddered. Crying out, Danielle collapsed under the sweet molten spasms as he continued to stimulate her clit.

She tried to move his hand, but he pushed her attempts aside. The waves of passion began to build once more and she ground against his hand, longing for the pleasure his magical fingers promised.

He slipped from her and she murmured, displeased, as he spread her thighs apart and thrust his cock between them, pushing deep inside. She received his length and rocked against the pounding, clinging to him. She wanted him. Her heart tugged with the feel of his naked body over her, in her and beneath her hands. The driving thrusts pounded against her clit as he fucked her.

"I love you, Danielle," he groaned as his body went rigid. The warmth of his come filled her and spasms seized her in strong grips of pleasure against his cock. She trembled in the second wave of release and hot sticky liquid rushed between her legs. She fell back onto the pillows as he rocked against her in the aftermath of his orgasm.

* * * * *

Danielle lay in Armondés' arms, pondering the events of the past week. Her old life seemed a dream, as though it belonged to someone else. She had forgotten what it felt like to get up in the mornings and go to work each day. Her time with Armondés seemed so much longer than her entire lifetime. How was that possible? How could he make her feel the things she did? What had she become? Nothing more than a vampire?

She traced the black curl that lay against his temple. He looked so human, almost boyish as he slept. He had said all vampires could read thoughts. How did one do that? Would he really teach her to read his mind? What man would risk such a thing? She rested her head on his chest and closed her eyes.

Scenes played against the darkness of closed eyelids. What was this? Dreams, the answer came. Dreams, filled with ancient times and battles. Blood. Lots of blood and screams. Grotesque scenes and then they stopped. A castle rose above a vineyard and there was order, calmness.

She sat up panting and quietly slipped from the bed, dragging on the new robe he'd bought her. Tying the sash, she parted the drapery and peered out at the sleeping city. It would be day soon. She looked back at her sleeping husband. The scenes had been his memories. Somehow she knew she'd managed to tap into those vampire abilities he had described. He lay sprawled across the bed, lying on his back, oblivious to her musings. But she knew. She had seen everything. Armondés had saved his people. He had nurtured a vision to bring them out of their baser selves to become educated and cultured and to find a solution to the enslavement to blood.

He had civilized his people and transformed them from hunters into artists, musicians, craftsmen, and scholars. Through his compassion and love, yes, love, he had raised them up from the base level of hunters into a new lifestyle. New appreciation for him as a man stretched beyond her former perception of the vampire who had transformed her. Armondés had honor and integrity. He was a visionary who had built a new world for his people. Tears welled in her eyes.

"Oh, Armondés, I had no idea," she whispered and turned back to the bed.

Chapter Seven

"You are so gorgeous," Armondés said and kissed her. His lips were firm and Danielle wanted to taste the depth of his kiss, but he pulled away. She shifted under the urgent need to rub against him. The memory of how he'd teased her into frenzied need only a few hours earlier licked jagged pulses to her groin.

She stared up at her husband, dressed in his tuxedo. He'd chosen a scarlet bow tie that matched the red handkerchief in his breast pocket. Her attention moved over the diamond stud buttons down to the gold and red cummerbund hugging his trim waist. He looked not a day over thirty-five. She lifted her stare and met his knowing one. Her stomach fluttered.

"I have something for you." He retrieved a long, slender, blue velvet box from the dresser drawer.

"What's this?" she asked, unable to rein in her excitement.

"For tonight," he said and opened the box. A large oval sapphire dangling from a row of diamonds sparkled from the blue lining.

"Oh my God!" she gasped and smiled at the gift.

"Here, let me help you with it." He lifted the necklace and placed it around her neck. She stood in front of the hall mirror, ignoring the faint reflection she cast. Instead, she focused on the magnificent necklace sparkling around her neck.

"Oh, Armondés, thank you. When do we have to return it?" she asked, assuming he had rented the magnificent necklace for the evening.

"Return? It's yours, Danielle. I bought it especially for our civil wedding ceremony and of course your presentation later this evening. It's just the first of many such gifts." He stood behind her. A sharp pang pierced through her. Was she falling in love with him? She ran her fingers over the diamonds and gathered the pendant between her fingers.

"I've never— Oh, thank you so much." She turned in the circle of his arms and stood on tiptoes to plant a kiss on his cheek. He moved his head and captured her lips with his. She responded to his passion, opening her lips slightly to allow his tongue entry into her mouth.

"My King, it's time," the guard said from the other side of the door leading to the hallway.

She needed to feel him in her arms and tightened them around his neck as though he'd leave. It had been nearly six weeks since she'd first come to his club and she'd not been outside their wing of the building. Reluctantly, she pulled from him.

"Your old life has fallen from you completely. Tonight marks the beginning of our life together." He held her to him, and kissed her shoulder.

"It's as though I've always been with you, Armondés. I can barely remember my former life. The memory grows dimmer each day."

"Is that so bad?" He cupped her face in his hands, looking for the answer in her eyes.

"No." She tilted her face to receive his kiss. His lips melted against hers until she moaned, needing to feel him inside her.

The rap on the door was louder this time. She jumped in response and jerked from him.

"Shh now. I have servants to assist you in your dress. Manicure, hair, makeup." He brushed his lips against hers again. "Remember, you are the Queen. They do your bidding, not the other way around." His words warmed her and stilled the nervous quivering in her stomach. She looked up into his dark eyes and found the confidence she needed within their depths. He had chosen her. She was his wife, his queen. No one could challenge her position or his devotion.

"Enter," he called and the door swung open.

The shorter man looked up at them, clearing his throat and adjusting his glasses.

"Where are the witnesses?" he asked, eyeing the large room and empty bottles of wine.

"Well, just how many do you need?" Armondés asked, hearing the man's thoughts about decadent parties complete with orgies, wine and who knows what else.

"I need at least two witnesses." The man fidgeted nervously, produced a handkerchief from his coat pocket and proceeded to mop his forehead. "I could have brought witnesses had I known there was a need."

Armondés was tempted to inform the man he was here to marry the heir of Armondés Wines, but decided it best to let the man think they were drunks and had decided to get married while in the throes of their stupor. It added to the drama of having called him here after-hours, even though he was being paid well for the service.

"Where are my sister and Fredrick? They were supposed to be here by now," he asked the guard, who had remained just inside the open doorway.

"I shall see what the delay is, my King," the guard bowed and left to do his bidding.

"King, is it?" The clerk began to tremble. "What country?"

"How many marriages have you performed, Mister—"

"Evans. Hal Evans. I have no idea. I lost count years ago." He looked around the room. "You have a nice place, here. This used to be a warehouse in the early 1800s."

"What is this?" Minnie's high heels clicked against the marble floor as she entered the room with her red silk robe fluttering around her.

"You need us?" Fredrick asked coming up behind her, struggling to button his shirt.

"We need witnesses," he answered.

"Oh, the civil service. How could we have forgotten?" She narrowed her stare on the Clerk of Deeds.

"Let's begin." Armondés stared at the flustered clerk.

"Ah…" Mr. Evans' discomfort seemed to grow by the second. "So this is it? A royal wedding and, I mean…yes, well, let's get started." He mopped his head one last time and then opened the small book.

"We only have five minutes," Minnie warned.

"The short version, please." Armondés took Danielle's hand in his, letting his stare move over her soft beige wedding gown. "You are so beautiful," he said and led her to stand in front of the man.

"Good evening." The clerk smiled widely at Danielle, clearly unsettled by her beauty. Armondés mused that the man would surely burst from his tight suit if he didn't hurry the ceremony along.

"Shall we get started?" he asked, squeezing her hand reassuringly.

"Very well then, do you, Danielle Louise Rivers take this man, Armondés—" he stuttered with realization widening his eyes. "Excuse me, Armondés Tresnávé to be your lawfully wedded husband?"

She looked up into Armondés' eyes and saw love in their depths. Tears burned her throat.

"I do." She smiled at him.

A doorbell chimed.

Mr. Evans stopped and looked up at them.

"Continue," Armondés said.

"Do you Armondés Tresnávé take this woman, Danielle Louise Rivers, to be your lawfully wedded wife?"

"I do," he said and pulled her into his arms.

"Very well then, I now pronounce you man and wife by the authority—"

The words drowned in her ears when Armondés pressed his lips against hers, sealing their marriage. She returned the deep kiss, longing to have the evening over so she could lie in his arms. It was strange having so many people around them when she'd spent the last weeks secluded in their quarters with just him.

She heard talking and movement as Mr. Evans was ushered from the suite.

The door closed and they were alone again. He released her lips, brushing gentle short kisses over them. She clung to each kiss, reluctant to release it.

"I already felt married," she whispered between kisses.

"Now we are married in both worlds. I love you so much, Danielle." He pressed a kiss on her cheek.

"I…I love you, Armondés." She searched his eyes and saw the joy reflected in their depths.

"I have waited so long to hear those words from you, my love." He twirled her around the room, lifting them from the floor, while crushing her to him. "This is truly the happiest day of my life." His kiss melted against hers.

* * * * *

They had an hour before Presentation and Danielle took the time to change her wedding gown. The Presentation gown was her favorite article of clothing. She had picked it out online and ordered it. The delivery had been made just that morning and she longed to surprise her husband with the deep blue silk, full-length gown. Multiple layers of folded silk formed an off the shoulders band. The snug fit outlined her curves.

She studied her reflection. Everything must be perfect for this night. Armondés had been called downstairs to attend to affairs of state, whatever that meant. She was too nervous to ask and had he told her doubted she'd have heard. She was too excited to take in anything beyond Presentation. Facing hundreds of vampires was disarming enough, much less to be presented to them as the new queen. She took one last look in the mirror, leaning forward and squinting at the foggy image. Would she ever get used to all this?

The door opened and Armondés entered their bedroom.

"It's time…" his voice trailed off when she turned around.

"I just need help with this," she said, holding out the sapphire necklace he'd gifted her.

"You—You are gorgeous!" His eyes glazed with the same passion stirring in the pit of her stomach. "You outshine the gown." He took the necklace and clasped it around her neck.

"Oh, Armondés, you're so handsome," she sighed, taking in the powerful image he cut in his tuxedo. His hair fell just past his shoulders.

He bestowed a soft kiss on her lips then held out his arm.

"Your court awaits. We must hurry." He leaned over and whispered as they entered the hallway, "Just you wait until later." His words fanned her ear.

"I can't wait." She tightened her hand in the crook of his arm and allowed him to escort her down the corridor. Her heart pounded harder, even though she knew it was impossible to feel it beating or for it to hammer out her excitement and anxiety, but it did. Their footfalls clicked along the marble floor, echoing in the unusual quietness as they walked the short distance to the elevator.

The guard fell in behind them and matched their pace. She glanced over her shoulder, recognizing the blond man in the tuxedo. He was the regular guard for their suite. Absently, she thought it odd not to know his name.

The three of them entered the elevator, and Armondés pressed the button for the lobby. She licked her lips and tried to still the raging emotions. Sensing her tension, her husband placed a steady hand over hers and squeezed just as the elevator stopped and the doors opened. She stepped onto the balcony with him and looked down at the crowded club below.

Colorful strobe lights flashed across the room, contradicting the elegance of the floral and silver decorations. Her knees weakened, but she managed to step from the elevator with her king. The club fell silent. All attention riveted to them. The flashing lights stopped and were replaced by soft red ones that bathed the vaulted ceiling. Candles flickered from the tables and wall sconces.

Danielle looked around, realizing that the hundreds of people who now stood in silence were all vampires. Her clansmen. It was too much to comprehend. She stiffened. He tightened his hand over hers, giving her the confidence she lacked. They stood on the upper balcony, looking down at the dance floor. No one bowed to them.

Armondés had given her brief instructions on court protocol. It was simple. She was to forget most of what she knew of human royalty. Vampires had their own rules and loved to flout the fact they were not human.

"Good evening!" His sexy voice boomed over the room. "Welcome to Presentation."

Cheers and shouts of congratulations pounded out a loud din. He held up his hand and the room fell silent again.

"I am most pleased this evening to present your new Queen…Danielle. Please come welcome her to the clan!" he shouted and moved her hand from his arm, holding it in his. He guided her around in front of him, raising their hands up—a signal to form the reception line.

Danielle nodded and gave what she hoped was a warm smile. Suddenly, the guests began to rise from the floor. She was startled at first, but calmed her reaction, masking her fright with what she hoped was a regal pose.

The vampires lifted effortlessly toward the balcony, forming a floating line that spiraled to the floor. Dressed in their finest black-tie attire, one by one they stepped onto the balcony. Armondés introduced each one to her by name, usually offering a small tidbit about the vampire.

Danielle was amazed at her husband's knowledge of each guest. No wonder he'd continued to be King for thousands of years. He was loyal to his clan and certainly demonstrated his ability to make each member feel special. At first she attempted to learn each name, but soon gave up and aimed to simply bestow a sincere smile and show an interest in them.

After two hours and with several guests still waiting to be presented, Danielle's smiling muscles ached. She counted the remaining people left but soon was discouraged. Sensing her fatigue, Armondés drew his arm around her waist and hugged her to his side. His strength reenergized her. She glanced at the dance floor below, meeting the occasional upturned glance in their direction. Goblets in hand, their guests seemed to be enjoying the evening. The vast room was a loud, constant roar of voices, laughter and clinking stemware.

The last two in line were Minnie and Fredrick. Danielle had not had an opportunity to talk with her new sister-in-law. After the ceremony, everyone had rushed to see about various preparations. Danielle looked forward to getting to know her better. Perhaps they could find some time later that evening.

"Danielle," Minnie said and leaned in to give an imaginary kiss on either cheek. "It's a great pleasure to officially welcome you into the family. I trust the past few weeks have not been too difficult for you. Transformations can be excruciating."

"Armondés took great care of me," she said, wondering if the look Minnie quickly masked had been pleasure at the thought of her suffering. She looked deeper into the other woman's eyes, but met a wall. She made a mental note not to trust her new sister- in-law just yet.

"My brother can be surprising," Minnie clipped, then reached for him and bestowed an airy kiss on either side of his face. "Congratulations, brother. Your queen is ravishing."

"She certainly is." He smiled down at Danielle. She lifted her stare to his. Hunger flashed in his eyes. Heat swept over her. She cleared her throat and glanced past Minnie, focusing on the stranger waiting patiently behind her. The man smiled at her and she stiffened. He was familiar. Had she met him before? Minnie said something to her. She nodded her head, wondering what she'd just agreed to do. The man stepped around Minnie and clasped Armondés' hand, slapping him on the back.

"Danielle," Armondés said, "this is my best friend, Fredrick Van Cantrep. You may recall him. He was our best man."

"Fredrick. It's great to see you again." She offered her hand.

"My Queen." He bowed over her hand, clicking his heels together in a very old-world fashion. He kissed the air just above her flesh. "The ceremony happened so fast I did not have time to introduce myself. It was a very, well, short ceremony. Always the best kind of ceremony."

She saw the amused sneer flash over Minnie's face. What was up with her?

"I have served Armondés since he made me. I now serve you." Fredrick straightened.

His words struck a chord in her. They shared a strong bond in Armondés. Somehow, the thought was strangely comforting.

"You can depend on Fredrick, Danielle. If you ever need anything, especially something confidential, Fredrick is the one to seek."

She glanced up at her husband and nodded.

With the last guest greeted, champagne was uncorked and served to everyone. Danielle and Armondés stood on the balcony with Minnie and Fredrick by their sides. It was Fredrick who raised his goblet in a toast. Danielle examined her goblet, uncertain if she should try to drink champagne.

Sensing her concern, Armondés leaned over her.

"Just take a sip, eventually you can cultivate a tolerance for alcohol," he whispered then drew his arm around her waist, pulling her snugly to his side. She smiled up at him, grateful for his ability to know just what she needed. He was so handsome. Her breath quickened. She longed to wrap herself around him and taste his lips. Instead, she looked back at Fredrick, meeting Minnie's intense stare. If she'd not known better, Danielle could have sworn it was hatred, not love, blazing in her sister-in-law's eyes.

"A toast to our new Queen," Fredrick's voice split through the club. Everyone hushed and raised their goblets.

"To our Queen," they said in unison.

"Danielle," Fredrick addressed her. "We wish you a peaceful and happy reign by the side of your king. Welcome to our clan." He nodded then raised the goblet to his lips.

The guests cheered and downed their drinks as well.

Danielle nodded to Fredrick, raised her goblet to the room below and took a sip from it. The liquid rolled down her throat and crashed into her stomach. Nausea welled up in her. She leaned slightly forward, but straightened, knowing all eyes were on her.

She swallowed back the sickness and stepped up to the low railing, holding her goblet in a toast to her guests.

"I thank each of you for the warm welcome. I have much to learn, but know I will succeed in my role as your queen since I have each of you to assist me in my duties. May our clan remain strong and committed to the good of all."

The club was a roar of cheers and clapping. Armondés was by her side. Pride beamed over him like a spotlight as he hugged her to his side and pulled her into a kiss. The noise was deafening as the guests pounded tables with their fists and stamped their feet in approval.

The cheers were a dim echo in the wake of his kiss. She wanted to drag her husband back to their suite and fuck him until he could take no more. He had honored her better than she could have ever anticipated and for the first time, she truly felt she was his wife.

He released her, but she continued to stare up at him and reached to whisper in his ear.

"From this moment forward, I am truly your wife, Armondés. No regrets, no remorse. I fully embrace all it means to be your mate."

His dark eyes glazed with what she could have sworn were tears. He squeezed her hand and planted a hard kiss on her forehead.

"I love you, Danielle," he whispered.

His words seemed to enter her very body and swirled chaotic whirlwinds through her. Armondés loved her! She smiled down at their guests through teary eyes.

"Let the celebration begin!" he called out. The music blasted into the air, followed by a change in the lights. The strobes flashed a rainbow of colors in time with the beat. Their guests filled the dance floor. He turned to her and encircled her waist with his arms. His hard body pressed into hers. Her breathing was labored, giving away how his touch affected her.

"Let's dance, Danielle. Do you remember how to levitate?" he asked.

Before she could respond, he lifted her into the air with him and glided down toward the dance floor. The dance floor buzzed with comments as the crowd noticed their entrance. Couples elevated from the floor and joined them.

She clung to him, afraid if she attempted to solo she'd fall the two stories to the floor below. He didn't reprimand her for her lack of confidence. Instead, he held her tighter so she would feel safe. Each of his small acts of kindness and caring strummed her heartstrings. He twirled her through the air and for a brief moment she truly felt she was in a fantasy. They danced for what seemed like hours. Eventually, they landed on the dance floor and she wobbled to the nearby table.

"I will get you a goblet," he said.

"Mind if we join you?" Minnie asked. Not waiting for a response, she sat down beside Danielle while Fredrick headed for the bar. "Turned out to be a wonderful evening after all."

"Sounds as though you had your doubts." Danielle looked at her sister-in-law, trying to gauge if it was disappointment or surprise riding the tone in her voice.

"It's always a risk when dealing with one recently transformed." She must have seen how her words offended Danielle, for she was quick to explain. "I don't mean that in an accusatory manner, but a seasoned vampire would have less adjustment as queen."

"I can see how that would be true, but then again, a seasoned vampire could never be queen, if I understand the curse correctly."

Minnie shrugged.

"So do you have any regrets, Danielle?"

"About Armondés?" she asked, trying to mask the excitement created just thinking about her husband.

"Any of it. You've lost your old life."

"It wasn't really going anywhere I wanted to go," she admitted and met the other woman's look. She marveled at her own confidence and bravery. She recalled how intimidated she'd felt in Minnie's presence the night they'd met. It seemed lifetimes ago.

"That certainly is the attitude that will best serve you. I don't envy you, though. Being queen to Armondés' king is a painful job."

"Painful?" she asked with laughter bubbling past her attempts to stop it. "Dear Minnie, being Armondés' queen as you put it, is far from painful. I've never been so fulfilled and happy in my whole life." She leveled her gaze on her sister-in-law. The other woman's expression shifted from menacing to shocked then angry. Good. Now she knew her place.

"So are you getting to know each other better?" Armondés handed her a silver chalice. She appreciated his sensitivity in masking its contents so she would not have to see that it wasn't wine sloshing against the sides.

"Yes, my love," she said, emphasizing the endearment. "I'm getting to know Minnie very well." She tossed Minnie a challenging look, sensing the other woman's jealousy. Did Minnie feel her own position threatened by a new queen? Had the other queens threatened her as well? "Let's join the guests, darling." Danielle tucked her arm in his and glided away from Minnie.

"What was that about?" he asked.

"Just a little female thing, nothing of importance, my King." She tilted the chalice to her lips and sipped the nectar. It raced through her. It was like a secret power that worked its magic on her, pumping her up. It replaced her fatigue with renewed strength. She smiled at him and reached for his hand. He sat down beside her and they watched the dancers while sipping from the goblets. He nuzzled her ear.

"I want you," he whispered in her ear. His words tunneled against her ear, sending wild pulses all the way to her pussy. "My cock is hard for you. Here, feel it." He moved her hand underneath the tablecloth to the bulge in his pants. She let him brush her palm against him.

"What do you want me to do, sire?" she asked, feeling giddy from the goblet's contents.

"I want you to lie on top of the table and let me spread your legs so I can eat your pussy," he whispered.

She gasped and pulled slightly from him. Something moved behind them. She looked over her shoulder. Three men stood only a few feet from them. She saw the crossbow first, then the swords. Her scream ripped from her. It was as though all life stopped and became fluid, moving in slow motion. She was aware her husband had jumped from the table, and shoved her behind him, using his body as a shield. The crossbow sounded in front of them as the arrow was released. Armondés grabbed her by the arms and lifted her away from the danger. The arrow flew past her head and plunged into the wall. The other man flew toward them with sword drawn back.

"Armondés!" she screamed as the blade sliced the air only inches from his head. He dodged the movement and fell backwards onto the floor.

"No!" Danielle knew the blade would find its mark. Eternity without Armondés flashed in front of her. He struggled to rise to his feet, but the swordsman was too quick.

"Armondés!" Instinct took over, allowing her no time to think, only to act as the second swordsman charged. She lunged forward, throwing herself in front of the blade. Her only concern was to save her husband. The steel swished inches from her neck, barely missing her. Landing on top of her husband, she groped for him. Strong hands came up underneath her arms and Danielle found herself hoisted into Armondés' powerful embrace as he flew toward the balcony and their suite beyond.

"Save the King!" A shout blasted from the crowd. Several men rushed to their defense and tackled the assassins.

She glanced back as one of the attackers was stabbed with a wooden stake and disintegrated into dust.

"Oh my God!" she gasped.

"We're almost there," Armondés responded. Danielle sighed in relief and nuzzled against his chest. He was safe!

"I was afraid they had destroyed you," he said, kicking open the doors to their suite, not breaking his stride. "Close the doors and don't let anyone in," he barked. She peered over his shoulder realizing the guards had been behind them. Once in the safety of their rooms, he stopped and released her legs, letting her slide down the length of his body. He smothered her in kisses then tightened his embrace.

"Are you okay?" he asked.

"Yes, are you?" she asked.

"I was so scared." She buried her head into his chest. "Those were vampires weren't they? Not stalkers."

"Yes. Vampire assassins."

"I don't understand. Why were they trying to kill you?"

"I can't lose you, Danielle. I *won't* lose you." He smoothed back her hair.

"You won't. I promise."

"Tonight I nearly did." His eyes were filled with something she'd never seen in their depths, fear. Fear for her.

"I'm sorry, but I had to protect you. The sword would have struck you."

"No," he said and stiffened beside her.

"Yes, it would have sliced right through you."

"I was not the target, Danielle." He pulled her closer.

Chapter Eight

"Bonsoir, ma reine." The servant dressed in a gray uniform bowed then entered the bedroom.

Danielle frowned at the older woman who wore her gray hair in a tight bun. Did she ever do anything differently? Over the past months she had never seen the maid change her routine.

"Ingund, how many times do I need to tell you to quit calling me your queen? My name's Danielle."

"Mais non, ma reine. I have served the Tresnávé family ever since I was first turned, and I am aware of protocol." The older woman bobbed her head and set about her morning chores.

Danielle shrugged. It was impossible to make the woman live in the modern world. And no wonder... She looked about the room and stood from the makeup table. Just look at what they were living in—a castle, no less. She looked at her reflection in the mirror. Thankfully, the story about vampire's having no reflection was false. Although her reflection was rather faded, she did at least have one. She mused and tucked in her shirt, certain Ingund disapproved of her choice of jeans and tee shirt. Screw protocol.

Ingund drew back the long drapery, revealing a brilliant night bathed by a full moon. Danielle so loved such nights.

"A glorious night!" Ingund exclaimed and stood looking out the window.

"I love full moons," Danielle said coming to stand by her.

"No lovelier a sight," the older woman sighed and turned to open the other draperies. Danielle contemplated the woman. It was rare that one met an old vampire. Why had she been turned at such an old age? She was about to ask when Minnie burst into the bedroom.

"Good morning, Minnie," she said and sat down at the breakfast tray. "Ever hear of knocking? Ingund was just informing me about protocol."

"Knock knock." Minnie sneered and sat down at the table. "What's for *supper*?" She grabbed a glass.

"Blood and more blood. I think this evening's flavor is apricot."

"Oh yum, pour me some," Minnie said and held out her glass.

"You're awfully happy tonight. What's up?" Danielle poured the creamy red mixture into the glass goblet.

"Nothing. Trying to spread some cheer. I've been so damn depressed ever since arriving here. I feel like we're living in a tomb. I never did like this damned castle or this damned country for that matter."

"I thought you were born here," Danielle said.

"Oh gawd, no. Armondés moved us to this region during the second year of Charlemagne's solitary rule in 772."

"Solitary?"

"Yeah, before that he shared the throne, ruling the Franks with his brother for a couple of years, then his brother died, and he got the whole enchilada. Armondés felt Charlemagne would bring a renaissance to France that would bring great opportunity to those who lived here. Sorta like we could ride the wave and make a fortune. And of course, Charlemagne did just that, and we made a fortune."

"That's amazing, where did you live before that time?"

"Everywhere. We lived in Julius Caesar's Roma. Of course, there really wasn't a France back then as we know it now. It was called Gaul. And we also lived in Egypt for a while. Back then people knew what we were, and we didn't have to hide behind myths and legends. No one dared challenge us. And we weren't forced to live the way we do now. Our natural instincts were allowed full rein." She sighed with a wistful look glazing over her eyes. "Those were the 'good ole days', not at all like it is now. We're fricking prisoners here!" She stood from the table and started for the door, but it opened before she could reach for it. Armondés entered.

"So, what's this?" He looked from his sister to his wife then back to his sister.

"Dinner." Minnie held up the goblet and brushed past him.

"Minnie being social? She must be bored," he said and sat down beside his wife, nodding for the maid to leave.

"She was telling me about Charlemagne and how you came to live here."

"Did she now?"

"It was fascinating. She said you lived in Julius Caesar's Rome. Is that true?"

"Yes. It's not as fascinating as it sounds, though. Life is much better nowadays. We no longer have to hunt. Our clan is fairly civilized. And there are no plagues or crusades to contend with."

"Right, I can see how assassins are a huge improvement over all that," she said.

"That's why we're here, my love," he said and pulled her into his arms. "We are safe here. And until we can find out who is behind this, here is where we will stay."

"What if your second wife wasn't killed by a vampire stalker, but was a victim of those assassins? You said yourself there were just a handful of stalkers left. Maybe the assassins are after me for the same reason, because I'm now the queen.

"You said they wanted to kill me, not you. Why did you say that? What would happen if they did?"

"Other than devastate me?"

"Seriously, why would they try for your new wife?"

"I don't know."

"I think you do." She tried to probe into his mind, but it was as if she hit a blank wall. Could he block her searching?

"I would never place you in danger."

"I believe you, but I also know if you've lived over two thousand years then you've had time to develop a lot of abilities, such as lying, and twisting reality to suit your purpose. I love you. And I think my love can counter any of those abilities, but I can't win out over the truth."

"You are naïve then, my love. And that is why I adore you." He kissed her, tugging on her lower lip with his.

"Oh, you're insulting as hell." She moved from his embrace and settled on the window seat overlooking the vast vineyards. "Is that what you told your other wife? Charisse?"

"Why must we do this?" The irritation in his voice made her stomach flutter nervously, but she had to press on and find out what he was hiding from her.

"Because I want to know. It's normal to be curious about your husband's other wife, or in your case, wives."

"Charisse's death was not a result of vampires trying to dethrone me," he said and looked up into her eyes. "As I said, she was careless. She took a lot of risks and was stalked and killed."

"But how can you be sure?" She was not going to relent until she was satisfied he had told her everything.

"Yes. We found the stalker's body."

"But how did you know it was a vampire stalker?"

"They always have a tattoo on their left forearm, a Celtic cross."

"Okay," she nodded, finally satisfied he was telling her the truth. "And did you turn Charisse and Alexa the same way you did me?"

"Charisse was a servant in my house."

"You aren't answering my question, Armondés. Did you make her?"

"Yes, of course."

"And Alexa? Did you make her, too?"

"Yes. It is part of the curse that I must make my bride a vampire. You should know this." His voice tightened and she knew she was trying his patience.

"I see, so you put them through the same tests as you did me? With the champagne and the taste of the Private Label?"

"Yes."

"And so you consider yourself 'civilized'. Is that the word you used?"

"I am."

"Do you honestly think taking a woman like that and transforming her into a vampire, which she has no idea she has become until it is too late... Do you really think that's civilized?"

"What would you have me do?" His stare opened and she felt as if she were plummeting into those depthless eyes.

"I don't know." She looked away, focusing on getting to the rest of the truth. Her feelings for him made her want to end the questions and pretend it didn't matter, but she sensed it mattered a great deal.

"It's a little late to be arguing about all this." He cleared his throat and paced in front of her.

"I'm not trying to argue. I'm just worried."

"I understand."

"No, you don't. You couldn't. Before I met you, being civilized had a different meaning than it does now. It meant I lived in a world where people worked and lived together without worrying about assassins. It meant I didn't drink blood from a bottle instead of killing people for it. It just wasn't part of my 'being civilized' makeup. You're kidding yourself, Armondés." She looked from him, focusing her stare beyond the window. The protective shielding on the window that allowed her the luxury of looking out at the world bathed in daylight gave the night scene a bluish tint.

"You have much to adjust to, my Danielle. I understand this. But you must also realize what it was like for us before we adopted a civilized life." He stood in front of her and reached out to stroke her cheek with the back of his hand.

"Then tell me so I can understand."

"Before I moved my people to France, we ravaged the villages where we roamed. We lived by our base instincts. We enjoyed the hunt. No, we did more than that, we existed for the hunt. Craved it. Many had turned it into an art form. Some of my clansmen kept feeders, held them imprisoned, used them for sex and blood."

"It sounds familiar," she said.

"I was converting you, Danielle. There is a difference."

"Is there? I still don't see how it could be considered civilized." Still, she recalled the visions she'd had that night when she'd accidentally seen into his dreams. It had been the moment she realized she loved him. His voice interrupted her thoughts.

"Perhaps in your old world it wouldn't be considered a civilized act. Compared to my old world, it is very civilized. My people were out of control. They terrorized the world. It was clear to me that unless I did something, the humans would band together and try to destroy us. It would be a war, and the human race would lose. We are dependent upon human blood. As a race, we needed the human race to survive. It was too great a risk to allow a war. So I came here, followed Charlemagne's example of educating my people and encouraging their creativity. With these things I brought an end to the dangers of our very existence."

"How?"

"By discovering what we are outside the definition of vampire. I brought an end to the need to just survive. I provided my people what they required in order to sustain their existence. This freed them to become more. I gave them freedom they had never known. To your former world, it would be like giving everyone all the money they required with no need to worry or work for income. Do you see how that would free you so you could place that energy into something else, something creative?"

"Oh that is very profound."

He nodded.

"But when you're immortal, as you shall discover, life can grow boring unless you put effort into making new discoveries and adventures. Most of my clansmen are at least a thousand years old. Some are as old as Minnie and me."

"I can't imagine what it must be like for you. All the civilizations you have seen rise and fall."

"I am a witness to humankind, Danielle, but I was not part of it. That's the real problem for my people. We are outsiders. I have led them for centuries, into a new lifestyle, and some have begun to grow restless."

She struggled to wrap her mind around the endlessness of living for thousands of years. She could see how his people would grow jaded and be in constant search for new excitement.

"I don't understand why you selected me to become a part of this world," she said.

"You were meant to be my mate."

"And Charisse? Alexa? Were they meant to be your mates as well?"

"Was your ex-husband meant to be *your* mate? Do you wish me to be jealous that you loved someone before me?"

"I just want the truth, Armondés. I want you to tell me about Charisse, if it's not too painful."

"My pain surrounding her loss is not as you think, my Danielle. There was no love, so you are free to ask about her without concern. For it is the pain of failure and the loss of her life that haunt me, but not as a lost lover."

She nodded and continued. "Please tell me about the circumstances surrounding her death. Where was she? Did you find her?"

"She was discovered—"

"Discovered?"

"Sometimes, Danielle, when one becomes a vampire, it's not easy to adapt to this lifestyle I've created for my people. The hunting instinct is too strong and drinking from a bottle is too tame."

"Are you saying she was going out and killing people?" Newfound horror gripped her. If it had happened to Charisse—

"Yes. I could not curb her appetite. She thrilled in the pursuit itself. Her need to hunt and feed from a live victim, relishing the fear and terror her victims felt. This need overrode all other things. And after the first few months, she went into hiding."

"From what?"

"From me. She was watched at all times. At first, Minnie and I tried to train her to our lifestyle. We used ancient techniques I had discovered and adapted to fit a vampire nature to reprogram ourselves so the need to hunt would be eradicated, but it didn't have any effect on Charisse. She was *primal*.. I could look at her and see how I had been during my first few hundred years. I knew the driving compulsion burning in her demanding fulfillment that only hunting could appease. Then one night she escaped. Someone from inside helped her, of that I'm convinced. And her last would-be victim must have known what she was. Had followed her and entrapped her. Because of the tattoo, I know this man was a stalker. They are not careless, but they can be overpowered."

"What happened?" She bit her lower lip, gnawing on it, imagining how different her own transformation could have been.

"The stalker...staked her."

Danielle winced.

"I arrived too late. She was gone when my men and I finally tracked her down." He turned from her and stood with his hands clasped behind his back, staring out into the night. "Minnie tracked down and killed the stalker, but she was too late to save Charisse."

"That's horrible. I'm so sorry." She shuddered, knowing her predecessor's fate could easily have been her own had her own transformation followed the same path.

"It was bitter, but she would never have adjusted to our lifestyle. It's part of the risk in transformations. It's not something that can be predicted." He glanced over his shoulder at her.

"So I'm right, my transformation could have been like hers?" she asked and joined him by the window, longing to feel his arms around her. Instead, she clasped her hands behind her back.

"But your transformation was nothing like Charisse's."

"That's not the point. It could have been. There was a great risk in what you did to me."

He nodded then rushed to add, "I am sorry, my love. I would never risk your existence like that now. I didn't love you then. But my love for you is too great to ever allow any danger to threaten you. I hope you believe me."

"Yes," she said and met his heated stare.

"So tell me." She was too close to allow the searing need to feel his lips on hers to derail their conversation. Not yet. "Why do you need a wife?"

"Because I'm a horny king." He leaned over and kissed her cheek, pulling her into his warm embrace. Excitement rushed through her. She pushed gently from him and the fiery liquid his touch sent racing through her.

"Is needing a wife part of the curse?"

"Of course, what good is a curse without motivation?" he asked and brushed a faint kiss against her lips.

"Motivation?" she asked and returned his tender kiss. "I think I can motivate you, my King." She rubbed against him and his arousal was immediate. "Yes, I believe you are the horniest king I've ever known." She gasped when his hand slipped down her tee shirt and closed over her breast.

"And how many kings have you known?" He captured her lips with his and plunged his tongue into her mouth, moving it in and out. Breaking from the kiss, he grasped his shirt and pulled it over his head, quickly doffing his clothes so he stood naked before her. Without warning, he leaned backwards, tugging her with him as they floated about three feet above the floor.

"Have you ever heard of a Chinese basket?" he asked, peeling the jeans down her long legs.

She wiggled out of her panties and straddled him, sitting across his bare legs as he supported them in midair.

"Do you have one?"

"Sorta," he said. Grasping her buttocks, he lifted her into the air, positioning her above his erection.

"Oh my, now that is delightful!" she gasped when brought down onto his cock. It eased into her and she ground her hips, driving the hot cock deeper, but cried out when he lifted her slightly above him.

"You cannot move," he said, "that's part of the torture and pleasure. Imagine yourself in a basket, with a cutout, similar to a pair of crotchless panties. Now, bring your knees up to your chest and lock your arms around them."

She did and was lifted once more and brought down onto his cock. The pleasure pulsated though her as she was lifted up and down the length of his cock. She relaxed in his hold as the rhythm grew faster and faster. Excitement throbbed to her clit and she released her legs to straddle him. Her nub rubbed against each thrust, sending frenetic energy through her.

Each thrust down grew harder and harder. He groaned and fucked her with powerful thrusts. One last thrust and he shuddered in orgasm. She rocked against his throbbing erection with her feet dangling on either side of his body, her toes only inches from the floor. Heat melted between her legs, her clit throbbing in the wake of her orgasm. She cried out and fell forward, smothering him with kisses.

Chapter Nine

"I didn't do anything wrong," Minnie's voice echoed up the stairwell. Danielle leaned over the railing.

"…what happened… You were last seen with them. Tell me what you did…" Armondés' voice boomed.

"You told me…"

"What did you think that meant?"

"Oh please. You know damn well…"

"I meant you were to see they were not allowed… Do I have to spell everything out for you?"

Danielle strained to hear the conversation from the entrance below. The old castle carried the slightest sound, but the echo prevented her from understanding everything said. She silently cursed that she had no control over her newfound power. What good did it do to hear at a great distance when she could not filter out the acoustics? The conversation was muffled and disjointed, still she listened, trying to understand what they were fighting about.

"You're such a liar…cloak your meaning now that you've fallen in love with her."

"You're a fool, Minnie. Why would I want…"

What did it mean? Did it have to do with the investigation over Charisse's murder or possibly her own Presentation and the assassination attempt?

"You wanted th…brother, so you could…love slave."

The slap sounded as though it were beside her.

"You hit me!" Minnie screamed.

"You're lucky that's all I did. You know the penalty for hunting."

Danielle gasped. Minnie had been hunting. That was what they were arguing about. She was relieved it wasn't worse. Still, Minnie had broken the law if she had in fact been hunting.

"Do you think I fear destruction? Oh, bring on the sweet release from this prison you've built for us."

"You hunted…down, didn't you? I know you. You always enjoyed the 'sport'. You never agreed with my mandate that we no longer hunt…recent attacks? I received another report this morning…man's body…found…river."

"How dare you accuse me…been…castle every night since…I don't know…renegades… More power to them…live their lives in freedom. You've imposed this insane lifestyle…twelve hundred years. It's not…thwart natural instincts. Whatever gave…right to play our god?"

"I'm not going…over a thousand years…listened to your whining…natural instincts and unfair mandates. Whether you agree or not, those are the rules that govern our clan. It's long past time you got over it."

Danielle was relieved by the sudden clarity and hoped it lasted, unsure what she'd done to hear their conversation better.

"The way Charisse was supposed to get over it?"

"That's enough!"

"Oh it is, brother. More than enough. You cannot force your ideas over our entire clan and not expect rebellion."

A door slammed and she jumped. The shouting stopped. Quietly, she turned back into the suite.

"So you overheard my conversation?" Armondés asked, standing behind her.

"I'm sorry. I only heard part of it. I didn't mean to, I just started picking up bits and pieces."

"What did you hear specifically?"

"I don't know. Mostly that Minnie has been hunting and that she is angry about your law against it."

Armondés frowned at her, making her wonder what he was trying to figure out.

"I swear that's all I heard." She smiled stiffly.

"I believe you," he sighed, appearing relieved. "It's just that Minnie's headstrong."

"If she's hunting, then that could undermine your entire clan, couldn't it? I mean the king's own sister?"

"Yes, it could." He frowned and pulled her hand into his clasp.

"She killed a man?"

"What? I don't know. There have been two bodies discovered this week, both were bitten by a vampire, but they were not drained dry, which is what would have happened had they been attacked by a hunter. I'm not sure what it means."

"So there are no in-betweens with a vampire who hunts?"

"Generally, no. The need to hunt and feed are mindless acts that consume until there is nothing left to consume."

She shuddered.

"Don't worry, my love. I shall handle Minnie."

"I don't feel that is possible, Armondés. If that instinct is so strong, not even you can control her."

"I don't want you to worry any further about it." He showered her with kisses, each longer than the previous one.

* * * * *

Danielle was beginning to realize that life as a vampire had its own set of problems. The whole not going out during the day was one of the biggest adjustments. She had never realized how important the sun had been to her mental well-being. She missed it to the point of feeling as though she were in mourning. She missed sunrises and sunsets and so many other things she'd taken for granted as a human. Granted she could still see out the protected windows and enjoy the views, it just wasn't the same as sitting in the late afternoon sunshine reading a book.

And while her new world was less complicated in some ways, there were still rules. If she obeyed the few laws of her husband's vampire kingdom, life was very simple. But just like her sister-in-law, Danielle soon found it too confining.

The one saving grace was the passion and love Armondés so generously gave her. Her life was an adventure of new sensations and experiences, especially sexually. After a few weeks, their lives began to fall into a routine but the comfort she found in her husband's arms reassured her it would be all right. She could make a happy life as long as she had him by her side.

At night she often accompanied him to the production plant and learned about making champagne. The night workers were mostly vampires while the day shift workers were from the nearby villages. The vineyards and castle were situated in the Champagne region of France and covered hundreds of acres. She learned about grape varieties and how important the soil was, as well as the types of plant life that grew in the region.

It was after midnight as she walked with her husband from the plant underneath a canopy of stars, that she finally realized it felt like home. The path between the rows of vines was illuminated by a full moon. He held her hand as they walked side-by-side, with two burly guards walking a discreet distance behind them.

"It feels so ancient here," she said, squeezing his hand. "How long has wine been produced in France?"

"The making of wine predates recorded history. It's a subject of great debate," he said with a short chuckle. "In 92 A.D., the Emperor Domitian declared that *all* the vineyards in France be destroyed."

"Why would he order such a thing?"

"Politics. He wished to end the competition for Italian wines."

"So what happened? Obviously, he failed." She breathed in the succulent flavors of the grapes, appreciative of the heightened sense of smell as yet one more of her newfound powers.

"For over two centuries the Franks stubbornly cultivated their precious vineyards in secret."

"That sounds impossible."

"It was an impossible feat but they accomplished it, and here," he said, stretching his arms out in a gesture to the rolling hills of grapevines, "is the result of their refusal to be dominated."

"That's amazing." She hugged his arm, and they resumed walking.

"Nowadays, everything is regulated for our champagne production. All vineyards are classified. Only three grapes can be grown and harvested for champagne. Even the amount of grape juice from each pressing is controlled as well as setting the age when it can be sold."

"Is that a good thing?"

"Like all things it's a two-edged sword." He gently tapped her nose with his forefinger.

"I don't know if I will ever learn this business. It's very complicated."

"It helps to be immortal, that way you can become an expert." He kissed her forehead. "But I didn't ask you to go for a walk so we could talk about work. I wanted to discuss something with you, Danielle," he said and buried his face in her hair.

"It sounds serious." Dread invaded the magic of the moment.

"I want to teach you to defend yourself. I want to train you to fly beyond just levitating and floating."

"Oh, and here I thought those were just sexual aids," she giggled and squeezed his hand.

"You need to be able to defend yourself should you find yourself alone with an assassin. I don't think that would ever happen," he was quick to add, "but I would like to start tomorrow night."

"Sure, if it will make you feel better."

"It will. Come," he said and glanced over his shoulder at the two guards who walked behind them. "Let's fly back to the castle." He lifted from the ground. She released her mind the way he'd taught her, and she rose beside him.

It was a beautiful night. They soared over the vineyards. She marveled over the rows bathed in mystical moonlight as the late summer wind warmed against her cheeks.

"This feels like a fairytale."

"I promise it shall be a happily ever after one, my Danielle."

* * * * *

Once a month Armondés would meet with representatives of the clan at the production house to hear grievances and concerns. She could tell this month's meeting had him on pins and needles and felt his anxiety when he finally left the castle. She decided to make his homecoming erotic and set about lighting candles and selecting exotic music. She showered and drenched herself in his favorite perfume, then sat waiting for his return.

"You're late. Was there trouble at the plant?"

"No, everything is fine." He took the goblet she handed him.

She enjoyed the way his stare warmed on her. The dress was a success!

"Is that new?" he asked and pulled her to him as he let his stare travel down her.

"Do you like it?" She pulled away to turn around so he could see how revealing the thin material was.

"I do. Come here."

"No. I want to tease you a bit first." She pushed him into the chair and climbed onto his lap, taking the goblet from him to set it on the nearby table. His lips sought hers but she brushed against his kiss lightly then turned in his lap.

"Have you ever had a lap dance?"

"Not from you," he chuckled.

She wiggled and found the right spot and began to grind her hips into him, rolling them in a rhythmic circle. Her stockings slid easily against his slacks, giving her the ease of movement needed. His hand came around to cup her breasts.

"I'm the one who is supposed to be giving the pleasure, mister." She grabbed his hands and forced them to the arms of the chair. "Think Chinese basket only not."

"Hmmm," he moaned when she stood and picked up the remote. Before he could speak, sultry Mediterranean music rushed into the room, changing the mood dramatically. She moved to the music, twisting and squirming to the steps she had been practicing all week.

"What is this?" he asked with pleasure radiating in his voice.

"You like?" She held her arms in arcs above her head as she gyrated her torso and hips while floating back to his chair.

"Oh, I like a lot. Come here." He reached for her.

"No, sit back. There's more." She kneeled in front of him, still moving to the music as she pushed his legs apart and slipped between them.

A scream shattered the moment, clashing with the music, sounding as though it had come from the corridor. Armondés jumped from her, flying toward the door and into the hall, heading for the stairwell. Danielle ran to catch up and found him in Minnie's suite.

"What is it?" she asked, bounding into the room. The scene answered her questions. Several guards stood around the prone body.

"Minnie was attacked. The fucking assassins broke into my castle!" Armondés turned from Fredrick, who lay sprawled on the floor. He wasn't moving.

"He's hurt," Minnie wailed, pulling herself from the floor to lean against the bed. "They tried to destroy Freddie when he protected me."

"Oh my God!" Danielle rushed over to her sister-in-law and hugged her. "Were you hurt?"

"Get my army ready," Armondés ordered. The guards stood to attention and the older one left with his heels clicking against the marble floor. Armondés turned to his sister. "Did you see who did this?"

She shook her head.

"How many were there?"

"I don't know. Two, maybe three."

"How did they get in?" he demanded.

"I don't know." Her lips trembled. She looked at the body of her lover. "We were—" Her voice broke off, and she bowed her head. "I don't know what happened. I just know we were attacked." She dissolved into tears.

Danielle glanced at Armondés. She'd never seen him so angry. A big man entered the room.

"My King, the men are ready." He stood a foot taller than Armondés and wore a black leather vest with his muscular arms bulging from the openings.

"Hold fast," he ordered and turned to his sister. "Minnie. Where did they go?"

She pointed to the open balcony doors.

"Captain, have your men pair up. I want every known refuge searched, and every rogue vampire questioned."

The Captain bowed and backed from the room.

Armondés looked at Danielle then Minnie. Danielle wanted to cry, but the tears wouldn't come. Minnie pushed from her and stood up, bracing herself against the bed post.

"I'm putting an end to this terror, tonight!" He stood over them. "Who did this, Minnie? Did you see them? Tell me."

"If I knew I'd tell you, brother. They nearly murdered my lover. Do you think I'd protect anyone who did this? You're insulting as hell. Get out of my room, both of you." Her cold eyes were like stones. Danielle shivered when her icy stare riveted on her.

She looked at Minnie, knowing her anger was rooted in fear. She understood that fear. She'd felt it the night of Presentation when the assassins had nearly killed Armondés. Her heart tugged for her sister-in-law. Two guards lifted the motionless Fredrick and placed him onto the bed. Minnie sat down beside him and stroked his forehead.

"Escort the Queen to her chambers," he told the man behind him.

"I want to help," Danielle insisted.

"You can help best by staying where I know you're safe, with guards." Armondés grabbed Danielle by the arm and pressed a harsh kiss against her lips. For the first time, she was truly aware of his strength. His arm relaxed and she stumbled backwards.

"Keep your cell phone on. Call me if you need me."

She nodded, numb from the evening's unexpected events.

"Is Fredrick going to be okay?" he asked as two men moved from the bed.

"The wound is deep, but he'll heal," one of them said.

Armondés started for the balcony, followed by his guards. She watched him lift his arms and slowly rise from the balcony. The men followed him, soundlessly, as they flew from the castle. She stood watching them soar from the building. It was an amazing sight.

"My Queen." The mountain posing as a man bowed to her. She came to herself and pivoted toward the hall, giving Minnie one last glance, but the woman looked away and whispered endearments to Fredrick.

Danielle marched with her guards to her suite. One guard moved to take his post on the balcony outside the den, leaving the door ajar, while the other two took up station outside her door in the hallway. Realizing she was still wearing the revealing dress, she retreated into her bathroom to change into jeans and a top.

When she emerged, she sat down in the loveseat, tucking her sock feet underneath her and clicked though the hundreds of satellite stations, constantly looking through the French doors at the guard. He stood as though a statue. She had not been around many vampires since her transformation, and didn't know what to expect of them. The night of her presentation had seen hundreds of vampires in attendance, but since escaping the assassins and coming to France, she'd lived in seclusion.

Pondering the lives of vampires, she realized all she knew was what her husband had taught her and what she had learned during the brief contact she had with Minnie. Still, as a species, she found them to be very distant, and as clichéd as it struck her, cold. Their emotions seemed to run on the side of great passion, yet they had very little compassion or warmth for each other and certainly no emotions toward humans, other than as their next meal.

The one contradiction to her observations was her husband. His passion seemed to include genuine emotion. Still, she recalled how cold Minnie was to Armondés, and from what she'd witnessed he had little warmth for his sister. She settled back into the seat and continued to flip through the channels. How she'd loved watching horror movies, especially vampire ones. Now they seemed absurd. In fact, everything related to her former life seemed empty and of no relevance.

It was as though she'd lived in a fantasy world, completely oblivious to the truth. Absently, she wondered if there were other truths she didn't know. Since vampires were real, did that mean other legends and myths were also true? The niggling thought invaded her musings. It would stand to reason that werewolves and other mythological creatures were also real.

Her mind whirled with the possibilities. She hugged herself and picked up her cell phone, double-checked that it was on and the battery charged and dropped it onto the side table, continuing to scroll through the marquee, finally opting for a music channel.

The classical piece lilted into the suite, replacing the stagnant quiet. She propped her feet onto the square coffee table and closed her eyes. Oh yes, she must learn to fly better, she told herself, thinking how adept the men had been when they had lifted from the castle to give chase to the assassins. Armondés had taught her several techniques, but she needed more practice.

The knock on the door made her jump.

"Yes?" she called.

"Your evening meal, my Queen," Ingund's familiar voice, strangely, comforted her.

"Come in," she said and uncrossed her ankles. The shorter woman moved around the guard as he held the door open for her. Carrying a silver tray, two goblets and a black bottle with a gold crested label, Ingund placed the tray on the coffee table.

"Good evening, my Queen, your favorite—raspberry flavored," she said and set about pouring the contents into the goblet. Danielle noticed how the woman's hands shook.

"I'll do that, Ingund," she said, and took the goblet and bottle from the servant.

"I heard the Advisor was murdered," Ingund whispered as she struggled to control the tears by swiping at them with the back of her hand.

"No. He's injured, but will be all right," she assured the woman.

Relief washed over her wrinkled face, but the fear still shone in her watery eyes.

"Those close to Princess Minnie are always destroyed," she said and started to leave.

"Whoa, what does that mean?" Danielle was on her feet blocking the servant's exit.

"Nothing, my Queen. I should not speak out of turn."

"I insist."

Ingund hung her head.

"Tell me," Danielle insisted.

"Charisse… Queen Charisse was rumored to be hiding those last two months of her life. But I know she was being hidden, by Princess Minnie." She lowered her voice. "Queen Charisse was out hunting with the princess on the night she died, and now Advisor Van Cantrep was nearly killed. It just seems, well, I should say nothing more. Just be careful, my Queen, you're most vulnerable this night." She bowed and hurried past her and out of the room. Her warning haunted Danielle for the rest of the evening. Did Armondés know about Minnie hiding Charisse? She could not wait until he returned so she could ask him.

She tried to settle into watching an old horror movie but couldn't keep her mind off the danger threatening all of them. The film paled in comparison to her real life. She muted the television and pressed the button to call up the time. It was nearly five o'clock, and she'd not heard from Armondés. She tossed the remote onto the table and picked up her cell phone for the hundredth time. Turning it over in her hand, she resisted the temptation to hit the speed dialer for his phone. Instead, she placed it back on the side table.

The half-empty bottle was within easy reach so she poured another glass and quickly polished off the remainder. Sinking into the couch, she thought about how much she'd enjoyed the drink. Even though she still found the thought of sustenance by blood a disgusting way to live, she craved it more and more each day. Armondés' words about Charisse and how her transformation had been to a baser type of vampire, unable to adapt to his reformation techniques, plagued Danielle. Secretly, she feared becoming like her predecessor. Could she still change? Was it possible at this stage to revert to the lowest form of a vampire? Should she ask Armondés to teach her the techniques he had mentioned, just in case she was not past the danger point? Was there a no-return point after a transformation? She had so many questions.

She understood so little about what had happened to her and what she should expect. She certainly missed the pleasure of eating real food. She was so lost in thought she didn't hear the door open, in fact she didn't know anyone was in the room until the shadow flickered across the wall.

She jumped from the couch, poised to defend herself.

"Settle down, girl. It's just me." Minnie laughed and collapsed into the side chair, dangling her long legs over the arm.

"Don't you know how to knock?" Danielle asked and pulled the chenille throw around her as she settled back into the loveseat.

"I got lonely in my room, besides, I don't like the vibes in there. How about some blood?" she asked.

Danielle glared up at her.

"Oh please, you can't be that sensitive. You're a vamp. Get over it." Minnie stood and moved over to the sideboard. "What flavors do you have here? Ah, there's a new one, chocolate. My brother is really getting creative these days. Poor Freddie. He's in a deep sleep. He was so heroic." Minnie moved behind her and handed the goblet to her.

"I have one already," she refused.

"What, that raspberry stuff? Try this. It's much better."

Reluctantly, Danielle took the drink.

"Cheers." Minnie toasted, clicking her goblet against hers before settling back into the chair.

"Will he recover? I mean I don't know how vampires heal." She took a long sip of the drink, then sniffed it. It didn't taste like chocolate to her, nor did it smell like chocolate.

"Drink up, the flavor is delayed, it blooms once you've drunk about half of it," Minnie instructed and took a long sip, "as for my Freddie, he'll recover. He's a warrior." Minnie leaned forward. "So do you like our new flavor of the month—Dark Chocolate?"

"It's okay, although I don't taste the chocolate yet." Danielle took another sip. "Even warriors must find an attack like that unnerving." Her eyes fluttered closed and she forced them open. She hadn't realized how tired she was. "It's just so frightening to think about assassins attacking. I'm sure it was frightening for you," she yawned.

"It was. What would you do if faced with assassins?"

Her words prickled every nerve ending in Danielle's body. She stared at her sister-in-law, trying to gauge if her words had been a threat, or if she was truly concerned. Even in her groggy state, she knew Minnie loved to play with people like a cat with a mouse.

"That's a really morbid thing to ask," she said and clutched the throw tighter. She placed the half empty goblet onto the side table.

"I know. I'm sorry. It's just that unlike Fredrick, you've not been trained to defend yourself, much less fight another vampire." Minnie eyed the goblet. "These assassins are highly trained. They live for only one thing. To kill."

"How do you know that?" An eerie sensation raced over her flesh in a chilling path.

"Because I trained them." Minnie straightened in the chair.

Panic sliced through her like a knife.

"But we all have our purpose in life, Danielle. Mine seems to be the one who frees my brother of his wives."

"What?" Panic shot through her. What was she saying?

"I know it's a bloody nasty job. He wanted to set the stage for you."

"Who?" Danielle needed to call out for the guard, but first she must know what Minnie was talking about. Fear sliced through her and all she wanted was to flee.

"Armondés, of course. Gawd, he can be so dramatic. I thought Fredrick's little vignette was totally unnecessary, but how else could my brother explain leaving his bride alone."

"No. You're lying. He would never do this."

"Oh yes, he would. He's done it many times. Chasing imaginary assassins works nice enough. Of course, I'd have preferred something in your sleep. Easier and takes less planning, but he's the king and I have to do as he orders. Even if it means killing people. Your friends, for instance."

"No!" Danielle jumped from the couch and ran for the balcony door where the guard was stationed.

"Don't bother, he's gone. Sent him on a little errand."

She didn't believe her. Armondés had ordered the guard to remain. She opened the door and found the balcony deserted.

"I'm telling you, it's been planned from the beginning. The stupid assassin missed that night at the club during your little presentation ceremony, through no fault of your own—you clearly made yourself an easy target." Minnie stood and took a menacing step toward her. "My brother's acting is always so convincing. Don't you think?"

"He'd never harm me. Why are you doing this, Minnie?" she asked. Her attention shifted to the courtyard below. She'd not mastered the art of flying yet and Minnie had, still, it might prove her best defense.

"I told you, Armondés asked me to." Minnie's eyes darkened.

"That's a lie!" Anger surged with fear. Was she telling the truth? Had Armondés sent his sister to murder her?

"It's not a lie. The only lie is your marriage and your belief that he loves you. Wake up, Danielle." Minnie held up her hand.

"What's that?" she asked, trying to see the object Minnie held between her fingers, but her vision blurred.

"Don't you recognize it? It's Armondés' wedding ring. Kind of a twisted code between us. When he slips it under my door, I know he's ready to be free of his marriage. Simple really." Minnie took another step toward her.

"You're a liar. It was you who tried to destroy Fredrick tonight, wasn't it? And you destroyed Charisse. Why?"

"I told you, I'm following the orders of my king."

"Liar!" Danielle screamed and lunged over the railing.

Chapter Ten

She stiffened her arms by her sides, the way Armondés had taught her, so she could gain speed quickly. The screech behind her was that of a banshee. Goose bumps crept up her arms. She struggled not to look behind her. It would slow her down, and she needed every advantage she could get if she was to escape.

She plummeted down the side of the tall turret. She knew she needed to dive as close to the ground as she could before rising up the arc of her fall. Her night vision was sharper than ever, but her vision kept blurring. What was that shape on the ground? She squinted and immediately recognized the clothing. It was the guard.

The ground was getting too close. She extended her arms, driving herself upward in a steady arc. The effect was like a slingshot. She flew just above the treetops then descended, hoping to lose Minnie in the thickets of the forest. The night grew silent as she floated soundlessly down to the forest bed. Pine needles crept the soles of her feet. She padded about the rough ravine and climbed over a scattered outcropping of rocks. Lazy ferns and scraggly sprigs of juniper brushed against her feet. Larger boulders were set in permanent, tumbled patterns as though some past flood had carried them from the ridge into the valley.

Her legs were weak and she leaned against the hard cold granite. Minnie had drugged her! The world blurred around her. The wind rustled through the hollow, carrying unknown soft scents of the forest to her. Was it the forest's enchantment or the drug-laced drink Minnie had given her? She shook her head, trying to clear the fog seeping into her thoughts, and stumbled up the side of the gulley.

A dark shadow loomed along the wall of overgrowth. She fell against it. Briars and vines scraped against her arms. What was that? She reached into the vines and her hand met cold stone. She pulled the growth aside, revealing a mossy opening where cooler air stirred.

"A cave," she slurred. Was that possible or was it a hallucination? A wide fern draped from the natural ledge overhead and cascaded across the mossy opening. She peered inside, not wanting to startle a sleeping boar or some other animal. The screeching overhead was unearthly, and she knew it was Minnie, enraged over being foiled by a novice.

Trembling, Danielle ducked inside the dark cave and moved further inside the tight confines. The predatory squawks resounded. She flattened herself against the rock wall, knowing the stone mass would cloak her and prevent Minnie from sensing her presence.

She waited, fading in and out of grogginess, starting awake from a nightmarish slumber only to drift back into another. She opened her eyes and looked at the opening, drawing her legs to her stomach. It would be light soon. Minnie would be forced to retreat.

The first rays of day pierced through the cave opening. She moved further back, struggling to avoid the light. Minnie could not come back until night. Until then, she'd wait. In spite of her attempt to stay awake, she drifted off to sleep once more. Her dreams moved from nightmares to deep fantasy within the arms of her husband.

* * * * *

"I want you, Danielle," he said and deepened his thrusts as he pounded his cock into her. She moved under him, drinking his kisses. "You are my one true love. I shall never let anyone harm you."

"Armondés," she whispered and awoke with a start.

She groped for her husband, but her hand met the hard stone of the cave wall. Everything flooded back to her. She must warn Armondés. She stretched from the hard floor. Night had fallen. She'd missed sunset, which meant Minnie had the advantage. She scrambled from the narrow cave. A lazy evening breeze greeted her.

The moon shone high above the forest. Its silvery light filtered through the trees. It had to be close to midnight for the moon to be so high in the sky. She spread her arms and lifted from the ground, floating quietly toward the tree limbs. How would Minnie explain her absence to Armondés? She was anxious to confront Minnie in his presence. This was going to be a night Minnie would forever regret.

She flew through the countryside, staying in shadows whenever possible. The vineyards glistened under the moonlight, back-dropped by the chateau and its tall turrets. She stopped, hovering above the fields. Her stare widened on the dark castle. Why were there no lights? Her mouth dried. She leaned into the wind and flew faster toward her home.

The first thing she noticed was the open, ground-level balcony door. She straightened and floated down, careful to stay within the shadows. She stood along the castle wall, listening. Her mind traveled into the parlor and searched for occupants. It was deserted. With her heart pounding, she stepped inside. The night breeze followed her, lifting the gauzy draperies into the room.

She took a deep breath and stood listening. Papers rustled as the wind rushed ahead of her. Lifting slightly from the floor, she floated through the parlor into the great foyer and looked up the five-storied staircase that wound through the castle. Chills prickled over her. She'd never heard such *silence* before. Her ears rang in the absence of any sound. Where was everyone? Where was her husband? She lifted up the stairwell, circling to search the railed landings as she made her way to the top floor and the wing she shared with Armondés.

The double doors to their wing stood open. There were no guards standing outside the rooms. She dared not risk making any sounds, so she continued to float through the open doors.

There were no lights, no movements and no sounds coming from the sitting room or beyond.

She moved quickly through the series of rooms, heading for their bedroom. Her attention moved about the room, flashing from the balcony doors to the open closet, the dresser drawers pulled out as though someone had packed in a hurry. She noticed all of Armondés' suits were missing.

She hurried to the closet and jerked the door open. The closet was a mess with open boxes, partially filled with her clothing while the remainder were still on hangers. It looked as though something had interrupted the packing. She stooped over to examine the label.

"Consignment?" Armondés was having her clothes sent to a consignment shop? She reached out and ran her hand along the gown she'd worn the night she'd been presented to the clan.

Tears welled in her eyes. Could it be true? Had Armondés truly ordered Minnie to murder her? She'd not had time to examine the ring Minnie had claimed belonged to Armondés but it certainly looked like the one he'd picked out for his wedding band. She turned around in the room. What else could she think? A vampire who'd been vaporized would not need clothes. She didn't know how long she stayed, looking in each drawer, knowing what contents were no longer there. All her belongings, even her jewelry, had been left behind.

What would she do now? If he truly had wanted her destroyed, why had he abandoned the castle without proof? What had made them leave so quickly? How had Minnie convinced him without a body? Unless— Her breath latched in her throat. What if Minnie had accused her of planning and arranging Fredrick's attack? Danielle shook her head. She could not reconcile the man Minnie claimed had ordered her destruction with the man Danielle knew as her husband. The man she knew would not harm her. He loved her.

She collapsed onto the bed. It was too much to believe. He could not have made love to her the way he had and then tried to harm her. She didn't care if he was a vampire. He was not a monster. He had never revealed a baser nature to her. Minnie, on the other hand, had. Minnie could have lied to Armondés. She was capable of lying, she certainly was not happy with the lifestyle Armondés had chosen for the clan. Ingund's words haunted her. "Those close to Princess Minnie are always destroyed... Queen Charisse was out hunting with the princess on the night she died."

Perhaps it was Minnie and not Armondés who had planned all this. Of course, that was it! Hope rose in her. She sat up in the bed. Minnie was behind it all. She was the one trying to assassinate Armondés. And Fredrick must have tried to stop her. She practically ran to the phone. Her fingers trembled as she punched in Armondés' satellite phone number.

"The number you have dialed is no longer in service." The message surprised her. She hung up and redialed, careful to enter each number correctly. Once more the automated message answered. Taking a deep breath, she dialed Minnie's satellite phone and was not surprised when the same message played. They had fled and changed their numbers. Why would they change their numbers? They had international numbers to accommodate their traveling. There'd be no need to change them, unless something else had happened while she was in the cave. It could be anything. She would drive herself crazy asking these questions. She had to find answers.

The grandfather clock chimed once. She was too late. What would she do now? How could she survive? Her stomach rumbled. As long as she remained in the castle she'd have plenty of Private Label. The last thing she wanted to do was have to hunt for her food, but she could not risk going to the production plant to stock up. It would be suicidal to attempt to glean any information from the workers since she had no idea how deep the plot to murder her ran within the clan. Still, she had to find Armondés and warn him. His sister wanted him dead.

So where had they gone? Armondés would need another wife before the anniversary of her death. Danielle bit the back of her hand. The thought of Armondés with another woman enraged her. No, that was what Minnie would want. She must be levelheaded and calculating. Think. The most logical place would be to go back to Savannah. If she had been the real target of the assassination attempts, then there was no longer any reason for Armondés to stay away from Savannah. It was where she'd start, yet she couldn't just walk into the club. She'd never make it to Armondés. His sister would make certain she was finally destroyed.

Danielle rubbed her forehead. How was she going to do this? Minnie was a formidable opponent. She'd had thousands of years to develop her powers. In comparison to Minnie's skills, Danielle was less than a novice. She would be slaughtered if she had to fight her sister-in-law. It was luck that she'd escaped Minnie the previous night. She needed to be careful not to have another confrontation with Minnie until she had trained. That was it. She'd train and grow stronger.

Her stomach rumbled. But first, she had to make sure she had plenty of the Private Label, and she'd need a place to stay. Someplace close to the club. She had jewels, she would pawn them. As much as they meant to her, Armondés' very life was at risk. She would be on her own and needed all the resources at her disposal. She would practice and hone her powers before going up against Minnie. The key to regaining access to Armondés would be her intellect. It would take a flawless plan to outwit Minnie. She knew it would take time. First she would concentrate on developing the power to shield from the mental probing of other vampires. That would be her biggest challenge. When she felt ready, she'd test her powers out on an unwitting vampire. Then she would retaliate on her own terms.

* * * * *

"I know you had affection for her, but you can't lock yourself up in your rooms and forget the clock is ticking." Minnie shoved the Private Label bottle across the table, but Armondés simply sat, staring at it with dull vacant eyes.

"She was not like anyone I'd ever known. I loved her." He looked up at his sister. "Do you remember what that feels like? I'd forgotten. I'd forgotten so many things. Danielle gave me new life." He ignored her look of sarcasm. "Get out!" He shoved the bottle from him.

"I'm not going anywhere. We're all worried about you. It's been over ten months since she was destroyed. You've refused to even meet the candidates I've sent to you, and now you've stopped feeding. Consider this an intervention."

"I consider this an intrusion. Get the hell out." He jumped from the table. The chair toppled over and crashed to the floor. "I just want to be left alone." Couldn't she understand how devastated he was? He didn't want to live. He only wanted Danielle. How could she have been destroyed? Gone from him forever?

Minnie's footsteps sounded behind him in fast angry clicks.

"Look here, I've seen you through this before. I'll see you through it again. Ten months is long enough. Savannah is where we found Danielle and where we will find your next queen. I have five promising potentials, and you *will* see each one of them."

"No! I'm not going through it again."

"Oh yes, you will." She put her hands on her hips and stared across the dimly lit room at him. "You owe it to your people."

He shook his head and turned his back to her, peering out the window at the night skyline.

The door opened from the foyer. He didn't turn to see who it was. He'd sensed the man when he'd exited the elevator down the hall.

"What's going on?" Fredrick asked.

"He refuses to feed. He refuses to accept Danielle's gone. And he won't consider replacements."

Anger scorched him. He turned to glare at her.

"No one can ever replace my wife. Don't make that mistake again."

"Okay, so I chose the wrong words. I'm sorry, but the fact remains, you have to have another wife." Minnie folded her arms across her chest.

"Why? So the assassins can destroy her, too? And what about the next time and the next? We're approaching this the wrong way. Don't you see? We have to ferret out the traitor. That's how I will win back my kingdom and restore peace to our clan."

"You're right, my friend," Fredrick said and nodded. "I've been discussing a new strategy with your captains. I would like to have a meeting later this evening if you're free to join us in the conference room."

"New strategy?" he asked and glanced at his best friend. Fredrick seemed nervous and blocked his attempts to see into his mind. What was that about?

"I think you'll be very pleased."

"Good. Good." New power surged through him.

"Until then," Fredrick said and motioned the servant into the room, "you must feed and repair yourself. When you are full strength once more we can become the aggressors."

"You always had an excellent military mind, Fredrick. Charlemagne would have been wise to enlist you as his new general instead of condemning you to death."

"Bestowing such an honor on his worst enemy would have been suicide." Fredrick clicked his heels together.

Armondés chuckled slightly, feeling empowered.

"Now you must feed, my King." Fredrick motioned to the servant who placed the silver tray holding the black bottle and goblet down in front of him. "We take our leave until this evening." Fredrick bowed and practically dragged Minnie from the room.

Once outside in the upstairs foyer, Minnie jerked free of his hold.

"What the hell are you doing?"

"My duty." He started toward their wing.

"Your duty is to me, lover, or did you forget?" she asked, storming into the room behind him. She slammed the door.

"My duty, Minnie, is to myself, then you. Armondés needs to believe we have his best interests at heart. These are the methods I would take to save my king. Just as you would force him to feed and agree to resume the search for a new mate. That said, we will see these strategies through." He gathered her into his embrace. "Then, my love, we'll do what we do best." His lips covered hers. Minnie struggled to free herself, but his arms tightened around her. His lips demanded a response. She quivered, needing to taste him fully, but he broke from their kiss. She moaned.

"Come to bed and show me how you intend to win me over to your side," she said and pulled him toward the bedroom.

"I can't, not now. I have to meet with the men and make sure everyone knows their roles." He planted a quick kiss on her lips.

"You should be more concerned about pleasing me, Fredrick. I will soon be your queen."

"And I shall be your *king*." He gave her a peck on the cheek.

She looked up at him, unable to stop the slow smile spreading to her lips. She knew his ambitions. It was part of the bond between them, along with their mutual hatred for her brother.

"To finally be able to hunt in the open again. To not have to drink that putrid, flavored Private Label, but to savor warm live blood. Feel the fear coursing through our victims. Oh, Fredrick, the energy that kind of terrified blood has. My brother has perverted us into less than we were meant to be." She grabbed his arms, unable to control the excitement surging in her.

"Relax, my sweet. Don't let those baser passions get the best of you just yet. Since you were able to track down Danielle and destroy her, half our battle is won." His words sent streaks of panic through her. She could not be certain Danielle had scorched, but still she was a novice and not at all adept in the art of self-protection.

"Yes. Hers was the most enjoyable hunt and slaughter I've ever had." She touched her tongue to her lower lip.

"And so it shall be when I strike your brother. He's the vilest of them all. At last he shall pay for having claimed my life, condemning me to this enslavement. We shall soon have our freedom, and our revenge. But we must be careful. We have to be patient. Can I count on you?" he asked and held her in the circle of his arms.

"As sure as you know the sun shall rise every morning, my love." She blocked her thoughts from him. Poor Fredrick. He had no idea how expendable he would become once he completed his part of the task. She certainly had not endured all the past centuries to end up sharing her throne with anyone. Oh, there was the matter of inheriting the curse, but she could handle it better than her brother. A young man, transformed by her and kept locked away except when wanted was the perfect solution. Her brother had been too weak to recognize it as the only way to live with the curse. She was stronger than her sibling. What would she care if her mate was a sex slave locked away in the safety of the castle? Soon she'd be truly free of both Armondés and Fredrick. She chuckled and tossed back her head with deep laughter filling the room. Fredrick lifted her in his arms and swung her around the room, laughing with her.

Chapter Eleven

"There, I'm finished, look in the mirror," Sinclair Armstrong said, and held the mirror up to Danielle. She sat in front of the makeup cabinet with his makeup strewn all over the place. The plastic mold now gaped, empty. Her face felt hot where the prosthetic nose and chin were attached. She took a deep breath and held the mirror to her reflection, knowing it would be faint.

"Hold the mirror so the light doesn't reflect directly in it. It'll give a better image."

"I've never been a blonde before." She nodded, and the ghostlike image nodded back at her. He had also cut her hair so it now barely brushed her shoulders. Her nose was slightly bigger and upturned, her chin and jawline were now squared. Blue contacts completed the disguise.

"It's wonderful." She turned sideways to make sure no one would know her nose was fake.

"You're beautiful with or without it. Now have you practiced your accent?"

"I can speak English because my father vaz an American soldier stationed in Russia. My mother died when I vaz fifteen, and I vaz brought to the United States to be raised by my American grandmother."

"Wonderful. Wonderful. I'd never recognize you. Minnie won't know what hit her until it's too late." Sinclair, a man in his fifties when he'd been turned, had been more than willing to help her during the past months. He'd trained her to create more than just a mind shield, he'd taught her how to project the illusion of a mortal among other vampires. She would be able to use these new powers to gain access to Armondés and shield against Minnie's mind probing. She knew Armondés would be too powerful to project the illusion for long, but she only needed a few minutes with him. This disguise was the final step in her plan. It had been a long ten months, but the payoff was near.

"I've done a lot of disguises for undercover agents over the centuries, but yours is my best creation. Mind if I take a picture?"

"Do we photograph?" she asked.

"Oh yes, better than we reflect." The flash sent shards of light dancing in front of her. She turned from him, shielding her eyes.

"Are you okay?"

"Yes, just the flash." She squinted and rubbed the dancing lights from her eyes.

"So you're all ready, my protégée." He stood behind her, beaming like a proud parent. She covered his hand with hers.

"How can I ever thank you, Sinclair?" she asked. "I never thought I would find so true a friend as I did in you when I moved into this building. I'm so grateful."

"It's been said by wiser men than I, when the student is ready, the teacher will appear."

"So, I just picked up on your teacher vibe?"

"Tonight is your graduation, my Queen." He kissed her cheek and held out his hand.

She smiled up at him. He was the father she'd never had.

"You promise me now," she said, taking his hand, "that you'll not follow. I'm capable of doing this on my own. If you were to follow me, you could put my life in jeopardy. You realize that if they find out, then I'm dust." She spoke in a sterner tone than normal because she wanted Sinclair to be safe. She knew he might try to protect her.

"I understand, Danielle." He bowed.

"That's not good enough. I need your promise. You will stay out of the matter from this point forward."

"It's difficult to let the student leave the classroom, but it must happen to all. You're ready." Sinclair, pushed his glasses onto his bald head. "Now take this." He gave her the small tube of glue. "You'll need to use it every time you put on the nose and chin. Remember it's going to take you longer than it did me and if you need me to help, just call me, you have my number. If you decide you need me to do it for you each time—"

"Thank you, Sinclair. You've been a lifesaver." She kissed his cheek.

"Hey." He grabbed her upper arm. Her pulse raced. "Just promise me you'll be careful. Your sister-in-law is a very dangerous vampire."

"I promise. I have to go change and then I'm off to test my new look." She opened the door to the hallway.

"Just be *careful*," he called after her.

* * * * *

Danielle pulled on the crotchless panties and instantly was back to that night so long ago in the restroom with Lillian and Amy. She recalled how Minnie had made her so uncomfortable. Since returning to Savannah, she had tried to discover what had happened to Lillian and Amy, but the police had been no help. A missing persons report had been filed by each woman's family, but nothing had ever come of it. Her heart sank. Of course, she knew what had happened to them even though she'd hoped against all hope. Minnie had killed them. The thought seared through her and Danielle pushed the pain away. Her hands trembled as she slipped the black dress over her head and let it fall. It stopped several inches above her knees. Not too short, but not too long. She struggled to zip it up then turned to gaze at her faint reflection.

She needed the guards to recognize her as a vampire so she could gain entrance into the club. That should be the easy part since it was a sixth sense for their kind. Over the months, Sinclair and she had run over several scenarios of how she could set her trap and had decided being open as a vampire to Minnie was her safest route. It would require less energy to shield herself. She could play her role and gain a private meeting with Armondés, then her plan would succeed. She had an advantage. She knew what he liked. It would be okay, she told herself as she walked up to the doorman in front of Armondés' club.

The doorman looked as though he had stepped right out of a wrestling ring. He gave her a knowing nod and opened the door for her. The groans and snide comments shouted behind her reminded her of the night Minnie had led them into the club. They'd been so innocent following her into the erotic nightspot. It had been so easy for Minnie. She glanced over her shoulder at the partygoers. If they only knew what awaited them inside, their outrage would melt into gratitude.

The club looked the same, only this time her perspective was with the knowledge of its patrons and the reason Armondés had opened it. Strobe lights flashed across the undulating mass of dancers as they moved to the driving beat. She didn't recognize anyone from the clan. Perhaps Armondés didn't allow them entry as part of tightened security. The temptation to feed on the human patrons must surely prove too great a temptation for most vampires. A faint haze surrounded the humans reminding her of heat reflecting off a car hood. She looked about the room, trying to get her bearings. She focused on projecting this same haze around her to fool any vampires. Minnie had led them to Armondés' booth that fated night. It was a good place to start. She made her way across the club to the far corner but halted mid-stride. There, standing by the booth, was her husband. Panic threatened to undo all her training. She slipped into a vacant booth and willed the tears to stop. Relief washed over her. He was still alive. She said a silent prayer.

She stole a glance at him. He was as handsome as ever. A deep longing ravaged Danielle. Her stare traveled over his face, noting each tense line as he talked. His broad shoulders cut into the finely made suit, revealing just enough of his strength while promising so much more if one were to remove his jacket. She ached to feel the smooth linen shirt give beneath her fingers and free his flesh to her touch. She pushed the heat from her. She must separate herself from the emotions or she'd never be able to shield from him.

Minnie paraded a woman dressed in a blue sequined mini-dress through the crowd and stopped in front of Armondés. Danielle trained her senses the way Sinclair had taught her.

"This is my brother, Armondés, owner of the club. This is Jacqueline." She stepped aside and motioned for the candidate to step forward.

Danielle balled her fists in her lap. Her eyes scorched. The woman slid her arm through the crook of his arm and he led her over to the booth. She knew he was bored. Her husband did not tolerate mindless prattle which seemed to be what the brunette was doing. She looked at him. He appeared okay. Unharmed. White-hot anger seared through her. Just what was he doing? Did she mean so little to him that he was already trying to find her replacement? She suddenly felt insignificant, as though she were one of many wives. It wasn't true. He loved her. She knew that. But the worrisome thought dug at her confidence.

What if he had in fact ordered Minnie to assassinate her? She closed her eyes against the thought. It was not true. He loved her. Danielle jumped from the booth and pushed through the crowd. She wanted to feel the woman's flesh tear beneath her nails.

"Stop!" A voice pierced the searing anger as strong fingers grabbed her arm. She was spun around and pulled in the opposite direction.

She flashed an angry glare.

"Sinclair?" The rage evaporated. "What are you doing here?"

"Saving you." He shoved her into a nearby booth and ducked inside with her. "Your emotions are all over the place. You have to focus."

"I know. I'm sorry," she said and sniffed back the tears. "I haven't seen my husband in months. I was shocked and angered."

"And jealous?"

"That, too."

"And why I came. I knew the first time seeing him would be difficult. I want you to carry this." He handed her the round white stone.

"What is it?" She turned it over in her hand. The emotions drained from her. It felt as though they were being siphoned from her fingers right into the stone.

"It's my touchstone. You need it more than I. It'll keep your emotions below the surface. I didn't think about it until you'd left. I was afraid I'd not get to you in time."

"How can I thank you?" She reached across the table and grabbed his hand.

"Be safe." He stood as though to leave, but she knew he'd be nearby watching her.

She held the stone in her fist and took a deep breath, even though she no longer needed the habit of breath. Training her mind, she replaced her shield and looked about the club. Armondés was gone. Her heart sank, but the rising anger abated, passing from her into the stone. It warmed in her hand. She stiffened her spine and glanced about for Minnie.

Her short, tight, red leather dress flashed behind the man standing near her then disappeared, only to reappear several feet away. Danielle wove her way between the dancers, blocking the music from her mind. She moved in silence, slicing through the crowd as though she were water tumbling through a stream. She spotted the red dress just beyond a man standing with his back to the room. Danielle's attention sharpened when he put his arm around Minnie's waist and pulled her against him.

She'd seen that gesture so many times. She let her gaze travel up the man's back. He shifted and turned to whisper something in Minnie's ear. Danielle was grateful for the touchstone, for standing no more than ten feet from her was Fredrick Van Cantrep. The last time she'd seen him, he'd been lying on the floor, wounded. She still suspected Minnie had betrayed him just as she had all of them. Her mind reeled with the various scenarios she'd attributed to Minnie.

"Are you here alone?" a handsome man asked, standing over her, holding a goblet in his hand. Immediately, she smelled the blood and recognized him as being a vampire.

"No. I'm here to see Armondés," she said in her Russian accent.

"Oh, a Russian vamp. Welcome to America."

She glanced past him to Minnie. Fredrick had moved, leaving Minnie by herself. This was her moment.

"So do you want to dance?" the vampire asked, apparently not discouraged by her obvious lack of interest.

"No, thank you," she said in her best Russian accent and brushed past him. She began the visualization of raising walls around her, just enough to block her identity, but allow Minnie to sense she was vampire. She sensed Minnie's awareness as she approached. Her sister-in-law turned. She met the other woman's intent to read her mind by clutching the touchstone tighter and focusing her energy on fortifying her shield. It was working. She smiled slightly when Minnie started toward her.

"You're new here." Minnie stopped in front of her, blocking her path.

She looked at Minnie and was glad she'd worn the blue tinted contacts.

"Good evening," she said with a thick Russian accent. "My name is Maria."

"Oh my, Maria, you're a long way from home."

"I sensed this was the place for our kind. I have missed such places. There are many in Russia."

"All our fellow *comrades* come here," Minnie said. Her eyes narrowed as she let her gaze move over Danielle.

All I Need

"Unfortunately, I find clubs take the edge off of hunting. Don't you think? After all, it's the sport that makes being immortal such a thrill."

Excitement flickered in Minnie's eyes. Danielle knew her sister-in-law would be pleased to match Armondés with yet another huntress like Charisse. But part of the matching criteria was the woman must be turning thirty and of course a mortal. Still, she knew Minnie could find a way to introduce her to Armondés and come up with a plan to use her.

"Have you lived in the U.S. long?" Minnie asked.

Danielle could feel her probing and focused her attention on maintaining the wall around her.

"My father was an American soldier during the war, the second one. He stayed in Europe with my mother when released from the army. When my mother died, I came to live with my grandmother in Washington, DC. I was sent to a private school and became a forensics expert. That is how I met Sinclair. He was a suspect in a murder case. A man I thought was most fascinating and indeed he was," she said and paused to flash a quick look about the club, making sure Sinclair had left. She fought to maintain her shield against Minnie's interest.

"So this Sinclair is your creator?"

"Ya. Amongst other things," she said and gave Minnie a small wink. "He introduced me to my immortality, as it were. Unfortunately, he was stalked and killed. I am without a mate and now search clubs such as this in hopes of finding a male deserving of the kind of pleasure I can give."

"Deserving?" Minnie asked with laughter shaking her shoulders. She struggled to compose herself. "I don't mean to be rude."

"I understand. Sinclair was an ancient one and taught me many sexual techniques that are, shall we say, lost art forms. But he was careless. He underestimated me and truly believed I was his. He had no idea how much I truly hated the prison he had built around me. I wanted my *freedom*." She shrugged off

171

Minnie's wide-eyed stare. Good, there was nothing Minnie loved better than a mirror of herself. She had just made a friend.

"You're a brave one, aren't you? You destroyed your creator and have no worries about bragging about it in public."

"Why should I?" She leaned closer and lowered her voice. "I tell you because I sense you understand how I felt, being imprisoned and forced to live someone else's ideal lifestyle. I can see it in your eyes, even though you struggle to shield it from me. I recognize one like myself." She straightened, noting the way Minnie's expression fell. Appearing to be able to read Minnie's mind gave her the illusion of having exceptional powers. Just like she had planned. Another thing for Minnie to envy.

"How are you able to—"

"Penetrate your shield? As I said, Sinclair had lived several thousands of years, so long he had lost count. He taught me everything he knew. As a natural hunter you could benefit from some of my secrets, ya?"

"Possibly," Minnie said and folded her arms across her chest.

"What I want in exchange is not too great of a price." She let her gaze move from her sister-in-law toward the door leading to the private quarters. Minnie followed her stare.

"You want Armondés?"

"He's the one I seek."

"Why?"

"Why not?" she asked. "He's king."

"Yes, but he seeks a mortal. A very specific female."

"Ya. This I know. One who will soon turn thirty. That is when the soul becomes fully seated in the body."

Minnie's mouth fell open. She took a step backwards.

"What? You think that's secret knowledge?" Danielle asked, letting her lips curve upwards slightly.

"He'll know you're vampire. You can't fool him into thinking you are a mortal," Minnie whispered.

"You could not fool him, but I can make a vampire believe I am a mortal," she said.

"That's not possible. I sense you're vampire. So will he."

"You shall see. I have greater powers than I have revealed and you know me as vampire only because I allowed it. I am very good. The only difficulty is once I've revealed myself as I have with you, I cannot then disguise myself as mortal. So for you, Minnie, I shall always be *uncloaked*." Her words hit Minnie just as she intended. Her eyes widened and excitement danced in their depths.

"Very good, you even know my name."

"I know more than you can imagine. Sinclair taught me the ability to cloak myself. It requires much concentration, and if the person is powerful like your brother, then it may prove difficult to cloak from others at the same time. For this reason, I have come to you uncloaked. I sense you are stronger than your brother." She smiled at the way Minnie's eyes widened. "So when I meet the King, I shall need a controlled environment. If you help me do this, I shall see you are allowed to hunt again. Is that now what you seek? Your freedom? I can give you that."

"Why would you? And what makes you think I cannot free myself?"

"You tried twice and failed." She watched the color rise over Minnie's face and her hands clench into tight fists by her sides. "And I would do this for you because I have plans for our king. I have my own agenda, as it were. What do you have to lose? If he does not marry a mortal and make her his, then he ages to his true age, ya?"

"How can you know these things?"

"As I said, Sinclair taught me the ancient secrets, which I am willing to share with you should you be able to steal me into your brother's room so I can seduce him," she said, pausing to glance in the direction of his private quarters. "You will ascend the throne in a natural order without anyone suspecting you. At the rate you are going, you will be replacing his wife every year for all eternity."

Minnie seemed to bristle at this observation, assuring her the woman had considered the possibility.

"I don't understand how you can deceive him into believing you're mortal."

"It is a special power I learned. As I said, it does not work on those who have already recognized me as a vampire."

"Right, convenient that you can't test it on me."

"Ah, I understand now. You want proof that I have this power. Perhaps I could offer a demonstration," she paused. "Pick out any one of these vampires and introduce me. I shall show you so you have no doubt."

"Good, come along." Minnie led the way through the crowd and immediately Danielle realized Fredrick was going to be her test. Fear dragged from her into the stone as they stopped in front of the bar. Minnie touched his arm and he turned. Danielle willed all her power to the forefront and donned the visualization of being mortal just as Sinclair had taught her.

"Freddie, darling, I want to introduce you to Maria. She's going to meet Armondés in a few moments."

"Ah, Maria." He bent over her hand with a very European flare. She focused on the mental image just as she had trained so many times.

"It is my pleasure to meet you," she nodded.

"I'm sure Armondés will be very pleased to meet you, Maria," he winked.

Minnie's jaw dropped but she was quick to recover.

"Come here, Freddie," she said and pulled him to the side. Danielle listened intently.

"Are you telling me that you think she's a good candidate?"

"Well," he paused and glanced back at her. "Sure, baby, as good as any of the others. Did you taste her drink?"

"Well, I'll be damned."

"What?" His forehead furrowed.

"You think as a human she's a good possibility?"

"Well, darling, if she wasn't human she'd not be a candidate at all. What kind of a question is that?" he laughed.

"Never mind, I'll talk to you later," she said and walked back to Danielle.

"Well, that is quite impressive. But I am still not sure I can agree to go along with this," she hesitated.

"I see. I proved that I could do what I claimed, yet still you do no trust me. Perhaps further demonstration of the extent of my abilities is called for. Let's begin with Charisse and the last night of her life, when she was on a secret and forbidden hunt with you."

Minnie gasped. Her face hardened, and she glanced around to make sure no one had overheard them.

"Who are you? How do you know that?"

"As I said, I shall share with you later, once I have what I want." She studied Minnie and could tell she needed a little more convincing. "You are still not convinced? Then I shall probe further. Danielle was not destroyed in the castle as you claimed. The ashes you used belonged to those of an unfortunate guard. And why did you have to use his ashes?"

Minnie stumbled backwards coming up against the railing.

"Because *you* chased poor frightened Danielle into the forest. Instead of being an easy prey, she outsmarted you." She paused, taking great satisfaction in claiming Minnie had been outsmarted. "You were forced to return to the castle and create the hoax that she had fallen victim to the assassins. You stirred a sense of urgency and managed to convince Armondés to flee to Savannah."

Minnie grabbed her arm and dragged her to a private corner. Danielle jerked free of her talons, noticing Fredrick now sat in the corner talking with two men. He looked up from his conversation and frowned at them.

"You could not possibly know that," Minnie hissed.

"You waited until the last moment, flying over the forest, then fled, knowing the sun would finish what you started. And it did."

"How do you know that?"

"I was there," Danielle said, enjoying the panic she saw in her enemy's eyes. "I am everywhere. It is the greatest secret Sinclair taught me."

"How do I know I can trust you?"

"You don't. But you will because I don't need you, Minnie. I could go to your brother and tell him right now what I have told you, but I won't. I have my own needs to fulfill. When you own the secrets I own, your needs become very different. I want a clan. I have chosen yours. I want Armondés for my own reasons. You need not worry about the why, all you need to know is I will fulfill all your goals and the bonus will be the secret abilities I shall share with you. You just have one task to perform. Will you arrange for me to be taken to his chambers?"

Minnie looked at her, still trying to penetrate her armor. Danielle braced herself and focused all her attention on resisting the powerful assaults. Finally, Minnie relented.

"Come with me." She turned toward the private entrance.

"But wait, does not the King have someone with him? I saw Jacqueline go through these very doors."

"You know her?"

"No, I heard the introduction. I may be a determined bitch, but I do not want to interrupt and place the King in a compromising position."

"Oh, please, my brother isn't going to compromise anyone. If I know Armondés, we will meet Jacqueline on the way up," Minnie laughed. She stopped in front of the guard by the door.

"Is the King alone? Or is his guest still up there with him."

"No, my princess, his guest left out the back entrance."

"See? Come on." Minnie grabbed her by the arm.

The guard bowed as they passed and opened the door for them. Danielle reined in the excitement that threatened to tear down her shield. She could not afford any of her thoughts slipping past her walls. It was all so familiar. She was at long last home. She struggled against the emotions. Pressing the touchstone tighter in her hand, the emotions subsided.

Minnie paused and stared at her.

"You've been in these chambers before."

Danielle panicked, but quickly reinforced her shield against Minnie's probing. She couldn't afford to let her glimpse any other thoughts.

"How is it possible that you feel familiarity here? You're lying to me."

"I have been here, but not in body. Just as I was in the forest where you chased your sister-in-law."

Minnie narrowed her stare and considered the explanation.

"Come." She turned. Their high heels clicked against the marble floors. Minnie led her down the hall and to the elevator.

"An elevator?" Danielle chuckled. "You are truly a modern vampire."

Minnie seemed to bristle slightly and punched the top button. The doors closed.

"There is such a thing as discretion, Maria. We don't flaunt our abilities."

"The first thing Sinclair taught me was if we do not use our powers, we eventually lose them."

"I'm not losing anything." Minnie stiffened.

Danielle smiled slightly. She'd never seen Minnie rattled. To think she'd been so frightened of her that night in the forest. She bolstered her shield. The elevator doors opened. Minnie bounced out of the elevator, leaving her to follow. They headed down the corridor toward Armondés' suite. She recalled the first time he had brought her here. She restrained her emotions and focused on her Maria persona.

Minnie glanced over her shoulder.

"I know everything about him and what he does in these chambers," she said, hoping whatever Minnie had picked up had not been who she truly was.

"Yes. I see that." She opened the door and motioned for her to enter. "Make yourself at home. I'll send my brother to you."

"A word of caution," Danielle said with her Russian accent weighting the air. She reached out and clasped the woman's forearm. "I know how you pretended there were intruders that night and that they attacked your lover."

Minnie took a step back, pulling free of her hold.

"I also know other things I could reveal to Armondés should you cross me as I see you are planning, Minnie. You are not to tell anyone about our pact. Especially *Fredrick*."

"Just who the hell are you?" Minnie leaned forward as though she were going to snatch the fake nose and chin from Danielle's face.

"Stop there!" Danielle held up her hand. "If I wanted to destroy you, I would have done so by now. I recognize my kind. Oppressed. Entrapped in a lifestyle not of your choosing. I offer you freedom. Do you want it? Are you patient enough to wait for it? Your plan has yet to work after all these years. Your brother still rules, and you still suffer. My plan, unlike yours, will work, and you shall never be suspected." She watched Minnie's rage recede. It was quickly replaced with a look of apprehension.

"If you can do all this, Maria, then I'll be in your debt. But be warned," she said, taking a menacing step forward. "You may be privy to *secret knowledge*, or you may just be a damn good magician of sorts. I've not decided what you are, or what you truly want. Whatever you are up to—if you fail, if you cross me, I shall *destroy* you." She turned on her heel and closed the doors.

Danielle resisted the urge to relax. She knew Minnie was standing outside the door, waiting for that moment when she'd drop her guard. It was some time before she heard the elevator doors open and the car begin its descent.

She collapsed into the nearby chair by the soft glowing lamp. With her legs crossed at the knees, her long legs would be in full view when Armondés entered. She needed to plant a stronger façade than the one she'd presented to Minnie. Armondés knew her best. She could not risk letting him know who she was until she was certain he had not ordered her assassination.

Thoughts of her husband sent burning desire flickering to her groin. It would require all her control not to betray herself. She recalled all the nights she'd spent in these chambers, and the golden days making love behind drawn draperies. She wanted all that back. Lost in her musing, the sound of the elevator doors brought her to her feet.

His footfalls grew closer. She swallowed the dryness in her throat. He was coming. Her arms ached to embrace him. Her façade was deteriorating. She stiffened. Focus. She squeezed the touchstone. Hold the shield. She must maintain distance from him. He was too strong for her. The door swung open. She steeled her mind for the effect his presence always had on her. He entered the room and stood in the doorway staring at her.

Chapter Twelve

He wore gray slacks and a matching trim jacket over a rich brocade gray and tan vest. His crisp white shirt was studded with diamond buttons that reflected in the dim light. A gray and tan striped tie completed his impeccable appearance. The lines in his face were drawn tight. He looked ghastly. She shielded her sympathy. What had happened to the virile man she'd grown to love? She masked her thoughts and smiled in what she hoped as a seductive look.

"Good evening." He paused, staring at her and immediately, Danielle felt his probing. "I was not expecting a vampire."

"I know. And I apologize, King Armondés." Her husky Russian accent sounded authentic to her and hoped it fooled him.

"You're Russian?" he asked. "But have lived in America for most of your life?"

She shrugged, not daring to lie to him.

"That explains the oddity in your accent then." He walked over to her. "You fooled my sister then? How did you do that? And, why? What is it you want, Miss —"

"Maria. Maria Bovichski Jordon." She noticed how his left eyebrow raised at her name.

"Ah, your father was the American tie then? World War II and met your mother after the war?"

"Something like that." She avoided committing to a lie. It was difficult enough fooling him with this charade, but necessary. She had to know the truth.

"So what is it you wished to talk with me about? I am pressed for time and don't tolerate deceit."

"Yes, I know. I did not mean to deceive. It is a delicate situation I find myself in and it was urgent I speak with you tonight. Please, at least listen to what I have to say. I have a proposition for you, but it requires your patience to hear me out. It is a complicated matter of great importance that affects your future."

"Really? Well, I love intrigue as much as the next man, so I think I can accommodate your request as long as you don't disappoint me." His eyes suddenly sparked with interest.

"I assure you, I shall not disappoint." She smiled slowly aware his stare traveled over her. She forced her focus on blocking his powerful attempts to penetrate her shield. She could not resist him for long.

"So what is this all about, Miss —"

"Please, Maria. First of all, I did lie to your sister. I regret doing so. I do not make a habit of such tactics."

"Well, that's not an easy thing to get away with," he frowned. "Why should I trust you? You've already admitted you're a liar."

"Yes. But I do have honorable reasons. If you will hear me out."

"Very well."

"Thank you. It is true, I told Minnie I could make you believe I was a mortal."

"Now why would you do that?"

"I have my reasons, if you will allow me to tell my story, my way."

He seemed to consider her and Danielle allowed her shield to slip enough for him to read her sincerity.

"Would you care for something to drink?"

"I have not fed this evening, perhaps —" She looked down at her lap. She hoped the coy gesture would win Armondés' curiosity. When she raised her stare, she was rewarded with a look of intrigue sparkling in his eyes. Why should a vampire as powerful as he have cause to fear or worry over her? Of course he would find her a mystery and be intrigued enough to solve her puzzling appearance.

He turned and retrieved two goblets and the familiar black bottle with its gold crested label. He poured the vintage into the two goblets and handed her one.

"So you don't hunt?" He let his stare sweep over her.

"No." Danielle shifted in the seat so he could take in her curves. She reclined slightly and tilted her breasts higher. The move caught his attention for he paused as he poured the contents into the goblet. She blazed under his intense regard. Her need inched along her spine, traveling to her pussy. She forced her energy to sustain her shield of disguise. She wanted to reveal her identity to him at that very moment, embrace him, shower his face with kisses, but if she did, then she would be forever plagued with doubts. She must have no doubts before she told him the truth, and even though this deception tore at her, Danielle was determined to see it through, just as she'd planned.

"It's rare to find anyone outside my own clan who no longer hunts," he said.

"I never enjoyed it. Messy business and high-risk undertaking. I prefer to live as a shadow in the mortal world and not draw attention to myself." She sipped the drink.

"Indeed." He graced her with a crooked smile and took a long sip, still staring at her, earnestly trying to break through her barrier.

Danielle steeled herself against his assaulting probe.

"I see you do not believe me," she said.

"I find it odd that one so young would be so wise and naturally aspire to a higher level of lifestyle."

"I had a good teacher."

"Who was that?"

"No one you would know, I am certain." She shifted, grateful for the hours she'd spent practicing her shielding techniques with Sinclair. Armondés was much stronger than Sinclair.

"So what brings you here, Miss Jordon...Maria?"

"As I mentioned, I have a proposition for you, King Armondés."

His eyes glinted brighter.

"I told your sister I had great powers. Alas, in truth , I have very few, but I told her I could make you believe me mortal and then convince you to marry me."

His laughter was a low rumbling.

"I know it sounds preposterous."

"You are preposterous, Maria, if you think I would allow you to come into my home, and accept whatever you say, much less when you openly admit to deceiving my own sister."

"You see, I have heard the rumors about the assassins who plot against you and how you have lost two wives to them." She ignored his indignation, feeling her defenses slipping under his constant probing. She must be sure about this.

"What business is it of yours?" he asked not even trying to hide his anger.

Hope kindled in her. She knew she was treading on dangerous ground, but she had to know. Her strength to shield against him was weakening. He was much stronger than Minnie. His thoughts punctured tiny holes into her armor.

"My proposition for you, Armondés," she said in her most sultry tone.

His demeanor shifted. The look in his eyes revealed his sexual arousal. She didn't know if she should be jealous or flattered and pressed the touchstone against her palm.

Slowly, she uncrossed her legs and stood in front of him, sipping her drink. She managed to maneuver a stray drop of blood to appear as though it had accidentally escaped her lips. It trickled down the side of her mouth. She glanced up to see if he had noticed and met his stare. Taking great care, she caught the drop with the tip of her tongue and licked her lips.

"It is a good vintage. I especially enjoy the mango taste," she said.

"What's your proposition?" he asked, obviously growing impatient.

"I have heard rumors about who these assassins are and I believe I can help you discover the one behind their plotting. Not just the minions, mind you, but the one who wishes to supplant you." She paused, giving him time to contemplate her claim. She watched his handsome face as he considered her with those dark eyes. Her heart tugged and guilt threatened to defeat her. She could not turn back. It was too late.

"You know this?" he asked, releasing another deep laugh. "How could *you* possibly know anything? Or hope to discover this when I've not been able to with all the resources at my disposal?"

"First of all," she said, slowly closing the space between them, aware his stare was riveted to her legs and the purposeful swaying of her hips. She knew he guarded a sudden desire. Part of her hated him for the betrayal while another part enjoyed the excitement, knowing he wanted her. "Let me assure you, I am not one to play games."

He lifted his eyebrow again.

"Well, I do enjoy a bit of sexual play, but when it comes to dire matters of betrayal, I am very straightforward," she said.

"That's good to know, but again I ask you, Miss Jordon, how do you think you can succeed where I have failed?"

"Because, Armondés, I am not part of your court," she purred, gliding her hands over his chest. She moved behind him and pressed hard against his buttocks. It was a fine balance to maintain her shield against his intense probing when the flashes of desire roared through her.

"What does that have to do with discovering who is my enemy?"

"Just that I am not an insider." She rubbed her breasts against his arm, and raised her hand to his face where she traced his ear with her forefinger and grinned at the way he stiffened.

"And you feel an outsider has a better chance of discovering who the assassins are?"

"Yes, I do when they are part of *your* court."

"Just who are you?" He seized her wrist within the steel band of his hand. She cried out in pain, but continued to shield herself from his mental probing.

"I told you." His nearness threatened to unravel all her training.

He released her and stood staring down at her.

"So you did. And if I went along with this game of yours what would you get out of it?"

"I would become your queen."

"That's impossible."

"Why? You are here to find a new wife, are you not? Is not that the reason you came back in Savannah?"

"Yes. I must find another wife." He bowed his head.

"Then that wife will be me."

"No. She must be a mortal. I must transform her into a vampire just before I make her my queen."

Wrong answer. Disappointment threatened to betray her emotions.

"I know, but I was hoping we could make an arrangement." Anger threatened to tear down her shield. She tightened her grip on the touchstone and willed herself to calm down. She was going to put her husband through the final test, then she would know if he was guilty or innocent. She pressed full length against him and slipped the touchstone between the deep cleavage of her breasts. "Sit, please," she purred and he sat down in the chair. She kneeled in front of him and separated his legs with her hands. Holding onto his gaze with her burning one she spoke, "There are all kinds of ways to trick these curses."

"Oh really?" he asked and leaned back into the chair. His gaze never left her face.

"Yes," she said and ran her hands along his thighs. "You just have to know where to look."

"What do you want?" he asked, but his voice was deep with passion.

"Right now?" She looked up at him, letting her fingers trail over his groin. His hard cock startled her. How much of a grieving husband was he? She hastily masked the thought and trailed circles with her forefinger to the zipper. "All I need is to give you a little consolation, my King. Then we shall discuss what else I want." She looked up at him, holding his gaze in hers while she unzipped his pants and freed his hard cock. She held it in her hands and lowered her mouth to his shaft. Opening her mouth, she pressed him inside and sucked against the sides of his cock. He groaned when she circled her tongue around the tip of his cock.

His hips moved to afford her easier access. She grasped the base of his cock with her hand. Suddenly, he jerked from her and flew from the chair, landing in front of the window with his back to her while he zipped the pants. That was not at all the kind of reaction she had expected, especially after he'd admitted the purpose of being in Savannah. Renewed hope kindled in her as she straightened from the crouched position, unsure what to do.

"My apologies," she said.

"Get out!"

Danielle balked. She could not leave. If she did, everything she had planned would be for nothing.

"My King, please forgive me. I did not mean to offend you."

"I truly wish I could take you up on all you offer, but I find I can't." He bowed his head.

"I do not understand," she said and reached out to touch his arm, but he pulled from her touch.

"Neither do I. For the first time in my very long life, I fell in love. My wife, Danielle, was all I ever wanted for my mate. We were…we were so happy. And even though it shall mean I fall victim to the curse, I don't care. My sister brings me candidates but I reject them all." He bowed his head, and leaned against the tall patio door. "I was so enraged the first time she brought a young woman to me, I nearly killed the girl." His voice broke. "So, you see, Maria, regardless what you have to offer me, I cannot take it. Even if I wanted to, I couldn't because my love for Danielle is stronger than anything I have ever known. It rules me as though I were its slave. I can never marry again."

That was what Danielle had come there to hear. She hesitated, unsure how to let down her guard and approach him.

"Then I think I can truly help you, Armondés." She still spoke with the accent. "If what you are telling me is the truth and from what I can see by looking into your mind, it is…" She paused and took a cautious step closer to him. "We have a lot to discuss, Armondés," she said in her normal voice and dropped her defense.

He spun around so fast Danielle lost her balance, but he caught her.

"What is this?" He stared down at her.

"It's a disguise to get me past those in your court who are traitors. The ones who tried to murder me while you were out with your army on a wild goose chase."

"It can't be." He held her at arm's length. "Are you real? Danielle? I thought you were destroyed. Lost to me forever." He looked into her eyes, struggling to see beyond the disguise and her contacts. "Danielle, is it really you?" he asked and rubbed her cheek with the back of his hand.

Slowly, Danielle tugged on the chin and the glue gave slightly. She peeled it from her face, watching his eyes widen as she removed the nose.

"My Danielle!" He held her face between his hands. "I don't know how, and I don't care. You are real!" He covered the words with his mouth before she could speak them and kissed her hard.

It had been too long since she had felt his passion. Tears pooled in her eyes. She was back in his arms. She wanted him. She needed him beyond reason but pulled from him. His taste lingered on her lips.

"We cannot risk this. Not here," she whispered and held her hand to her trembling lips.

"Why not?"

"Your enemies, my enemies, believe I was slain. That's how it must remain for now. I came tonight because I wanted you to know I was not destroyed. You do not need to marry another to avoid the curse."

"Danielle," he whispered, clearly beyond controlling his reaction to their reunion. "I need to make love to you. I need you to know how precious you are to me."

"I do, my love. You told me just a moment ago when I was a stranger to you."

"My Danielle," he said and took her into his arms again. "I love you."

"And I so love you, Armondés, but we must be wise in our next move. We have to force the traitors into revealing themselves. We haven't much time, Armondés. I need to repair my disguise and leave before Minnie comes back."

"But she'll be so relieved to know you've survived."

"No! No one must know. You must block this from everyone. Even Minnie."

"But why?"

"You must trust me, Armondés. In order for us to entrap the assassins, the ones who orchestrated it all, we must keep my identity secret."

"Yes, of course, whatever you wish, my love, only do not deny me." He pulled her against him again, but she stepped from him.

"Come to me just before sunrise. Spend the day in my loft."

"Yes, where is it?"

"I have one on the third floor over on Broughton Street, in one of the refurbished buildings."

"How civic-minded of you to be part of revitalization of the downtown area."

"Someone else did all the work. But you're right, it's an active area most of the night, at least until around three or four. It feels good to be around night people. I'll leave my window open. Come just before sunrise so no one can follow you. And I shall welcome you back into my bed, my love." She touched his face, stroking his jaw with her hand. He felt so good.

"I'll find you."

The rap on the door startled them. Danielle evoked her shields, praying it was not too late and that the heavy doors had protected her from being detected.

"Armondés?" Minnie's voice called from the hallway.

Grabbing her purse and hastily pressing the nose and chin back into place, Danielle kissed his cheek, and then opened the balcony door. She blew a kiss at him.

"Sunrise," she whispered and lifted from the terrace. He watched her ascend over the buildings. Minnie knocked on the door again and opened it.

"Armondés?" She peered into the room. "Where did Maria go?"

"She left," he said and turned his back to her. "Don't send any more up to me this evening. I'm tired."

"What about Maria? Did you already test her?"

"No."

"Will she be coming back?"

189

"Don't push it, Minnie. I haven't eliminated her."

"Good. I'm relieved. The sooner you find a new mate, the easier we can all rest." She paused in the doorway. "You only have few weeks left before the one year anniversary, you know. I don't want to see you walking around like a skeleton." She slammed the door before he could respond.

Laughter rumbled in him. Danielle was not destroyed! For the first time in months, he was happy. Danielle was unharmed. It was too incredible to be true. He wanted to shout it to the world. His beloved still existed! He had so many questions he wanted to ask her. It was maddening she had left so quickly. He glanced at the grandfather clock—it was only three o'clock. He had nearly three hours to wait. How he longed to fly to her right then—damn the chance of being followed. He held his arms to his sides and lifted from the patio, but drifted back down. He would respect her request. Why had she waited so long to contact him? Had she been hurt?

She had seemed so frightened that she'd be discovered. And who did she believe the traitor was in his own court? He would not jeopardize her life. He would wait. He paced through the door into the parlor and moved about the room, constantly glancing at the clock. Every second that passed was an eternity.

* * * * *

Danielle washed the glue from her face and set about repairing her makeup. She then removed her new negligee from its tissue and held it up. The purple netting was nearly transparent. She pulled it over her head, letting it fall over her body. The lace top was strapless and hugged her breasts, accentuating her cleavage with its heart-shaped design. She turned sideways and inspected the way the thin material revealed her buttocks. It was enough to cover her nakedness, and reveal just enough to please Armondés.

She wanted their reunion to be perfect. Later, she would break the news to him that Minnie was behind the assassination attempts. Until then, she would enjoy her time with her husband free of the fear of being discovered. Minnie would be retiring to her suite with Fredrick. No one would suspect Armondés was not in his suite.

Giddiness threatened to tear down her composure. She was exhausted from the effort it had required to prevent Minnie from penetrating her thoughts. She was grateful it had only been a short time with Armondés. He would have broken through her barriers easily. All her planning was going to pay off. She twirled through her bedroom into the den and lifted from the floor. She giggled and floated about the room, enjoying the freedom of flight. She shifted toward the balcony and froze in midair.

"Armondés!" she gasped, and flew across the room.

He lifted from the floor and embraced her. His lips covered her delighted squeals.

"Oh, I missed you!" She held his face between trembling hands and scattered kisses over it.

"My Danielle." He pulled against his shirt and the material gave under his strength, tearing from his hard body. Her stare riveted to his muscular chest and arms. Fire seared her throat.

"Oh, how I've missed you. When I thought you were dead—" He dropped the tattered shirt and ran his hand through her hair, smoothing it from her face. "You're so beautiful."

"I love you. I've missed you so, Armondés!" Her nostrils flared with his scent. Memories flooded back of his taste, his love, everything about him. Her pulse was riotous when his lips touched hers again, sending lightning streaks in the wake of his touch. His kiss was hard with urgent need as his tongue darted inside her mouth. Her deep moan seemed to fan his passion. Armondés pressed her tighter against him.

Molten fire erupted and flowed to the warm moistness throbbing between her legs. She ached for his touch, his kisses, knowing his hard cock could ease the desperate rawness pulsating from her clit.. The burning surged from that hidden place only he could find and breathed to life. Danielle jerked at his trousers, but her fingers trembled against the metal zipper and his hands covered hers to ease the metal down the zipper's length. His pants fell to the floor. Her pulse thickened. Every nerve ending screamed in response as his hard cock, freed from confining pants, throbbed against her. Her fingers tightened around the thick shaft.

"I want you," he rasped, brushing his lips against her ear. "I want you naked beneath me."

"Armondés," she gasped with shivers of delight shuddering all the way to her feet. Her gown fell to the floor as his hands moved over her hips and to her ass. He cupped her buttocks and lifted her to his waist.

"When I thought you were destroyed…" his voice shook.

"Shhh."

"I dreamed of this moment, my love." He pulled her legs around his waist, slipping his cock into her.

"You are so exquisite." He enfolded her in his arms, crushing her breasts against him.

He lifted from the floor, deliberately, twirling around the moonlit room as he moved in and out of her. She found herself lowered to the bed. His low groan became a caress over her cheek. His throbbing cock penetrated and plunged into her pussy.

She inhaled sharply, her hungry lips seeking his, demanding fulfillment. All of her desires were unleashed with wild abandon. The roaring passion he'd first fanned to flame consumed them. She fucked him with hard fast thrusts.

Armondés moved in and out of her, riding the wave of urgency. He kissed her, held her, and touched her, whispering words of love and promise. She clung to him, moving with each thrust. Her endless aching finally met, her bare legs around his waist, urging, pulling him deeper, panting words against his kisses until at length she quivered under him, clinging to him fiercely.

His heat broke out in rivulets of sweat along his flesh and he shuddered, a groan rushing from him along with the wave of release. He mumbled something, but his words were lost in the roaring in her ears. Spent, Armondés collapsed onto the mattress beside her. She lay with her arms and legs about him, entwined eternally. Contented. Fulfilled. At long last peaceful.

The sounds from the street below filled the room.

"I can't believe we are together." She opened her mouth and sucked his tongue then darted from his playful twists. His fingertips stroked her.

"Danielle," he breathed. "I'm so happy to have you back in my arms."

The sudden banging on the door jarred them from the bed. Danielle found herself plastered against the ceiling staring down at the room as he moved to the door.

"Don't open it!" she whispered. "It's the guy down the hall. He's drunk." She floated back to the bed and sat in the center of it, watching him.

"Does he do this often?"

"Afraid so," she sighed and let her gaze travel over his strong arms, his chest flexing as he stood near the door. Heat scorched up her thighs to her clit. She moved her hips and spread her legs so he had a clear view of her pussy.

"Come back to bed," she whispered and he turned from the door, giving her an appreciative lopsided grin.

"You are gorgeous."

"Fuck me, Armondés. Take me now. I'm burning for you."

He stood with his hand wrapped around his hard cock and slowly walked over to her, while stroking it with his hand. He stood over her, masturbating, and reached out to touch her breasts.

"You're so beautiful, Danielle." He moved his hand up and down his cock, while pressing her nipple between his thumb and forefinger. "Do you see how easily you arouse me?"

"Hmmm," she said, plunging her finger into her mouth, wrapping her lips around it as she stroked in and out of her mouth. She lifted her hips and rocked them forward then back.

"When you do that, it makes me want you so badly." He let his fingers trail over her stomach and stop just above her pussy.

She ached to feel his touch and lifted her hips higher, attempting to force his fingers closer.

"You want me?" he asked.

She nodded and looked up through burning eyes.

He moved his hand and cupped her pussy, and she writhed under his strokes, needing more. She pressed against him, but he continued to tease her. Grabbing his hand, she flattened it out, guiding his forefinger to her clit and moaning at the contact of his flesh against hers.

"You need to learn to wait," he said and lowered himself to the bed, supporting his weight with one arm.

"You need to learn when I need relief, not play." She wrapped her arms around his neck and then her legs around his waist, pulling him to her, closing her hand around his hard cock to guide him into her pussy.

"We will play later," he said and thrust his cock into her.

She groaned and grabbed his buttocks, pulling him deeper as he gripped her hips and pounded into her. She met each thrust. His lips were moist against hers—tender touches contrasting with his fierce taking. He drove in and out of her pussy, each thrust welcomed, fire rising higher from her pelvis, snaking up her spine. He lowered his face and captured one of her nipples, sucking it. Pleasure arced through her, intensifying with each nibble. She cried out. Her clit pulsed against each movement he made, and, as she tottered on the edge of climax, heat raced from her pussy and shot in hot, electrical currents to her head, bursting bright against closed eyes. The walls of her pussy clamped around his cock. Tears streamed from the corners of her eyes and she hugged him, wanting to get closer. Warmth radiated around them. She was home.

He collapsed against her.

"I love you, Danielle. Welcome home," he said and gathered her into his arms, kissing her forehead and stroking her hair.

* * * * *

She awoke to find her legs entangled with his and her arms wrapped around him. She nestled her nose into the hollow of his throat with a satisfied moan.

"You're awake," he said and kissed her forehead. He tightened his arms around her and rolled her on top of him.

"What time is it?" she asked and strained to see the bedside table. "It's noon already?" She rolled onto her side.

"I was thinking about a shower," he said and nuzzled her, planting short kisses on her breasts.

"That sounds nice," she said and draped her arms over his shoulders.

He picked her up and she tightened her arms around his neck, thinking how much she loved the way it felt to be in his arms again. He carried her to the bathroom, and let her slip down the full length of his hard naked body. His rigid cock pressed between their bellies.

Excitement scorched through her. He reached to turn on the water, and she captured his lips with hers as the water burst from the showerhead. His wet hand fanned against her back, slipping to the curve of her buttocks where he cupped a cheek in his hand and pulled her into the shower with him. He lifted her legs and pressed her against the smooth tile wall as he pumped his cock into her, the water pounding against them as he took her slow and hard. She begged him for release, but he teased her, sometimes stopping completely while other times he moved his cock in and out of her so slowly she cried out.

Incited beyond control, he pounded harder, driving deeper into her until she cried out and shuddered against him. He groaned and ground himself into her until he jerked and liquid heat rushed into her. He held her against the wall, panting, licking the water from her shoulder.

"I love you," he said and wrapped her in a towel. Slowly, he carried her to the bed, pausing to enjoy a small kiss before lowering her onto the mattress where he dried her with the towel, letting his fingers trail over her body.

"I can't believe you are here," he said and kissed a nipple.

"I love you, Armondés."

"Where have you been all these months?"

"Preparing for this moment."

"Seriously." He looked down at her and traced the line of her jaw.

"Seriously, I have been in training so I could mask my identity from our enemies."

"Ah, as Maria. I want to hear everything. Every detail of what happened and where you have been and why you didn't let me know sooner that you were alive."

"Yes," she said and laced her fingers through his. "What I have to tell you is going to be difficult to hear, but you have to know the truth."

* * * * *

He kissed her goodbye, leaving a faint trail of his energy as he pulled from her. She didn't want to let him go, but he floated through the open window and out of her reach. She stood watching as he crested the rooftops and disappeared.

Dread overwhelmed her. Would he be smart and keep the secret to himself? He had agreed to go along with her plan, but she had felt his pain upon learning it was Minnie who was behind the attempted coup. He had not realized the extent of his sister's obsession or the depth of her unhappiness. Oh, he'd had his suspicions, but to actually have them proven was quite different.

She sat down in front of the dresser to apply the disguise, but was hindered by the faintness of her reflection. She tried turning on more lights, but it only made the reflection fainter. She hoped she could see well enough to make the disguise as seamless as Sinclair had. She was tempted to seek him out, but knew it was time to rely on herself. If she was gong to pull this off, it would have to come from her, not Sinclair.

Her thoughts wandered to the blissful day she'd spent with her husband. She smiled at her faded reflection. The mere thought of Armondés' powerful body sent excited flutters to her pussy. The memory of his complete possession of her sent streaks of pleasure throbbing through her. She licked her lower lip, still able to taste his kisses.

"Stop it," she said aloud, mentally shaking herself. She must remain focused and begin putting up her shield against Minnie. Dressing in the new red gown, she let it fall to her feet. It sported two very long slits to each thigh. It was not her choice, but a gown Armondés had given her in France. No one had ever seen it on her, except him. She loved wearing it for him, but was self-conscious about wearing it in public. Still, she knew it was an excellent choice for the Russian vamp role.

She caught her blonde ringlets into a hair clip on the top of her head and let the short tresses cascade over the sides of her head, barely touching her ears. It was a good style for the thin velvet strap V-neck gown. The silky fabric hugged her curves and accentuated her best features—her rounded breasts, narrow waist and feminine hips. She turned around to glance at the low back where the material cascaded in seductive folds just below her waist. She imagined how Armondés would react when he glimpsed the small of her back.

She rubbed her legs together, enjoying the pulsing heat between them. Since becoming a vampire, she'd learned to dread the sunrise, but now she could not wait for its return so she could be back in Armondés' arms. She slipped into the red high heels.

Pausing by the open window, she was tempted to take flight, but thought better of it. Besides, it was a nice evening and she wanted to enjoy the city. The walk would give her additional time to raise her shield against any nosy vampires. She battled all the worries of what could go wrong. Minnie could not be trusted, but as soon as they discovered who was helping her, they could end this charade.

* * * * *

"I don't need you to tell me about my duties." Armondés glared at Minnie, growing more than a little irritated.

"Well, someone needs to, you only have three weeks left to find your new wife." She paced to the other end of his den. With arms folded, she turned to face him. "The year has nearly passed and you've not made any real efforts to find a mate. Just like last time."

"I've been busy with other things."

"Yeah, I've heard the rumors, brother. Out flying around just before sunrise. That's a risk you should not take. Rumors are you fly to be with a woman. What are you doing? You should be finding a mate, not screwing around with some whore. What happened to Maria? She was an excellent candidate."

He leaped from his place and grasped her by the throat. One swift movement of his hand and she would be destroyed. Anger raged inside him. He blocked the knowledge pressing toward the consciousness of his mind that she was the betrayer.

"Do not speak of things you now nothing about. You try my patience beyond what I would allow even for you."

Fear etched across her face and mingled with the deep-seated anger shining in her large eyes.

"I meant no harm. I'm worried, that's all," she said, struggling from his powerful clutch.

"You're to attend to the affairs of the clan and find my new bride. Nothing more. Understand?" he asked and released her.

She fell back against the fireplace, rubbing her throat.

"I understand you're not yourself. I brave to comment further that your own clansmen are whispering."

"And your bravery is stretching my patience. I know you've had me followed. Or should I say attempted to have me followed. I saw the remnants of your two spies in the alley tonight. They weren't quite fast enough to beat the sun. You wasted two good men."

She turned her back to him again and cleared her throat.

"They weren't spies, but guards. I'm worried because you don't take any guards with you. You could be ambushed."

"Perhaps," he said and moved to stare out the window at the lights glimmering from the river. He masked the rising thought about the day spent in Danielle's arms and immediately replaced it with the thought of the guards.

"I have one more woman I'd like to send up to you. She's an excellent candidate. You should test her immediately. We're running out of time, brother. You must remarry. Soon, we'll mark the anniversary of Danielle's—"

"Again, do not remind me of what I must do. Send the woman up. I'll see her now."

Minnie straightened her shoulders and walked across the room to the door, where she paused.

"If you wish to have a lover, there's no harm in doing so. But you can't continue to reject every woman I send."

"None have passed the tests. What else would you have me do?" he asked, holding his arms out to his sides.

Minnie frowned at him and slammed the door behind her. He pushed all thoughts of Danielle from his mind, replacing them with thoughts of Maria. It was something he had begun to practice, calling her Maria, should his thoughts become too strong and he not be able to block them from Minnie.

A sharp rap on the door interrupted his thoughts. He turned just as Minnie opened it and the blonde woman entered. She was shorter than Minnie and wore a pink floral dress.

"Please enter," he said and moved across the room to greet her.

Chapter Thirteen

"He did the same thing last time," Minnie said, looking up at Fredrick, longing to taste his lips. She had started out using him, but now she needed him. Was she in love with him? Was that even possible?

"Yes, he did but he also found his mate at the eleventh hour, literally." He turned toward the elevator and pressed the button. "You just have to continue to select candidates who can't remotely be a match."

"That's why I've included the second test in *my* initial screening. As long as he doesn't find out, we'll achieve our goal this time," Minnie purred.

"We better. I'm weary of the whole process. The first test is conducted during the interview, correct? Unknown to the woman."

"Yes, I drink after her. Since I'm his blood, I can tell by taste if she's a good candidate to be transformed into a vampire. I did it with Danielle at the bistro, but her drink was watered down. But, the second part was strong enough to ensure failure."

"And the second test is the screening?"

"My brother scans their minds for compatibility, but I scan for an unhappy marriage or love affair."

"Why?"

"Part of the investigation into Charisse's transformation addressed the emotional stability of the candidate in relationship to transformation. The court scientists now believe that emotions play a more significant role than we first realized. The candidate's emotional state is the determining factor whether it will be an easy transformation or one destined to be problematic or, as in Charisse's case, disastrous."

She brushed against him, wanting to take him right there. Instead, she focused on their mission. "Charisse had a string of unhappy love affairs, and for whatever scientific reason, it dictated her transformation. As for your transformation, dumb luck worked in our favor."

He stroked her arm with his forefinger.

"Keep the candidates coming. We don't want him finding a mate secretly. If he does, I'll simply kidnap him and chain him in the sun. I'm through with being discreet," Fredrick said as the elevator doors opened and he motioned for her to enter first.

She laughed.

"How can you think this is funny?" He pressed the Lobby button.

"I don't, really I don't. It's just, you sound so desperate." She cleared her throat and composed herself. "There's no need for desperation, Freddie, love. I know the identity of the woman he's with every night."

"You do? When did you learn this?"

"Last night. I followed him. I nearly burned to a crisp, but managed to find a room in the attic of the building."

"Who is she?"

"Do you remember the odd Russian woman who made the proposal to me about getting rid of Armondés in exchange for certain favors?"

"Yes, but she never returned."

"I think our little Ruskie decided to work without us and has seduced my brother and placed him under her spell."

"What do you plan on doing about her?"

"I'm not sure, but I'm going to pay our friend a visit this evening. As soon as I hear about this last candidate."

"Like some company?"

The bell chimed and the elevator doors opened into the loud club. She hooked her arm through his and waltzed down the corridor into the vaulted dance area. It was a typical evening, already set to a high energy with plenty of Private Label bottles mixed with Armondés wines.

"My princess." A man dressed in the uniform of leather slacks and tight-fitting vest, bowed to her with his fist slamming against his chest. "You asked to know if the blonde Russian returned."

"Where?" she asked, shooting a look of surprise and excitement toward Fredrick.

"I had her wait over there," he said and nodded toward the bar.

"Good." Minnie hurried past him with Fredrick following her. He grabbed her by the elbow.

"Whoa there, Minnie. What are you going to do?"

"I want to talk with her. Find out what she's up to."

"Not so fast. I think you should play it cool here, let her come to you. She's obviously here to see you and not your brother. Let her make the first move."

Minnie considered him.

"Let's dance. She'll see us easily that way and not become suspicious. Just be cool. Let her take the lead," he said.

"I knew there was a reason I chose you to be my partner." She moved with him onto the dance floor and swayed to the rhythm of the salsa. The music snaked up her spine and she moved against him, pressing and twisting—grinding into him. She was rewarded when his groin hardened. His excitement aroused her. The music pounded in her chest until it consumed her. She reached up and kissed him. He responded by jerking her against him, moving with her, seeming oblivious to the dancers around them.

"I had no idea you could dance like this," she said, admiring the way his muscles rippled underneath his clothes. She leaned closer. "I want you."

"I think she spotted us." He glanced over her head.

She prickled under his slight, but brushed off the sharp pangs of hurt.

"Good. Let's move closer," she said and pulled him forward.

The music crescendoed to an end. She leaned into him, fighting the urge to continue to grind against him.

"That was very enjoyable." He buried his head in her hair.

"Let's sit over there," she said, determined to avoid being so vulnerable to him again.

They wove in and out of the crowd, all the while pretending they had not seen Maria.

"Minnie?" Her Russian accent sliced overhead.

Minnie turned, feeling as though she'd rehearsed the scene. She knew exactly how she would manipulate the other woman.

"Do you remember me?" she asked.

"Yes, I do. It's been a couple of weeks, though. Come," she said, and nodded for Fredrick to leave them alone. She led Maria toward the booth near the door that led to their private quarters.

She allowed Minnie to sit down first, then sat down across from her.

"So, I thought you'd gone back to Russia. All that bold talk about how you were going to take control of my brother and free us from his tyranny."

"And you think I turned out to be using smoke and mirrors? Is that it?"

"Yeah, something like that."

She leaned in to whisper. "Discretion is my greatest gift. In case you have not noticed, your brother has been very distracted. Just as I promised, I have kept him occupied so he has no interest in your candidates. I keep him consumed with only thoughts of me day and night. Perhaps you did not realize he slips from his suite just before sunrise every day? Or if you are aware of this, then perhaps your snide remarks are an attempt to discredit what I have accomplished?"

"Don't be absurd. I just wanted proof it was you who had captivated my brother."

"And who else would it have been? Why do you feel I have not lived up to my part of our agreement?"

"I don't. I'd just like a little more information."

"Such as?"

"Timetable? Plan of action. What's your fee? What do you expect from me once you have prevented my brother from stopping the curse?"

"Ah, we never did talk about my fee. I have none."

"What?"

"I shall get all I want when Armondés and I marry in a few weeks."

"I still don't understand. You certainly will not be queen, if that is what you are thinking."

"That is just it, is it not, Minnie. You do not know what I am thinking," she laughed.

Minnie clenched her jaw tighter.

"Look, I don't care what your game is, bitch. I just want it clear you'll do as you promised and that you have reasonable expectations about your payment."

"I'm going to overlook your insult because I know you are frightened, Princess. You worry I may come after you once I finish with your brother." She leaned back in the seat.

Minnie jutted her chin out.

"I do not want anything once I have Armondés."

"How stupid of me, of course, you're out for revenge. That's why you don't require payment from me. I don't have anything you want. You have all these special powers, so what could I give you?"

"Armondés shall marry me and when midnight strikes, he will realize too late I have duped him. I shall have what I want. And you will have what you want, his kingdom and your freedom." Danielle smiled.

Minnie shook her head.

"Something else worries you?"

"I just don't understand how you can deceive him into thinking you're mortal. He's with you all day. Do you not have to feed? Doesn't he ask why you don't go out in the sun? Doesn't it require a lot of energy to master such a cloak of disguise?"

She chuckled and let Minnie stew a little longer.

"My magic is not something I explain. You shall see its power on the anniversary of Danielle's death."

Her sister-in-law sat back in the booth with a dumbstruck look washing over her.

"Do not try to make this a complicated matter, Minnie. It is not."

"If you're lying to me. If you try to betray me—"

"What point would it serve me to lie?" she asked.

"I don't know. But I'll destroy you if you do."

"Ya, I recall your threats." She stood from the booth. "I have no patience with this silliness. Now that we understand each other, I hope I can be with Armondés from now until it is time for the ceremony without constant questioning? And secrecy? You will not follow me anymore, ya?"

Minnie jerked her head in a nod.

"Good. Would you be so kind as to tell the guard to let me into the private quarters?"

"Ah, he's a bit indisposed at the moment." Minnie's grin widened.

"A candidate for my position as his vife?" Danielle struggled to contain her anger and keep her shield held firm against Minnie's, who was intent on forcing her into an emotional outburst and being unable to maintain her shield, leaving her vulnerable to Minnie's probing.

Minnie shrugged.

"Well ve shall see about this, shall ve not?" She walked past her toward the door.

"Is the King still busy?" Minnie asked the guard, placing emphasis on the last word.

"No, my princess, his guest was escorted out the back entrance soon after she arrived, like all the others."

"See there," she leaned over to whisper in Minnie's ear. "Vonce more, you have underestimated my power over your brother."

* * * * *

"And she didn't question you further?" Armondés asked, amazed.

"Oh she wanted to, but Maria's persona is too strong. Minnie believes Maria has great powers because she knows so many details. I told her how she chased Danielle into the forest and left her to the sun."

"I should just kill her now." His arms tightened around her.

"Shh," she said and kissed his lips, molding her naked body against his. "We need to entrap all who are with her. Only then can we be safe."

"I cannot bear the thought of anyone hurting you. I never thought my own sister would betray me."

"Let's forget about Minnie," she said and nibbled on his ear. "I still think we need to keep moving every night. I don't trust her. Your quarters are probably bugged and who knows what else. This hotel is nice, I wish we could stay here, but she'll find us. She won't uphold her word to stop following me. At least tonight she knew we would be in your suite, only—" she giggled.

"Only you lured me here. My sister has gone insane." His body went rigid.

"She's like other vampires, Armondés. A hunter by nature. Can you truly force her to be less?"

"Are you saying I'm wrong?"

"Not at all. But I don't know that you can fully blame Minnie. I don't think she can help what she is."

"I blame her fully for what she has done to you. What she did to Charisse. And what she is planning for Maria."

She nodded, not wanting to have their night ruined by a discussion about Minnie, but it was too late. She moved from the covers.

"Where are you going?" he asked, sitting up in bed.

"I'm hungry. Would you like something?"

He shook his head and shifted onto his back, putting his arm underneath his head.

She stood staring down at him. He was so sexy, lying there. Her stare devoured his hard muscled body and all thought of food fled.

"I thought you were going to get a bottle of —"

She rested on the mattress with her weight on one knee, admiring the way he lay spread out in front of her. His partially erect cock rested against his balls. Her stare followed the thin line of hair leading from his groin to his trim waist.

"You were in your thirties when you were transformed?" she asked, knowing the answer.

"Yes."

"You had a master?" She stroked his bare leg.

"No. My parents, our parents were vampires. We are the genuine article born and bred. As such we chose the age of our complete transformation."

"I see. I didn't realize vampires could have children."

"Only those of the original bloodline can sire children. There were but a handful left even during three hundred A.D. I believe Minnie and I are the last. Would you like to have my children?"

"I could?" The thought of having his child filled her with a radiating warmth.

"Oh, yes. You can."

"And your other wives couldn't?"

"Wouldn't." He bowed his head.

She decided to change the subject and asked, "How did vampires come into being?"

"I don't know. Perhaps they were created about the same time of Cyclops and the unicorns. When the world was less restricted and creativity flowed naturally to all."

"Is that what happened? The world became restricted?"

"It was necessary. Too many rulers. Too many demi-gods. Chaos ruled."

She crouched forward and crawled toward him, flattening her hand against his leg. She delighted in the taut, muscular calf. The dark hairs on his shin tickled her fingertips as she glided her hand up his smooth, hard thigh, pausing inches from his cock.

"I would have loved to have known you then," she whispered.

"We have eternity." He reached for her and pulled her on top of him. She flattened full body against him. He turned her over. They floated from the bed, hovering just a few inches above the mattress. Her hair fell around her, suspended in the air. He planted tender kisses along the side of her face and down the column of her neck. She moaned.

He lifted his hand and stroked the air. The tapers along the walls ignited, their flickering flames dancing along the ceiling.

"Armondés," she sighed and drew her arms around his neck.

He whispered something before covering her lips with a fierce kiss. His groan vibrated in the room, sending excited streaks racing to her clit. The kiss deepened and firm hands massaged her erect nipples. His long bare leg twisted over her and leveraged them into the air, twirling above the bed.

"I want you, Danielle," he said.

"You have me."

He shifted above her and spread her legs apart to receive him. His hardened cock brushed against her thigh before he slipped between her legs and entered with a powerful thrust that sent them floating across the room to the other wall.

Bumping their heads against the painting, she broke from the kiss, giggling as the canvas crashed to the floor. She met dark eyes filled with naked passion. Sizzling currents shot through her. The contact of cool plaster against her ass sent streaks of raw pleasure cascading over her. He threaded long strong fingers through her smaller ones and lifted her arms above her head. Passion seared between them and melted until it was hard to tell where she began and he ended.

"You are so beautiful." He brushed cool lips against her trembling ones, teasing with excited tongue flicks against the soft kiss. She moaned and opened her mouth to receive the deep thrusts as his tongue moved in and out.

The fervor grew and stretched. She drew bare legs around his waist and rolled her hips into each powerful thrust as he pumped his cock into her. Arousal was a frenzied need. It grew in heat and fused together. They rolled suspended in the air, bodies entwined and twirling to the rhythm of their lovemaking. She moaned, tasting complete happiness in his arms. He broke from the kiss and stared down at her.

"What is it?" she asked.

He looked past her toward the row of windows in their hotel suite.

"The sun," he whispered and reached to pull the drapery closed.

"Can you stay tonight as well?"

"I can," he said and lowered them to the bed where he pulled the sheet over her, planting a kiss on her shoulder.

Warmth washed over Danielle, reminding her of hot summer days spent lounging on Tybee Beach with the ocean lapping at her feet. She snuggled against his chest, almost able to hear the seagulls crying overhead.

"Do you think we can keep dodging Minnie until next week?" she asked. "She'd love nothing more than to be able to destroy Maria."

"She won't, I promise. I won't let her." He kissed her forehead. "We only need another week. Then we can trick her into revealing if anyone else is involved. Is Sinclair ready?"

"Sinclair is eager to start his part of the ruse. I'm glad you asked him to help us," she said.

"We couldn't pull it off without him. I just hope he's as good as you claim."

Chapter Fourteen

"You can't continue to send guards out only to let them be destroyed. We're not that many," Fredrick said.

"I want them found!" Minnie seethed and flounced across the room, stopping in front of him. "You don't understand how serious this is. My brother believes she is mortal, so he will marry her. That is not even a question anymore."

"But that's what we want, isn't it? Armondés will miss the deadline. He will age and his strength will be gone. Weakened, I will be able to overpower him easily and can destroy him, then you can claim the throne."

"Don't you understand? My plan was for Maria to distract him long enough for him to miss the deadline. I never planned for him to marry that bitch! If he goes through with the ceremony, regardless if she is mortal or vampire, Maria will be the queen. It won't matter that she's a vampire when he takes her, because she will still be his mate."

"Oh…" Fredrick ran his hand through his hair.

"We have no idea what she has planned once she's queen. There's no telling what that insane vamp will do."

"Then we just destroy her, too."

"Are you just not listening to me? Where have you been these past weeks? Do you not understand the kind of powers she has? Trying to assassinate her *after* she is queen will be impossible." Minnie wrung her hands together and paced the length of the room.

"I've never seen you frightened of anyone, Minnie. What is it about this creature?"

"I'm not frightened." She glared at him.

"You're scared, Minnie," he said and put his hands on her shoulders, leaning down to her. "You're very unnerved by Maria. Tell me what it is."

She shook her head. No way was she telling him what Maria had known about Danielle. Besides, Minnie had told him how she had personally destroyed Danielle with a stake through her heart. She looked deeper into his eyes. Fredrick didn't need to know any differently.

"She's a wizard of sorts, Freddie. She has all these secret powers. Or claims to, I'm not sure if it's power or just magic. But she has yet to tell me why she's doing all this and what kind of revenge she seeks against Armondés."

"We'll take care of Maria immediately after the ceremony. They will both be destroyed and then," he laughed, encircling her with his arms, "you and I will celebrate with one of the biggest hunts in history!" He picked her up and twirled her about the room.

The knock on the door interrupted their play. Minnie pulled from him and straightened her dress.

"Yes?" Fredrick's voice boomed across the room.

"Princess Minnie." The servant entered the room and bowed. "A visitor requests an audience with you in the club."

"Visitor?" Her heels clicked against the marble floor as she walked toward the hall. "Who might this visitor be?"

"He asked that I give you this." He handed her the black business card with gold embossed letters.

"Sinclair?" she asked, hearing the shock in her own voice.

"Who is this?" Fredrick jerked the card from her hand.

"A ghost," she said and motioned for the servant to see the visitor to her suite. "I need to talk with him alone."

"I don't know what's going on, Minnie, but I don't like it. Who is Sinclair?" he asked, holding the card in front of him.

"He was Maria's creator, only she claims she destroyed him."

"I'm staying," he huffed and sat down in the chair by the window with his arms folded over his chest.

"Look, I think he'll speak more freely if it's just me. Please, Freddie, baby, go into my bedroom. You can hear from there. Please?" she coaxed, aware the elevator doors had opened.

Reluctantly, he did as she asked, leaving the door slightly ajar.

Minnie hurried over to the sideboard and willed the nervous fluttering to calm. If Sinclair was anything like Maria, he would immediately read all her jumbled panicky thoughts. She focused and raised her shield then steadied her hands to pour her guest a goblet of Private Label.

"Princess, this is Mister Sinclair," the servant said behind her. Minnie deliberately ignored the man, and continued to pour the goblets with her back to him.

"Have a seat, Mister Sinclair."

"Your Highness." His voice vibrated with strength and volume.

In spite of her composure, she pivoted to look at him. Her gaze widened on him, shocked. She'd envisioned a tall muscular man, instead, he stood only a few inches taller than she. She recovered quickly and lifted the goblets.

He appeared to be in his late fifties, bald and clean-shaven, dressed in a white shirt and dark slacks. He was trim and reasonably fit for a man his age, but he was nothing like Maria's version of a strong and powerful vampire.

"I took the liberty of pouring you a glass of our Private Label. We find it more favorable than having to hunt for our food."

"Thank you," he said.

"Please have a seat." She handed him the goblet. He waited for her to sit then sat down in the chair across from her. She sensed an air of urgency and expectation around him, but like Maria, his shield was too strong for her probing. She frowned.

"What may I do for you, Mister Sinclair?" she asked and sipped from the goblet.

"It's what I'm going to do for you, Princess," he said in that same irritating, superior manner of his protégée. She straightened in the chair.

"You want to do something for me? Why?"

"I recently discovered that my mate has visited you."

"Your mate, sir?" she asked. Minnie shifted under his intense stare. His gray eyes seemed hard—like chips of granite. The power she had dismissed as being myth emerged from him as though a separate entity.

"Maria has been here many times. I can sense her presence in this building. She visited you probably no more than a couple of days ago."

She tried to hide her surprise but knew by the look in his eyes she failed.

"I have met a Maria on a couple of occasions. What is this about, Mister Sinclair?"

"She probably told you she had destroyed me and that I was somewhat of a tyrant to her?"

Dread overwhelmed her. She did not like the arrogant tone in his voice. She also didn't like the fact that Maria had lied to her.

"I'm not sure I understand," she said, trying to force him into revealing more without admitting to any of his conclusions.

"You have chosen the wrong partner in this plot to supplant your brother."

She choked and put the goblet on the side table, clearing her throat.

"I assure you, Mister Sinclair, I have *no idea* what you're talking about."

"Your shield is too weak to block my mind, young one. I know what my Maria has been up to. She has become unstable over the past few years. I try to keep her close to me, but every now and then she manages to escape even my control. I always find her, but this time she has been very wise. She moves about every day, staying in different places. It makes it difficult to pick up her scent."

All her worries and fears burst to reality. She clasped her hands together, struggling to maintain her composure.

"What exactly do you mean? Unstable?"

"Maria is mentally unbalanced. Oh, she does in fact have great powers, but she does not always react in a rational manner. It makes for a lethal combination. I know she used the gifts I shared with her to manipulate you. I don't blame you."

"Excuse me? You think I'm so easily manipulated? I don't think so."

"I don't mean to be insulting, Princess. But she's a clever one. She can probe into the strongest minds. Her powers often alarm me. She grows more and more advanced each day. But this time, I fear she has crossed the thin line separating sanity and insanity."

Minnie sat numb, unable to say anything.

"She has this plan to marry your brother and become queen. She thinks if she does this, then she can somehow eventually restore her mortal self."

"What? That's absurd."

"Exactly how I feel. If she manages to accomplish this marriage, then she will destroy your brother and all who pose a threat to her plans, including you."

Minnie laughed, but her sudden amusement died when she met his cold stare.

"Look. I didn't agree to any of her plot. She wanted an audience with my brother, which I reluctantly granted."

"Your first mistake. Now she has him in her power. She will keep him from you until it is time for the ceremony. Yes, I know about the curse. I know everything she knows. You must get past your doubts about my abilities. I am her teacher. I taught her everything I know and I can help you."

"I'm listening."

"She will see they perform the ceremony in private and once complete, she'll turn on him like a praying mantis and consume him. Once she has made herself queen, she'll come after you and all those close to you. She's completely out of control, you see."

"I'm beginning to. My God! What can we do?" Minnie could no longer hide her fear. If this man could stop the crazy Russian, then she was willing to do whatever he suggested.

"I can stop her, but I need your help. You will provide me with men to track her down."

"I've tried that."

"But you were following your brother when he left, and tonight he has not come back as usual. He won't. She plans to keep him away from you until it is time for the ceremony."

"That little bitch!" Minnie jumped to her feet. "I *knew* she would betray me. I'm going to destroy her."

"No, you aren't," he said with calm certainty.

"I'll do whatever I damn well please. I don't know who you think you are—" She turned on him.

"I'm the only one who can find them. I can track her. I just need enough men to help me once I find them. How many can you spare?"

Her thoughts tumbled over in a frantic jumble. What could she do? That creature was going to destroy everything she'd planned.

"I don't have many left. We were never a large group. Around twenty. We're now only twelve in strength." She wanted to snatch the words from her mouth the moment she said them. He'd tricked her. He now knew exactly how many were in her rebellion. She mentally shrugged. It didn't matter.

The only thing that mattered was stopping Maria. Then she'd deal with Sinclair.

"I'm prepared to hunt tonight. Have your men meet me on the roof." He stood and made to leave.

"Wait, I have questions. How do I know I can trust *you*? What is it you want from me once you find them?"

"You? I don't want anything from you, Princess." He looked at her as though she were insane. Anger sparked in her. "I just want Maria back. That's all."

"How do I know that's true? Maria said the same thing. She only wanted to marry my brother."

"As you can see, I am not Maria. What you do in your little kingdom means nothing to my world. I simply want what belongs to me. I need your guarantee she will not be harmed by your men."

"That's all?" she asked, still not certain she trusted him. "I can't believe you don't want something from me."

"What more could I want?" he asked and took a sip from the goblet. "Unless… Actually, there is something I could use."

"I knew it," Minnie nodded.

"I could use several cases of this." He held up the goblet. "Not having to hunt my food will mean I have more time to track down my mate and if I had a nice supply on hand—"

"That's it?" Minnie was relieved but a little disappointed. It was a simple request and easily fulfilled.

"You can take a case with you now and if you'll give me your address—"

"I prefer to take it all with me tonight if it's the same to you. I don't stay in one place very long and if I have this once I capture Maria, it will make life easier."

"Very well, I'll see to it."

* * * * *

"Did you leave something for Sinclair?" Armondés asked and grabbed for Danielle's hand as they lifted above the city.

"I left a scarf. My favorite one at that," she sighed and drifted closer to him and held onto his waist with her arm draped over him.

"I'll buy you a hundred like it."

"So where are we going?" she asked, looking at the brilliant lights below. The Savannah River sparkled from the lights reflecting along its winding shore.

"It's so gorgeous."

"Where would you like to spend the week?" he asked.

"We can't leave Sinclair to do this alone," she insisted.

"I'm teasing you. We won't. I have some ambushes planned. We will weed out the traitors and ultimately only Minnie and those who have remained in the club will be all that's left of the rebellion."

She closed her eyes, longing for it to be over. She was weary of moving from hotel to hotel. The only advantage was the romantic days she spent with her husband.

"Are you a member of the Mile High Club?" she asked, gliding her hand to his groin.

He laughed and shifted the duffel bag onto his back. The Private Label bottles clinked with the movement.

"Come on, baby, let's show them how it's really done. Without a jet." She rubbed his slacks, feeling his cock underneath the material.

"I can think of nothing I'd rather to do, but until we are past this current danger, we must take minimal risks." His response disappointed her, but she saw the wisdom in what he said.

Reluctantly, she didn't press further.

"I have a very lovely suite reserved for us this evening. Come." He guided her back toward the city. They glided through the trees into Oglethorpe Square. The Spanish moss-covered trees afforded great shadows to cloak their descent from any possible witnesses. She landed beside him and he reached up to tug a small piece of moss from her hair.

"Where are we staying?" she asked, looking about the deserted square. She glanced at the Owens-Thomas house recalling her grade school class tour and how the Regency period home had captivated her imagination. It seemed a lifetime ago. The things she had been so connected to now had a different meaning, except the city. Savannah would always resonate as home whether she was mortal or vampire. They walked through the square, their footfalls seeming loud against the brick walkway, and continued down Abercorn. When he slowed at Broughton, she froze.

"We aren't going back to my flat, are we?"

"No, I'd not risk that. I have a reservation under Black at the Marshall House."

"Oh, that's wonderful. I've never stayed there." Excitement momentarily replaced fear. She had spent a semester studying the great buildings of the city and their respective history. Suddenly, the pang of a normal life struck her. How she would have loved to spend the night at Marshall House when she'd been mortal. Yet, she squeezed his hand, having Armondés was worth whatever she must sacrifice or leave behind.

He led her toward the back entrance. She raked her hands through her hair and tugged on the waist of her slacks. She had only one other pair of slacks and a shirt in the duffel bag he carried. If they were going to be on the run for a week, she'd need more clothes.

"I need to go shopping sometime," she informed him.

"Then we're staying in the right place, since all the shops are here."

"I better not go through the front entrance. I've lived here all my life, I might run into someone who knows me. The last thing we need is to attract unwanted attention and questions I can't possibly answer."

He nodded and escorted her through the back entrance. The antebellum hotel had been renovated a few years ago with great attention to detail, including the rear entrance. They traveled down the servants' back hallway and paused in front of a door. He opened it and peered around, then bowed for her to go first. She was surprised that they emerged into the side entrance of the lobby. She'd been one of many locals who had toured the hotel soon after it reopened its doors.

"Did you know this hotel was named a National Historic building in 2000?"

"Guess I could be named historic?"

She giggled.

"I love this city, so much. It's only been about twelve years since The Savannah Development and Renewal Authority was chartered and began the revitalization of Broughton Street."

"You miss your old life," he said with sadness riding his words.

"Some. But I love my life with you." She hugged his arm.

He planted a kiss on her forehead as they walked across the lobby. It was a flash of color and architectural motifs carved into white woodwork. Yellow plaster walls back-dropped tall columns supporting an oval ceiling. She glanced at the lovely black and white checkered floor, noting how the squares had been put together to form large diamond patterns. She wandered into the deserted library just left of the staircase while Armondés registered.

Her feet padded against the red, yellow and blue modern design rug complimented by a large semi-circular blue sofa that reminded her of a barrel. Gold upholstered chairs created an intimate seating in front of the fireplace. The red walls and white woodwork pulled the room together. When she'd toured the grand hotel on opening day, never would she have imagined the one time she spent as a guest would be as a vampire. She covered her smile with her hand. How her life contrasted with her old one.

Her beliefs about life and what was real had shattered the night Armondés had turned her and taken her as his wife. She ran her hand along the bookshelf, noting the book titles. How many people had lived oblivious to the reality that vampires walked the same streets, shopped the same stores and moved throughout the world blending in. While the rest of the world aged and decayed, she would continue. Panic roiled in the pit of her stomach. What would it be like to live forever? She stared at the room, realizing her brief trip of nostalgia had lulled her into forgetting how dangerous it was for them to be out in public like this.

She turned back to the lobby, staring at the gold tiles angling through the center of the checkerboard effect. He joined her at the bottom of the staircase and cupped her elbow in his hand. His face was drawn with worried lines along the corner of his eyes.

"What is it?"

"Nothing," he whispered.

Their footsteps were cushioned by the thick red and green runner. Once on the second floor, he pulled her into a service alcove with his finger to his lips.

Panic gripped her when he pushed her behind him and stood waiting.

"Where'd they go?" a male voice whispered.

"They must have used the elevator."

"No, I saw her in the library. I was across the street and had a clear line of vision."

"They must have escaped through the back then."

"She didn't see me."

"I know he saw me. Come on, we're going back on the street, now." Their running footfalls sounded down the stairs.

She collapsed against his back.

"Come on," Armondés said, dragging her behind him toward the elevator.

"Where are we going?"

"To our room. My sister's minions are lurking about downtown." They got off on the fourth floor and he quickly unlocked the door.

The suite was calming with blue, the trademark white woodwork and pine floors. She walked across the den to the bedroom, noticing the elaborate iron headboard and colorful blue and yellow quilt.

"This is beautiful, but are you sure we'll be safe here?"

"They won't be back." He folded her into his embrace and pressed his lips to her forehead. "Just a few more days, and then it's over."

"One way or another," she said.

"There's only one way for this to end. We'll be fine." He lowered his face to hers and captured her lips in a deep long kiss.

She relaxed in his embrace, knowing she could trust him. He had kept them safe so far. She worried about Sinclair now being part of their plan. It was one thing taking the risk for herself, but quite another to involve an outsider who had nothing at stake.

"Sinclair will be fine, Danielle. He's a very wise man."

"I know." She nuzzled his neck and nibbled at his flesh.

"Do you want to bite me?" His voice was full of desire.

"Did you bring enough Private Label to compensate?"

"Enough for tonight, my love." He stretched his neck and she clamped down, sinking her teeth into his flesh. Desire raged through her, coiling down her spine to her groin. He groaned and she sucked harder. His blood surged through her.

"I want to fuck you," he groaned and slid his hands to cup her ass, pulling her hard against him.

Chapter Fifteen

"How could six of my men be destroyed in only four days?" Minnie asked, glaring at Sinclair.

"That's something I have asked. Your men seem reasonably trained in self-defense, but every time we draw close, they end up getting themselves dusted." He collapsed into the nearby chair and took the goblet the servant offered. He drank the sweet liquid, mentally noting he could grow accustomed to such easy living. He lifted his stare to the woman pacing in front of him. She was a bundle of nerves and fear. How could someone so easily manipulated be such a threat? He took another deep sip.

"I think you're to blame for this."

"Me?" he asked, not trying to hide his amusement. "You were losing men before I offered to assist in the search. You have a bunch of incompetent oafs, Princess. They're awkward and don't know how to be discreet.

"Just the other night two of your goons rushed inside the Marshall Hotel, claiming they'd seen the king and Maria in the lobby. Now I ask you, do you think Armondés would be out in public casually checking into a hotel?" he scoffed and downed the remainder of his drink.

"They ended up dead like the others, but somehow, you always manage to survive. Why is that?"

"I'm smarter and have certain advantages," he said.

"Oh yeah, those secret powers," she said, letting the sarcasm drip from her words.

He stood.

"Where are you going?" she asked.

"I think this plan's a bust. I'm going it alone," he said and started for the door.

"Wait." Her voice shook with uncertainty.

He turned slightly.

"Rethink this. We only have one night left in which to find them."

"Exactly." He turned the knob.

"You will not abandon our plan!" she said.

"It was my plan and I'm calling it off. Your men have cost me most of the week. I'm going to salvage what I can." He slammed the door behind him. He stood outside the door, relieved his part in this charade was over. He tucked in his shirt and whistled as he walked toward the elevator.

The man standing inside pressed the button.

"Ah, no, I'm going down." Sinclair said. The burly guy grinned widely as the doors closed.

Sinclair lunged for the doors, but he was too slow. The wire came around his neck, cutting into his flesh. He pushed his fingers under the wire, trying to protect his neck.

"The Princess wants you to know before you die how she deals with traitors," the vampire hissed.

Sinclair pushed his feet against the elevator wall, struggling to free himself.

* * * * *

"Sinclair never showed," Armondés said as he climbed in through the window of the eastside motel.

"Oh no." Tears welled in Danielle's eyes.

"It doesn't mean he's been destroyed."

"Yes, it does. He took too many chances trying to eliminate Minnie's men. I knew it was too great of a risk."

"Not necessarily. It could be Sinclair is in hiding. You must have faith in him."

"I do, but he took too many risks." She was inconsolable. He gathered her into his arms and held her for what seemed hours. Whispering in her ear, he rocked her and planted small tender kisses on her cheek every now and then.

Emotionally spent, she fell asleep. Her dreams were filled with ghastly scenes of Sinclair being attacked by Minnie. She screamed for him to run, but he always stood and fought. She jerked awake, but was shushed by Armondés. The room was dark, with only a faint glow from the streetlights outside slipping past the heavy draperies, partially pulled against the night.

Something bumped against the wall, and she realized it was in the room with them. Her nostrils flared and the scent of blood filled her senses. Fresh warm blood. Her stomach gnawed in response.

Armondés tightened his arms around her and slowly levitated them from the bed. The dark figure moved from the window, stealing around the chair. He crouched in the shadows for what seemed forever. She looked down at the humanlike figure as it crept toward the bed.

Armondés released her. She maintained her height above the room as he floated soundlessly toward the intruder. The man turned just as Armondés slammed into him, throwing him against the wall. The prowler fell to the floor and didn't attempt to stand.

Danielle lowered to the floor and hastily turned on the lamp. Golden light flooded the room, washing past Armondés to the crumpled form draped in dirty bloodied clothes. She rushed over to stand by him.

"Who is it?" she asked. He leaned forward and rolled the man over.

"Sinclair!" she gasped and rushed to cradle his head in her lap. "Get some towels, his neck's bleeding."

* * * * *

"I have found my bride, Minnie." Armondés winked at Danielle. "I met her at the club. The Russian you sent up to see me. Maria."

"Oh, well, that's wonderful news. When shall you be coming home? I've been very worried about you." Minnie's voice echoed from the cell phone.

He cut his eyes over at Danielle.

"We'll be there tonight. I trust you went ahead and made the usual arrangements. Is everything ready for the ceremony?"

"Oh yes, I have. I know how you like cutting it close. Just you and your bride be safe." Minnie's voice blasted in his ear.

"We couldn't be safer."

"Excellent. What time should I expect you?"

"Just before midnight. We aren't taking any chances."

"Very good, brother. We're all looking forward to this being over."

"As are we." He flipped the cell phone closed.

"We have several hours to wait," Danielle said.

"I have reserved the room next door. Sinclair can recuperate here. Come." He pulled her behind him. "I plan to spend the day in your arms, not waiting for that old fart to wake up."

"That's not nice."

"But you are," he said and opened the door to the room next door. "Now come in here and show me how grateful you are to me for saving your friend."

"You're horrid!" She shoved him against the wall and molded to him. "I've forgotten what it feels like not to hide. I'm so looking forward to our freedom."

"I am to a point. I've enjoyed having you all to myself."

"I can still spoil you once it's over."

"Prove it," he said and spun her around so her back was against his chest. He cupped her breasts in both hands. Hot flutters quivered in her stomach.

"I love you," she said.

"I believe you." His voice filled with emotion.

"I also love it when you touch me."

"Which touch do you like best?" he asked, nuzzling her neck.

"I like that one very much," she said and tilted her head sideways so he could reach her better. He kissed her neck, tracing tiny patterns with his tongue. Delightful shivers rippled down her.

"Umm," she said. "That's a wonderful touch too."

He thrust his tongue into her ear, flicking erotic strokes that moved through her body. She rolled her hips and pressed her ass against him. He still wore his slacks, but his arousal was hard against her.

She sank deeper into his spell, writhing beneath his seductive touches. His hands released her breasts and groped among her clothing, seeking the zipper to her slacks. The material gave and she gasped when his fingers dipped beneath her panties. He massaged her pussy, releasing its heat and moistness, driving her beyond care. Her pants fell to her ankles and her panties followed. He buried his lips into the crook of her neck and moved his finger against her clit.

He stroked her harder, turning her sideways so his other hand could cup her buttocks, and then slid his fingers between her cheeks and slightly into her anus. She moaned at the new sensation this created and pumped against the forefinger rubbing her clit. He shifted around so she faced him, playing his magic touches to all of her hot, achy spots. He lowered his face and captured one of her hard nipples with his lips and tugged against it. She moaned and arched on her toes, receiving him from both ends.

"Oh, Armondés!" she cried as the first waves jerked through her body, sending new sensations through her. He released her and pushed her to the mattress. His cock entered as the second wave of orgasm gripped her. His entry aroused her and she pushed against him, rolling on top of him. Grinding her hips, Danielle caressed his chest, lifting slightly from his shaft, then down again.

"Danielle!" He grasped her hips and rammed his cock deeper. She rode him harder, and he shuddered, slowing his pace. His eyes glazed with pleasure.

"Bite me," she said and lowered her neck to his mouth.

"I could hurt you," he argued.

"It's our anniversary, my love." His bite was gentle at first, almost a nibble. The walls of her pussy clenched tighter and he released a deep groan with his teeth sinking further into her flesh. Pleasure mingled with pain until the distinction between them blurred and all that remained was Armondés.

* * * * *

She looked up from the dresser when he entered the room.

"He's resting well," Armondés whispered and pulled against the tuxedo bow tie.

"Good. I want him to remain here until this is over."

"I laced the Private Label bottle with sleeping powder. He should be out until sunrise." He grinned, obviously proud of himself.

She nodded her appreciation at his reflection. He stood behind her, running his hands through her hair. A frown creased his handsome face.

She followed his stare to her neck.

"It's nothing," she said.

"It looks horrid. I would never hurt you."

"It didn't hurt. Besides, we want Minnie to believe we went through with the ceremony, remember?"

He dropped a kiss on her shoulder and lingered.

"Do you remember our first kiss?"

"Yes, I do. I also remember the first time you made love to me. I've had a passion for marble ever since." She giggled and brushed her cheek against his hand.

"You look ravishing." He held out his hand, lifting her gently to her feet. She wore a black, strapless dress. The layers of sheer material floated to her ankles. His stare was riveted to her neck, making her feel self-conscious.

"It'll heal. Too quickly. We need to leave."

"Yes, come." He led her to the window. "Watch out for snipers," he warned as he stepped out into the air.

She took his hand and joined him. The night was brilliant with the lights of the city and the canopy of stars overhead. A soft breeze stirred through the trees below.

"Regardless what happens this night, I want you to know I love you, Danielle." He tweaked her fake nose. "And Maria."

She chuckled, but quickly grew serious.

"And I love you, my husband. Please be very careful!"

* * * * *

"Where are they?" Minnie paced the length of the room one more time, pausing to double check the Private Label and goblets.

"They'll be here," Fredrick said for the fourth time. His patience seemed to be wearing thin, too.

"I wish I had the ashes of Sinclair. I'd love to rub them in her face, the lying bitch."

"I can get the ones I put in the dumpster if you like, I'm sure she'd not know they were mingled with the guard's."

"Oh, she would. Believe me, she would. That creature let me believe she'd destroyed her master." Minnie growled under her breath, gritting her teeth against the need to scream her outrage. She'd waited a long time for this night and every emotion she'd ever suppressed seemed to be surfacing. She stopped to look at the grandfather clock. It was one minute to midnight. "This is so like my brother, always waiting until the last minute."

"You think I stage it to the last minute?" Armondés asked and stepped from the long velvet draperies.

"There you are!" Minnie spun around. Immediately her eyes hardened on Maria. "And there *you* are." She immediately saw the bite mark and marveled at the woman's ability to dupe her brother. "I see you have completed most of the ceremony."

Self-consciously, Maria raised her hand to her neck and seemed to blush.

"All we need is the toast." He moved toward the sideboard and nodded to Fredrick.

"Evening, my King. Congratulations on your new mate." He bowed and poured the two goblets.

"Thank you." Armondés turned to Maria and offered his hand. She glided across the room and placed her hand in his. "May I present my wife, Maria."

"Enchanté." Fredrick feigned a kiss over her hand.

"Yes, well, enough of the social graces. Drink up you two, the clock is about to strike."

Armondés handed Maria a goblet. She watched her future sister-in-law, ready to drink to seal the union. The first chime broke through the awkward moment. The couple lifted the goblets to their lips. Minnie held her stare on them, jumping from one face to the other, awaiting the expected reaction. Both dropped the goblets and spewed the wine from their mouths.

"What the hell is this?" Armondés took quick strides to the sideboard and picked up the bottle. "Where is the nuptial vintage? Minnie!"

"Yes, brother, that's right. There's no nuptial vintage. Not this time. I'm exhausted from your last minute jaunts to beat the curse. This time you lose. Your bride over there happens to be a vampire, you silly fool. If getting rid of your other two wives was not taxing enough, trying to keep this crazy woman in line has driven me to near insanity myself."

"You, Minnie? You killed Danielle?"

"Yes."

"And Charisse?"

"Creative, wasn't I? Oh, I was very patient with the first one, but after Alexa, I wasn't going to wait for something to happen to Charisse. She was easy. She was insane. But Danielle, now there was a clever girl."

"*You* were the one behind the assassination attempts!"

"Oh, I am the one behind *all* the attempts on your life. I'm disgusted with this life you've forced us to live. You've robbed me of my true nature and held me to a lifestyle I abhor. From this moment forward, our clan will resume its natural instincts to hunt. Your reign is over, brother." She turned to Fredrick and held out her hand.

"Fredrick?" Armondés seemed surprised, but Danielle knew it was just good acting. They had feared Fredrick was involved but had to play out this charade to be certain. "The two of you have plotted together? Why?"

"Are you serious?" Fredrick stepped around Minnie. "You robbed me of my honor, my dignity, my death."

"Are you insane as well? You were too brilliant to die simply because you were on the wrong side. Charlemagne grieved over having to send you to your death."

"I didn't ask for this life. I had chosen my path. You interfered."

"All these years and you never said a word."

"Why should I? It was done."

"So you've hated me and waited for this moment?"

"I have *dreamed* of it. It's all I've wanted ever since that first time I hunted down a human and drank his blood."

"And you, sister? Do you have a fading memory like your lover?"

"Fading memory?" Fredrick yelled.

"Yes, that it was you, Fredrick, who came to me and begged me to save you from Charlemagne's wrath."

"I asked to be spared the execution."

"And so I spared you. There were no stipulations made in regards to the sparing."

"I did not give you the right to turn me into this!" he yelled with the veins popping out along his temple.

"You did. You begged for me to spare you. I did. The only way I could."

"I didn't know vampires existed, and I certainly didn't know you, the Chief Justice, were one."

"At the time, you didn't care. You clung to life like a suckling baby to a teat. You would have bedded the devil to remain in this world."

Fredrick released a savage scream and lunged forward as Armondés jumped toward him. They collided in the air and rolled toward the end of the room. Danielle watched in horror. Her heart ached when Fredrick hit Armondés and he slammed into the far wall.

"Stop it!" she screamed at Fredrick. She looked at Minnie, who stood watching with wide eyes. Fredrick grabbed Armondés by the arm and dragged him across the floor, hurling him into the air and into the fireplace.

"Stop it!" Danielle cried out with tears streaming down her cheeks. This was not how it was supposed to be.

"Why isn't he changing?" Minnie rushed over to Fredrick and tugged on his arm. "It's past the time, he should be aging."

Armondés pulled himself from the floor. Danielle ran over to him and hugged him, trying to dab the blood from his face with the hem of her gown.

"Why isn't he aging?' Minnie screamed like a banshee and jerked against Fredrick, who stood numbly looking on.

Danielle moved toward Minnie, but Armondés tried to stop her. She disentangled from his weakened hold.

"I'll tell you why," she said, and smiled slowly at them. "You thought you had destroyed yet another wife of your brother's, only Danielle was not destroyed."

Fredrick mumbled something.

"That's right," she said in her normal voice and pulled on the fake nose until it gave.

Minnie's gasp echoed in the room.

"I hid from you, Minnie." She tossed the nose to the floor and tugged on the chin until it too gave way. She took a bold step toward her sister-in-law. "I hid from you inside a cave and when the sun set I returned to the castle, only you had spread your lies and I was too late."

"No!" Minnie cried. "You can't be Danielle." The realization of the coup thundered with waves of emotion, changing her expression.

"The only special power I had, Minnie, was the ability to outwit you. And you made it so very easy."

Minnie screeched like a wild animal and lunged for her. She was prepared for the woman, but Armondés stepped between them and held his sister's arms behind her back.

She screamed and struggled against his hold. Insanity danced in her wide eyes.

"You stupid bitch! You let her trick you!" Fredrick cursed.

"Armondés!" Danielle cried when Fredrick jumped for him once more. Armondés turned just as the man sailed across the room heading toward him. He lifted his foot and planted it into Fredrick's neck, sending him crashing to the floor. He pushed Minnie into the chair and leaped to the fireplace, drawing the sword. Danielle cried out to him just as Fredrick threw a knife. It missed and plunged into the mantel. The Royal Advisor lunged for him, but Armondés was too fast and sailed over the man.

Fredrick pivoted and yelled then jumped toward him again. Armondés sliced the sword through the air. Danielle thought he had missed, until Fredrick froze. With a surprised look clouding his face, his head wobbled sideways and toppled to the floor, crumbling into dust. Danielle screamed.

Minnie just sat, staring, as his body fell forward and disintegrated before it hit the floor. A low growl rose and exploded into a yell as she leaped for Armondés, slashing the air with her long nails. He grabbed her by the throat and lifted her from the floor.

"Your lover is destroyed! But you, Minnie. What am I to do with you? How could I have been so blind to your ambition? I should have seen this coming."

"What are you going to do with her?" Danielle asked, afraid he would destroy her like he had Fredrick.

"What can I do? She's my sister." He frowned and released her. Minnie fell into a limp heap on the floor, wailing.

"I think you could see that she is put away so she can do neither of us any harm ever again," Danielle suggested.

"Destroy me!" Minnie seethed and glared up at them. "I don't want to continue to live in your world, brother."

"I shall not let you have so easy an out. Not for the pain you have inflicted. You murdered one queen and attempted to murder another. You must pay for your crimes. You have plotted against your king."

The door to the hall burst open. Sinclair stomped in with an army behind him.

"My King," Sinclair said and looked at Danielle.

"Sinclair, I thought you…" She looked at her husband, who shrugged. "As always, Sinclair, your timing is perfect," she grinned.

"You!" Minnie tried to claw at him, but the guards quickly restrained her. "You liar! All of you are liars! You had no special powers! Damn you to hell!" she screeched.

Sinclair motioned for the guards to remove her.

"What about her accomplice?" He looked around the room.

"I dealt with him. He's been destroyed." Armondés reached for his wife and drew her into his embrace. "Will you see that my sister is taken back to France, Sinclair? I know of no other I would entrust with such a task."

"It would be my honor."

"Secure a wing in the castle and fit it to accommodate her. Give her whatever she needs to be comfortable, but she is never to be allowed outside the confines of her own suite."

Sinclair bowed. He started to turn from the room, but Danielle ran after him.

"Sinclair," she said and he pivoted just in time to receive her hug. "Thank you."

"My honor, my Queen," he said and kissed her forehead. "Do you think you can see about getting me some of that Private Label on a regular basis?" he asked with a wink, then left to do the king's bidding.

"It's over," she sighed and slowly turned back to Armondés. She longed to taste him.

"Yes, my love, it is over." He held out his hand to her.

"So much has happened in the past year. I just want to rest for the next few." She reached out and clasped his hand. Electrical currents shot through her.

"We have all eternity, Danielle."

"Yes," she said and stepped into his embrace. It felt right to be in his arms as though she had always belonged there. What would their lives be like now that the threat was gone? Instantly she heard his thoughts. Blissful.

"Tell me what I can do to make all this up to you, my Danielle." He held her face between his hands. "What do you need, my love?"

"Armondés, you're all I ever need." She tilted her face to receive his hungry kiss.

About the author:

A native North Carolinian, Sally lives with her husband, daughter and cat, Bow, in the Blue Ridge Mountains.

Growing up just outside Charlotte, NC, Sally spent summers playing on the beaches of the Carolinas and learning to 'shag' — a form of beach dancing.

Born in the South and into an Irish/Scottish family meant storytelling was as natural as breathing. Everyone had their own repertoire of jokes and stories and growing up in North Carolina, famous for its ghost stories, meant scary ones, too. Sally knows a lot about ghosts since she's lived with them all her life. In 1987, she was asked to participate in a three-year paranormal research project she at long last embraced her Celtic seer heritage and even runs an online paranormal workshop featuring paranormal research professionals.

Trained in commercial art, she discovered writing fulfills her creative energies, especially Romantica™. When not writing, she can be found tending to her flowers and jungle of houseplants, studying all kinds of subject matters, and setting out on new adventures with her soul mate husband.

Sally welcomes mail from readers. You can write to her c/o Ellora's Cave Publishing at 1056 Home Avenue, Akron OH 44310-3502.

Why an electronic book?

We live in the Information Age—an exciting time in the history of human civilization in which technology rules supreme and continues to progress in leaps and bounds every minute of every hour of every day. For a multitude of reasons, more and more avid literary fans are opting to purchase e-books instead of paperbacks. The question to those not yet initiated to the world of electronic reading is simply: *why?*

1. *Price.* An electronic title at Ellora's Cave Publishing and Cerridwen Press runs anywhere from 40-75% less than the cover price of the <u>exact same title</u> in paperback format. Why? Cold mathematics. It is less expensive to publish an e-book than it is to publish a paperback, so the savings are passed along to the consumer.

2. *Space.* Running out of room to house your paperback books? That is one worry you will never have with electronic novels. For a low one-time cost, you can purchase a handheld computer designed specifically for e-reading purposes. Many e-readers are larger than the average handheld, giving you plenty of screen room. Better yet, hundreds of titles can be stored within your new library—a single microchip. (Please note that Ellora's Cave and Cerridwen Press does not endorse any specific brands. You can check our website at www.ellorascave.com or

www.cerridwenpress.com for customer recommendations we make available to new consumers.)

3. *Mobility.* Because your new library now consists of only a microchip, your entire cache of books can be taken with you wherever you go.

4. *Personal preferences are accounted for.* Are the words you are currently reading too small? Too large? Too...**ANNOYING**? Paperback books cannot be modified according to personal preferences, but e-books can.

5. *Instant gratification.* Is it the middle of the night and all the bookstores are closed? Are you tired of waiting days—sometimes weeks—for online and offline bookstores to ship the novels you bought? Ellora's Cave Publishing sells instantaneous downloads 24 hours a day, 7 days a week, 365 days a year. Our e-book delivery system is 100% automated, meaning your order is filled as soon as you pay for it.

Those are a few of the top reasons why electronic novels are displacing paperbacks for many an avid reader. As always, Ellora's Cave and Cerridwen Press welcomes your questions and comments. We invite you to email us at service@ellorascave.com, service@cerridwenpress.com or write to us directly at: 1056 Home Ave. Akron OH 44310-3502.

Printed in the United States
73594LV00002B/196-225

9 781419 952302